Allegiance

— A NOVEL —

Allegiance

— A NOVEL —

PAUL MARTIN MIDDEN

PUBLISHED BY

Wittmann*Blair*

ISBN-13: 978-0-9859223-5-1

Written by Paul Martin Midden
Published by Wittmann Blair
St. Louis, Missouri
wittmannblair@charter.net

*Never doubt that a small group of thoughtful,
committed citizens can change the world.
Indeed, it is the only thing that ever has.*

—Margaret Mead

Prologue

After the piercing whistle of the missile and the resulting explosion, a strange sense of quiet hovered over Washington, DC, for several minutes. To the shocked people near the Lincoln Memorial, which was the missile's target, it seemed like a perpetual moment, the kind you couldn't forget if you wanted to.

Officer Carly Mason had just turned her squad car onto Henry Bacon Drive from Constitution Avenue, headed toward the monument. She not only heard the explosion but saw it through her front windshield. And felt it, both in the ground, which shook beneath her vehicle, and in her soul, which was trying to digest an attack on one of the most sacred sites in the capital.

The ethereal silence was broken by the sound of rapid gunfire heard from some distance at first, but then getting closer. Officer Mason saw tourists and Washingtonians turning their heads from side to side. What are they doing? she wondered. Then she realized that her windows were closed and the air-conditioning was running hard. She rolled her window down so that she could hear better, and she knew immediately that they were trying to determine the direction of the gunshots. Sound is a funny thing in a built-up city like Washington. She pulled her car over to the side of the road and got out, straining to determine where the danger was coming from.

Carly Mason and the vast majority of people in the District that morning knew nothing of the events that led up to the first attack on the capital since the War of 1812. Prior to this moment, only a few government workers were suspicious, tipped off by an improbable informant.

Across the Potomac, Max Grabel, the CIA chief, was in his office. He was one of the few who knew. He learned just weeks prior to the attack that something was likely to happen, although he had no indication precisely what that might be. Max was also one of the first to understand that communications within the federal government had been compromised, and this sharply limited his ability to bring the full weight of the Agency's resources to bear on the problem. Because doing nothing was not an option, he turned to trusted contract workers Samantha Stranger and Marie LeBrun. None of that seemed to make a difference just now, and the pain in the pit of his stomach took on a distinctly sour feel.

What Samantha and Marie uncovered gave no comfort. They learned that a small group of fanatics had stitched together a grand conspiracy: to break apart the federal superstructure in the United States and replace it with autonomous states or smaller amalgamations of regional governments. They played on smoldering resentments based on race, religion, and the perennial American favorite: greed. These served as the groundwork for the insurgency, and modern technology and weapons development bequeathed to this small but influential group a fighting force many times as strong as absolute numbers suggested.

The driving force behind the insurrection was David Blinder, a wildly wealthy scion of a self-made father; his brother, George, assisted him in the preparation for the final showdown. He was allied with Adam Wilson, an unscrupulous academic with broad connections among right-wing religious groups who believed they were seeing their faith attacked on every front. The Blinders were also connected with Abner Bellamy who, for deep personal reasons, found it his special mission to resurrect the old Confederacy in the South.

The military muscle for this enterprise was provided by a group called the Sovereign Citizens. The SC paraded as a weekend-only group of obviously deranged "militants" who took part in weekly drills for the pleasure of doing so. Beneath the wing-nut façade, however, lay a powerful, disciplined, and deadly serious military organization put together by Winslow Parker, a West Point graduate and career US military until he switched sides at Blinder's behest.

When Max Grabel unleashed Marie LeBrun and Samantha Stranger to learn more about the conspiracy, he knew he was sending no insignificant force. They were two strong women with major skills in espionage, communication and technology, weapons, and counterinsurgency. They started in the Midwest, but their mission was soon uncovered by the insurgents.

Samantha and Marie found that the rebellion was much further advanced than anyone anticipated. While tracking down those responsible, they came across Cherie Keenan, whose husband was part of the conspiracy until his gruesome death. Cherie had turned to Darrin McAlister, the police chief in tiny Rolla, Missouri, for help, and McAlister joined the investigation.

To Officer Carly Mason and Max Grabel, it appeared the efforts of these patriots were in vain. They both saw the smoke rising from the Lincoln Memorial, they both heard the gunfire and knew more trouble was on the way. They both knew that in this moment they were being called to march toward danger, not away from it. The young police officer and the experienced CIA chief took deep breaths; both committed themselves to the fight; both didn't care if they survived the sacred fight or not. It wasn't personal. It was about the country they loved and served.

amantha Stranger stared at the live news feed of the mayhem in Washington, DC, with a crushing sense of guilt. Such feelings were not common for her, as she had dedicated her life to the pursuit of accomplishment by unremitting discipline and focus. She had been working feverishly over the past few weeks to prevent just what she was watching on the screen, and seeing it play out despite her best efforts nauseated her.

As far as CNN could tell, the Lincoln Memorial was badly damaged, and hostile troops, hostile *American* troops, were storming the White House and other government buildings. Confusion and gunfire were everywhere. The police, the FBI, the Marines guarding the White House were returning fire, but it was difficult to determine who the enemy soldiers were. Innocent people were being shot for doing anything suspicious. Chaos was clearly in charge.

Samantha knew that this fit in perfectly with the purposes of the subversives. They were not looking for a military victory as such. They were looking to decapitate the federal government if possible; but their real aim was to create chaos by highlighting weaknesses in the federal system to buy enough time to implement other elements of their plan. The goal of that plan was to replace the federal government of the United States with a number of smaller, more "manageable" nations that would take the place of the sprawling federal superstructure. They had options for what to do then, and they knew that the federal government had only one: to find them and use force to crush them.

But the feds couldn't crush what they couldn't find. Even though the insurrectionist troops were spreading chaos and violence throughout the District, they were masters at deception. They wore no uniforms and identified each other by various, nonstandard tattoos on their bodies, the significance of which was known only to other troops. Their strategy was to attack, disperse, and reassemble at another attack point. Nor were they limited to a single agenda: they could attack any number of targets of convenience among a list of many in the DC area. The defenders would have a hard time mounting a defense with such random targets.

Nonetheless, Samantha believed she saw the outlines of a battle strategy in play on the small screen: subversive Sovereign Citizen troops were snaking their way toward the White House, the Supreme Court, and the congressional office buildings, attacking, scattering, and reassembling.

Samantha could see regiments of men in T-shirts, jeans, and loose-fitting jackets that had been a military phalanx a few moments before and was now an amorphous crowd, apparently no different from other crowds of terrified civilians searching for cover. She could see members of the regiment blending in with the general population and then reassembling at another point. Seeing this did not help her nausea.

Samantha Stranger was not alone watching these events. She was in the Public Hotel in Chicago, along with key team members she'd been working with to prevent this very cataclysm from occurring. Marie LeBrun, her compatriot and close friend, was there, as were Cherie Keenan, a woman who fled from her husband's lead role in the insurrection, and Darrin McAlister, the police chief of tiny Rolla, Missouri, who had helped Cherie find refuge after her husband was murdered, and threw in his lot with her and with the federal agents who were working to preserve public peace.

There was silence among the team members. They were all entranced by what they were seeing on the screen, and each in his or her own way was sickened by it. Cherie Keenan's face was streaked with tears; Darrin McAlister sat stone-faced watching the small screen. Marie LeBrun was taking deep breaths to control the rage she felt in her soul.

Samantha tore her eyes away from the screen and looked at the other members of the group. She got up then and walked over to Marie and put her hands on her shoulders. It was a sign of support and affection, along with some mild impatience.

"We will get through this, Marie," she said softly. "We will hunt these bastards down and kill every last one of them." There was not a trace of irony or hyperbole in her voice.

Marie turned a tear-stained face to look up at her friend. "Yes, we will, Sam," she said. "Yes, we will."

Sam turned to the others in the room. She did not see herself as a leader, more a highly competent worker bee. But she couldn't stand the inertia and felt she had to say something to get the group moving.

"Listen up, everyone," she began. "We lost this round. We were unable to stop this from happening." She paused a moment and glanced down at the floor. "We knew something like this was in the works, and we did all we could to prevent it . . . but, despite our best efforts, it happened anyway." She looked at each person in the room directly in the face. Each looked back and nodded slightly.

"We all hate this. Now, it's also true that we are in a better position than most to keep this fight alive. We know the players, we have a good idea of how they are organized, and we have solid intel about the whereabouts of most of the principals." She paused again and looked around. "We also have a good idea of what they're up to. And we have a window to stop this thing before it goes much further." She looked at the television screen and frowned. "What you see on that screen is not the end. It's the beginning of a fight. Whether or not these people succeed is up to us and to people like us. I want each of us to keep doing what we've been doing and shove these sons of bitches back into whatever holes they came out of before they permanently wreck our country."

There was a collective sigh among the small group. It was not so much relief as it was a break from the trance induced by watching unbelievable images on the small screen. Each battle-weary person in that room knew that Samantha was correct and that the time for grief and shock would have to be postponed. There was work to be done.

cross the country, Max Grabel was having similar thoughts. He too had to fight back the rage he felt in his gut in order to do what he had to do: kill this thing before it went too far. More than anyone else at Langley, he knew it would not be easy.

Max was too busy to call the team in Chicago, even though he imagined they would be furious at their failure to prevent this naked assault on their country. He had been directing that team since he had first gotten wind of the rebellion. Ever practical, he knew the Chicago team had the same information he had, for the most part, and he trusted their instincts. Although he wanted to reconnect with their small, tightly knit group, at the moment he had bigger fish to fry.

He had just spoken to Bob Mueller, head of the FBI, who told him the President and the First Family had been taken to a safe location. Max doubted that: this attack on Washington was a surprise, and the President and his family were no doubt still in the White House. Max hoped and assumed they were in one of the safe rooms belowground. Whether or not that was a "safe location" was yet to be determined.

In the ten minutes since he learned of the attack, Max had assembled nearly a hundred agents to counterattack. He imagined, quite rightly, that the few troops on station in the District would hold out as long as they could, but they were few and the attackers were many. He figured it would take the military some hours to mount a counterattack, and by that time, it might be too late.

Any counterattack would be difficult at best. He knew some things about the men they were facing: he knew they were dressed like civilians and were known to each other only by small tattoos on their bodies. He knew their goal was not to take over Washington but to kill key government leaders and create confusion, terror, and panic. He was aware that the element of surprise took them some way toward achieving that goal.

He divided his agents into groups of ten and commandeered ten Sikorsky helicopters to take them into the District. The agents were equipped with whatever arms were readily available. Since they were in a CIA facility, those were substantial.

"Wheels up in five minutes," he yelled into his headset. He wanted more than anything to be on one of those copters so he could have the pleasure of capturing or killing one or more of the evildoers who invaded his country, but he knew his spot was behind the monitors, directing action in the air and on the ground once the copters arrived on what was now a battlefield.

He tried to condense all that he had learned in the previous weeks to share with the warriors at his disposal.

"Okay, gentlemen and ladies," he said. "We are facing a fanatical group of heavily armed men with no uniforms. Their standard garb consists of jeans and T-shirts. The one telltale sign is a small tattoo somewhere on the body, but visible. These tattoos are not all the same but they are located in the same area." He glared at the men and women, brave to a person, arrayed in front of him. "One spotter on each copter will identify the men with the tattoo as you approach. Shoot to kill.

"Once on the ground, shoot anyone with a weapon who is not military or police. Don't bother to ask questions." He looked around the room. His tone became slightly more relaxed but even more sober. "This is war, my friends. Let's win it."

And with that bit of encouragement, one hundred brave souls boarded the waiting helicopters.

Max took a deep breath as the Sikorskys lifted off and headed northward. He was also monitoring live feeds from traffic cams and other surveillance devices spread throughout the District. He knew he was sending his agents into a firestorm with little direction, but that was what he had to work with. By the time the copters got there, it would be hard to identify the invaders from the general population, most of whom were standing around in shock at the smoke and noise and devastation around them. He could see the regiments break up even as he was watching the monitors, just as his colleagues in Chicago were seeing them. He hoped the face recognition on the webcams was up to the job of tracking these evil people.

He had a minute. He picked up his mobile and punched Marie's number.

"Are you seeing this?" he said more gruffly than he intended. He couldn't contain the rage he felt, but this was the team that had worked tirelessly to prevent this very thing from happening. Given the short time frame, there was no one blame. Nevertheless, his frustration with himself extended to all involved in that futile endeavor, and he could not disguise it.

"Yeah, I see it, Max." Marie's own rage was not far from the surface. "What can we do to help?"

"I want you to stay on top of what you're seeing and be ready when I call. I'm sending my people in now."

"Will do, Max." She clicked off. She knew Max was just trying to give her some solace in an inconsolable situation. She looked over at Samantha and nodded in appreciation of the well-intended but pointless gesture. She did not need consolation. She needed revenge. She needed redemption.

amantha and Marie began reviewing what they knew. They had tracked the nature and the scope of the brewing insurrection, only to learn day by frustrating day that it was more advanced, better funded, and better organized than anyone had dreamed. The US government was more prepared for an attack by old Soviet bloc nations or by Al-Qaeda than by its own citizens, especially an attack as sophisticated as this.

Marie LeBrun pushed back from her monitor and stood up.

"What do we do now, Sam?"

It was not an idle question.

Rather, this was step one in an exercise they had performed many times together: developing an action plan. They would gather information, evaluate options, decide what to do next, and implement the plan. Simple, on paper.

Sam thought for a moment. "We know they have money, we know they have advanced weapons, we know they have a large fighting force that is mostly invisible to the federal troops." She paused. "And we know this attack is only the first step.

"But there's even more that we don't know—for instance, the chain of command. We can assume David Blinder is orchestrating this, but we don't know how or through whom." She frowned. "That's a big disadvantage."

Marie listened intently. She knew Sam was right; there were many more things they didn't know. But they had to take action on the basis of what they did know. To do nothing did not even seem like an option. While Marie admired how meticulous Sam was with facts, she also knew she was sometimes stymied by them. But this wasn't the time for splitting hairs. "Okay," she said. "What are their weaknesses?"

Samantha thought for a moment. "I believe we have degraded their communication somewhat," Samantha replied calmly, "but the extent of that is unknown." She was silent for a moment. "And I think the puppet masters, the Blinder brothers, are split. We know that George Blinder left the family compound yesterday, and we are tracking his movements. And we know where David Blinder is."

She looked directly at Marie. "We could take him out."

"If he's the guy we think is in charge," Marie replied, "then that seems like a sensible plan."

Both women knew that getting David Blinder would not be as easy as it sounded. Yes, they could locate where he lived, but the last two agents sent to interview him had not been heard from for days. They also knew the Blinders' enormous rural estate was crawling with Sovereign Citizens, the military arm of the insurrection about which the US government knew precious little, including their numbers. What they did know was that the SC troops were well trained, well equipped, and fervent in the pursuit of their goals. It would take more than the two of them to penetrate the compound.

Marie considered the suggestion for a few seconds, then she looked straight into Samantha's eyes. "How could we do that?"

Sam thought for a few moments. "We have a reason to treat the Blinder compound as hostile, as they have apparently detained our agents." She paused again, wondering if the two agents were still alive. "If we can collect enough agents in the area, we could mount a direct assault on the compound itself. That would be the most direct way."

"Dangerous," Marie replied. "We don't know how many men he has on the grounds or how they are equipped. We also may need him alive. We'd have to check with whoever is in charge down there." Her voice trailed off. Taking action under these conditions felt nearly as impossible as doing nothing at all. But she felt compelled to act.

"Look, Sam," she said. "Let's head down to Texas and figure out the specifics in the air. I know it's not optimal, but we are useless here, and we have information that federal authorities are just now learning. We are the tip of the spear." She looked at her friend, whose eyes seemed to be glazing over.

Marie looked at Samantha askance. It wasn't like Sam to lose focus. She was a planner, an implementer, an action-taker. She was not given to hesitation when she was clear about her goal. Marie found herself annoyed with her friend and colleague.

"Sam!" she cried. "We need to do something."

Samantha shook her head. The momentary lapse of focus vanished, and she was clear-eyed again. "Okay, let's get down to Texas. We'll plan on the way."

Marie felt a measure of relief at Sam's return to focus, and she was grateful. She looked over at Cherie and Darrin.

"What do you guys want to do?" she said simply. She believed in her heart that these two had gone way beyond duty to help the authorities track this thing down. It was an honest question.

Darrin spoke first. "I'm in," he said. "This makes me sick."

Cherie Keenan, a mother and homemaker and a dutiful if former wife, hesitated a bit. "I don't know what I would have done without you guys," she said. "And I don't know how I can help." She exhaled slowly. "But I will do anything I can to help stop this and bring these people to justice."

Four heads nodded around the room.

"Let's get packing," Marie said.

Cherie and Darrin got up to do just that and walked into the bedrooms of the large suite. Marie and Samantha continued their conversation in low voices.

"What about Max?" Samantha asked. "He wanted us to be ready if he calls."

"We'll be as ready in Texas as we are here," Marie replied. "Maybe more so."

"While you are getting ready, I can do some preliminary work," Samantha said.

"It's not as if we can call the Texas governor to use his militia," Marie said. "It is more than likely that he's in on the insurrection."

She peered down at Sam's laptop. "How many agents can we collect in the area? CIA, FBI, ATF?"

Sam thought for a minute and then turned and consulted her laptop. "I imagine we could have about fifty agents readily available."

As she was speaking, she was working her computer, checking available resources in southeastern Texas. "By the time we get there, we can probably have another fifty agents."

"Good," Marie replied, even though she had no idea if that was a sufficient number. The trouble was that they just didn't know how many Sovereign Citizen troops were on the Blinder estate, which ranged over eighty thousand acres with lots of trees and other forms of cover.

Sam found some preliminary data from a satellite feed that suggested around three hundred or four hundred SC troops on the estate. Both Marie and Samantha were aware, however, that they had no idea of how many more were nearby and could be readily utilized. This was not going to be a walk in the park.

Marie didn't care. She had to act, and she had to act *now*.

4

While the two federal contract workers were in Chicago deciding how to collect him, David Blinder was sitting at the center of a console in a windowless, sealed room in his sprawling estate in central Texas. From the moment the attack started, he had been on the phone with contacts in various state governments, starting with his own state of Texas, which would soon, he planned, be the Commonwealth of Texas and would include Oklahoma in its territory. He could barely take his eyes off the television news, he was so excited that the day he had planned for had finally arrived. He was talking to the governor of Texas.

"Mr. Regis," he said. "The day has come. As you can see, the federal government is no longer able to protect itself from its own dissenters." He paused for effect. "This isn't an attack from an outside force; this is an attack by patriotic Americans who want their country back. The way it was supposed to be, the way it used to be: free and proud with a small government. As you and I know, the role of government is to maintain order, and it is clear that the bureaucrats in Washington, DC, are incapable of doing that."

He could not help but smile at the aptness of what he was saying. He knew exactly what was going on in Washington; it was he who had orchestrated it. He also knew what was happening at other key sites, particularly Fort Knox. Ah, gold, he thought.

But these thoughts were interfering with his conversation with the governor.

"As I was saying, Mr. Regis," he continued, forcing himself to turn away from the television monitor, "this is not an errant event or some half-baked effort by pitchfork-wielding discontents. What is happening now is real, it is well coordinated, it is momentous, and it calls for courage on all our parts."

"What do you have in mind, Mr. Blinder?" Edwin Regis asked, feigning an insouciance he neither felt nor had any right to.

"Come now, Mr. Regis," Blinder replied. "You know precisely what I have in mind. I want you to call the Texas legislature back into emergency session and declare independence for the Republic of Texas." He paused for a moment, mostly for effect. "I want you—I want us to be the first in the line of new nations."

There was silence on the other end of the line. Edwin Regis did in fact know exactly what David Blinder was talking about; they had discussed this prospect several times over the past few months. Regis was not unsympathetic to the cause. But he was also a politician, and he had to feel secure in the knowledge that the entire plan would actually work. Otherwise, he was facing a trial for treason, a crime that carried with it at least a long prison term if not worse in addition to the likely destruction of his political life.

"How are the other governors responding, Mr. Blinder?"

"With iron in their blood, Edwin. With real leadership."

Edwin Regis closed his eyes. He had never been able to withstand Blinder's aggressive manipulation. He opened his eyes and nodded even before the words came out of his mouth. "You can count on me, David," he said simply.

"Good," said Blinder. He hung up without saying another word.

The governor of Texas took out his address book and started thumbing through the pages in the order he would contact people. He had been laying his own groundwork as soon as he and Blinder began discussing the possibility of secession months ago. He had a list of those he could count on, those who were on the fence, and those who would stand in the way of what even he, careful and cunning as he was, felt genuine excitement about: the rebirth of Texas as an independent state, that glorious country that for some reason fell for the siren song of a coast-to-coast national government in the days of US expansion. That was then, he thought grimly; now it was time to reestablish his beloved country.

He started making calls to the first names on his list. It was they who would break the news to the second group and lean on them to join the movement. Together they would devise a plan to neutralize those who would have them continue to be an appendage of the United States.

David Blinder, meanwhile, made similar calls to other key players. He called Tad Grover, the governor of Oklahoma, and gave him the same message he had given Regis: the time for talk had ended, and the time of action had begun.

Then he placed a call to Abner Bellamy, the man who had been coordinating the states of the old Confederacy to reassert their righteous claims to sovereignty. And he called Adam Wilson, who had devised an ingenious plan to marshal the power of his tight-knit evangelical group to bolster the insurrection. All would use their substantial influence to compel the emergence of new geopolitical structures on the continental US land mass: the Commonwealth of California out west, the newly reconstituted Confederacy in the South, the reborn Republic of Texas, and Vermont in New England. All the other states would have to fend for themselves once the shackles of federalism were broken.

It was Abner Bellamy's response that bolstered his sense of accomplishment the most.

"We are ready, sir," Abner said with absolute conviction in his voice.

"How long before you anticipate the announcements of secession?" Blinder asked.

"Within forty-eight hours, Mr. Blinder." Abner trusted the men he had worked so hard to place in key positions.

"Impressive," said Blinder. "Keep me posted of developments as they unfold."

"I will do that, Mr. Blinder."

Abner Bellamy gave David Blinder something he craved, even as he took it for granted: absolute allegiance.

Blinder's call to Adam Wilson was nearly as fulfilling. Wilson had been behind the idea of his group of influential men disappearing from their prestigious positions, a move calculated to add to the general sense of confusion and uncertainty. It would take federal agencies weeks before they sorted out what had happened to twenty of the most influential figures in American life. By that time, the political restructuring of North America would be a *fait accompli*.

Blinder returned his gaze to the television. Smoke, gunshots, and other evidence of warfare were readily apparent, and CNN and the other news outlets were struggling to find a suitable direction in which to point their cameras. As far as David was concerned, the more coverage the better. When this day ended, the whole country would know that the federal government was no longer completely in charge of its own destiny. That control was returning to the people.

hile David Blinder was on the phone working his sources and enjoying what he regarded as a show, the attack on Fort Knox was just getting under way.

It was said that Fort Knox was impregnable, but that was an old term. These days, nothing was impregnable given enough money, talent, creativity, and outright deviousness. And no one knew this better than Winslow Parker.

Parker, a tall, solidly built man from a military family, had been an Army Ranger in his early career. He was born in Mississippi and was an early adopter of the insurrection movement. He knew he had the skills needed by the insurrection, and he offered them wholeheartedly.

Part of his motivation was heritage: he grew up in a Mississippi that was widely derided by the elites of New York and Washington. He resented that, especially in light of the advanced culture of the state that had been nearly destroyed by the War Between the States.

Parker loved that culture. He was raised on an old plantation just south of Jackson, and his well-heeled family hewed to old traditions as much as possible. The farm workers were mostly African American, the house staff wore tuxedos and neatly ironed dresses, and the overseers were all white. All the way it used to be. All the way it should be.

He was delighted to have been placed in charge of the assault on Fort Knox. Kentucky was truly a state of the Confederacy, even though it was touch-and-go throughout much of the War Between the States. He believed securing Fort Knox was critical for the success of this new insurrection. And finally and most importantly, he believed his plan had every chance of succeeding.

Parker also knew that the amount of actual gold in the vaults of Fort Knox was half of what resided under the streets of Manhattan in the Federal Reserve vault. But Fort Knox held such a commanding position in the national imagination, it so symbolized the hard-currency wealth of the country, the symbolic and cultural impact of its loss to the federal government would have decisive and devastating implications. It would alert the nation and the world that this is no fringe group movement; it would alert them that America is no longer synonymous with Washington, DC. This enormous transfer of wealth would announce the birth of new nations.

Parker felt delicious irony in the plan, particularly in the use of the huge MOAB weapons that would initiate the engagement. These enormous but non-nuclear bombs were truly shock-and-awe weapons that would for the first time be turned against a federal target on federal property.

The defenses at Fort Knox were substantial. Thousands of GIs were available for its preservation, as were numerous civilian personnel. The armory itself would be the envy of any third-world dictator, housing the latest military technology. Finally, the layered security for the bullion store was complicated and known to only a few select personnel.

Just the kind of challenge Parker relished.

He had begun planning for this day more than a year prior to the actual assault. While he was respectful of the resources available to the Fort Knox defenders, he was equally impressed with the resources he had been able to assemble using the Blinder brothers' money and connections. He had secured the latest high-explosive ordnance. Just a few weeks earlier, he had successfully derailed shipments coming out of Fort Leonard Wood in Missouri and had appropriated them for his own use. That is to say, for the use of the insurrection.

He was looking through binoculars from two miles away, but he had a clear view of the front of the depository building. He saw the defensive arrangements: fencing and barbed wire, a guard post, and a free field of fire in every direction. He knew there were surveillance cameras panning everything 24/7. He also knew that, in just a few minutes, none of that would matter.

Eight thousand SC troops concealed in regiments on either side of him were waiting for the airbursts of the three MOABs that would strike all around the depository building. They were being carried by a World War II–era B-29 that had been restored and retrofitted precisely for this task. As soon as the bombs exploded in successive airbursts, the tightly surveilled barbed-wire fencing, the field of fire, and the guard posts—even most of the building itself— would simply evaporate, leaving an open avenue leading up to an unprotected front door of the most closely guarded gold depository in the world. The bombs would create a moat around what was left of the building and destroy its thick outer walls.

At that point, his troops would have open access to the depository and to the personnel who knew how to access everything. They understood the now-useless technological security systems and they knew which personnel had all the information to access the vaults manually. Parker also knew that it would be hours before the US Army could get its mind around what was happening and respond in force, and by that time, Fort Knox would be a building devoid of its actual purpose: the protection of American gold. That gold would be in the hands of the insurrection.

6

A bner Bellamy looked out the window of his downtown Atlanta condominium with a profound sense of satisfaction. The television news that had grabbed the nation's attention was playing on a wall behind him, but the sound was turned down. He had been waiting for this day for years, and he wanted to relish every moment of it.

This was the culmination of a special mission he had received years earlier, after he had a short but profitable career in the ministry and had tried the traditional marriage route. Now he was past all that and engaged in what every cell in his body knew was the right thing. He was acting out his true life's mission: to return the South to its former independent greatness.

At the moment, there wasn't a lot for him to do. He had his men in place in their respective Southern states. Each was fully trained and briefed about what he needed to do. They had collectively been working behind the scenes in preparation for this very day. It was their job to persuade, cajole, intimidate, or otherwise threaten the Southern governors and legislators to do what they had been cowed into not doing for more than a hundred and fifty years: declare the independence that was their right and heritage and throw off the milestone of the federal bureaucracy that had impeded their progress for the last century and a half.

Abner had been up with the sun. He signaled his men to implement their plan the night before—the one they had been working on for years—and he figured he wouldn't hear anything until later in the morning. He poured himself a bourbon neat and glanced at the television before turning his attention back to downtown Atlanta. He had no doubt the assault on Washington would succeed. In fact, the bar was low: the SC troops did not have to conquer and hold the nation's capital, they simply had to create chaos and eliminate as many top officials as they could. No matter the outcome, they would withdraw. But their actions would create a vacuum of power and an atmosphere of uncertainty and ambiguity into which the states would insert themselves by declaring their independence. The District would never have the same aura of invincibility in the minds of Americans or of other inhabitants of the planet.

As he gazed out at his favorite city, he imagined it, as he often did, as the seat of government of the reborn Confederacy. Yes, the states of the Old South would each be independent, but they would be in confederation for their own protection—especially against their former co-nationalists—and the seat of power of that Confederacy would be Atlanta. It would be like the *primus inter pares* status of the pope in Rome, a bishop himself who was recognized as the first among equals.

Abner had already spoken to David Blinder and given him the assurance that his men would do what they had been planning to do: finish the job of having the governors and legislatures of the original eleven Confederate states declare independence. He figured they would be working all day and late into the night.

Abner turned back toward the television. He noticed something amiss. He walked closer to the screen and picked up the remote to increase the volume. Helicopters were swarming over the heads of the SC troops. There must have been a dozen of them. And they were firing down into the regiments.

How could this be? Abner thought. His men were not dressed in any kind of uniform, and their weapons were compact and easily hidden. He stared more closely into the screen. Blinder's men—his men—were dropping like flies.

Anxiety grabbed hold of Abner, who until this moment was completely assured of success. Who are these people? He figured it wasn't regular military; they took time to get themselves on the ground. He looked closely at one of the helicopters that came into view. The occupants were wearing protective gear, but they weren't military. Federal agents! Maybe FBI, CIA, ATF—he didn't know. All he knew was that someone had alerted federal agents too soon.

He saw one of the helicopters start smoking, and he presumed with some relief that the SC men were firing back. But he also noticed that the agents in the wounded helicopter were still firing, even as they were losing altitude.

Their loyalty touched Abner. He didn't like to see people hurt or killed, but he respected the kind of loyalty these men were show-ing. In a silent salute, he raised his glass to them. They would all be dead within minutes.

Abner turned back to his vision for the future. He wanted to call Judith, his lover, but they had been on the outs since events ramped up during the past few weeks. She was with him until bloodshed threatened. Then she not only pulled away from the plan, she pulled away from him. Jumped ship, he thought bitterly. The truth was he didn't really know how she felt about any of this. She made one ambivalent remark, and Abner found himself dismissing her in his mind. He hadn't talked to her since.

Instead, Abner began calling the men in his group who were working the politicians. He wanted to connect with like-minded souls. He dialed the number of the lead man in Alabama.

"How's it going, Jake?" he asked.

Jake Rosner hesitated for just a second. "It's going great, Abner," he replied. "I've spoken to our key supporters, and they are spreading the word. We'll have a declaration by morning."

Abner sighed in relief, but the moment's hesitation was not lost on him. He couldn't help himself. "You were a little hesitant, Jake," he said simply.

The voice on the other end of the line chuckled. "I'm balancing three phone lines here, Abner. Sorry for the split-second delay." Then his voice softened. "Don't worry, Abner. Things are looking really good here."

"Thanks, Jake. Keep me posted."

He felt real relief when he put the phone down. He had not realized just how keyed up he had been.

He continued calling his contacts in the other states, and the responses were all sounding the same.

Morning would bring freedom.

7

From his command center in Virginia, Max watched the video monitors closely. He could see his men expertly taking out SC troops on the ground and generally avoiding taking much fire.

It appeared that the invading group had limited themselves to small arms—AK-47s and the like. They were not precision weapons. The officers in the helicopters, on the other hand, had the latest precision weaponry and the experience and skill to use it.

He was waiting for a call from General Dempsey, the chairman of the Joint Chiefs of Staff, who was with the President last time Max spoke with him. Dempsey was working to get US boots on the ground to clear the capital of the invading forces.

Max's phone rang. "Grabel."

"Max," General Dempsey said. "I see your men and women are doing a good job. Thanks for the rapid response." He hesitated a moment. "But the invaders are surrounding the White House, and we are short-staffed. We need to bring in more troops to clear the area along Pennsylvania Avenue."

Max did not hesitate. "I can direct all officers there right now, if you wish, General," he said.

"Good," said Dempsey. "My troops will be there within an hour or two."

Max grabbed the microphone. "All units converge on the White House lawn," he barked. Even as he was speaking, he could see the

Sikorskys shift course toward that destination. "Damn fine people," he whispered.

As he watched, he saw that some of the helicopters were landing in defensive positions, using the machines themselves for cover and for optimal use of their onboard guns. Others were landing behind them, no doubt in case they had to evacuate White House staff, including the President.

As the copters were landing, the officers were still picking off SC troops. Even the helicopter that went down did not crash: it landed harshly in the middle of an intersection. The men and women inside continued firing as long as they could.

Within ten minutes, however, superior numbers won out, and all the officers in that copter were shot, presumably dead. Heroes to a person, Max thought bitterly.

He grabbed another phone to rustle up more agents and more ways to get them into the District. Meanwhile, small cadres of officers were making their own plans. They brought them to Max for approval.

"Go, go, go," he said in rapid succession, glancing at each plan for just long enough to catch its intent. He needed more personnel in place and soon. "An hour or two" is a long time in a modern urban warfare scenario, and he needed to keep his men in the battle and well equipped.

"Drop supplies in behind the agents at the White House," he radioed to a copter taking off. He was concerned that they would be running short of ammunition.

Agents and officers scattered to do what Max had ordered them to do. Max's eyes were still on the monitors.

He adjusted the angle to give himself a broader view. He saw more SC troops pouring over the Fourteenth Street Bridge. He was trying to estimate how many troops his officers were up against. Hard to tell when they were still entering the District.

He turned to Marybeth Mayer, a tech assistant working the monitors. "Marybeth, look at these men. Try to follow where they are coming from. It's got to be someplace close," he said.

It was only then that Max realized he had taken officers out of their normal security duties at Langley to send them into battle in the District. This awareness hit him at the same time he heard gunfire coming from just outside the CIA headquarters. Shit! he thought.

"Marybeth, forget that. Sound the alarm!"

Everyone in the building knew what the alarm meant and what he or she needed to do. The CIA building was under attack, and every man and woman in the building became a defender. Automatic steel doors shut down all access to and from the outside world. Max unlocked what looked like a file cabinet and withdrew two assault rifles and two handguns. He handed one set to Marybeth. He knew he shouldn't leave his post, but he had to move.

"All units, all units!" he shouted into his microphone. "We are under attack. Stay at your posts in the District. We will get you reinforcements as soon as possible."

Max knew that the White House had its own ammunition stores, and he hoped his agents had access to them.

He turned to Marybeth. "Keep an eye on this and keep me posted if anything—and I mean anything—changes," he said in a voice that was way more aggressive than he intended. He was fond of his tech people and Marybeth in particular, but this was not a time for sentiment.

Max ripped his headset off, grabbed a radio, and started checking the defensive positions. He ran around the perimeter of the building, dodging office personnel who had been trained for this possibility but never, ever expected it to happen. Young men and women were carrying guns they were officially trained to use. Probably not a single one had ever fired a shot in anger or combat. He could not help but notice the fear in their eyes.

"Man your positions," he said every time he encountered a new group of people. And they did just that.

After making the circuit, Max returned to his station at the video monitors.

"They're coming in from different places, Mr. Grabel," Marybeth said. "I can't pinpoint a specific location." The tech was unable to squelch the disappointment in her voice.

"It's okay, Marybeth. We have a situation on our hands right here."

He gazed at the monitors. His mind was racing. He had one helicopter heading toward the White House with supplies. He hoped and prayed it could land.

He called Dempsey. "General," he said. "We are under attack, and the insurgents are sending in reinforcements. Where are your men?!"

"On the way, Max," General Dempsey said. "They will be coming up behind the White House attackers any minute."

Max shifted the camera angle to a broader view and, to his great relief, saw regular US Army units coming up behind the SC troops. He realized with great satisfaction that the no-uniform feint was not working. The Army troops began attacking the insurgents without quarter.

"Thanks, General. Can you spare us some reinforcements?"

"Doing it right now, Max."

Max heard helicopters in the distance. He hoped they were US Army and not SC troops.

He picked up an intercom link. "Hold fire on those copters until we get positive ID," he yelled. He walked to a room with a bulletproof window, picked up a pair of binoculars, and panned the horizon. He saw helicopter gunships with standard US markings, but he wasn't ready to take anything for granted. He yelled back to Marybeth: "Get General Dempsey on the phone to confirm the numbers of those copters."

Marybeth used Max's cell to call the General. He answered and she relayed Max's request. General Dempsey handed the phone to his aide to provide the needed information.

Marybeth typed furiously as she received the tail numbers from Max. At the same time, she was shouting the numbers back to Max for confirmation.

"They're ours!" Max said finally. "All units. The helicopters are ours. I repeat, the helicopters are ours." He thought he could feel relief spread through the facility, but he also thought maybe that was what he was feeling. It was small recompense for the guilt he felt at failing to prevent this attack in the first place.

8

Hundreds of miles to the north of events in Washington, DC, His Eminence Richard Cardinal Levine, Archbishop and Primate of All New England, sat in his private study drumming his fingers against an inlaid mahogany desk. The spacious room was window-less, and access was granted only by special request. Thorough soundproofing made it deathly still in the room, and the locked steel-reinforced door and constant monitoring for electronic sur-veillance made it as secure as could reasonably be expected in an age where privacy was beginning to feel like a historical curiosity. His gaunt, ascetic figure in the sparsely furnished room could have been mistaken for a funereal set piece.

Cardinal Levine was watching disturbing events taking place in Washington, DC—events that were beyond the imagination of the vast majority of American citizens, who could not fathom the concept that the capital of their country could be overrun by discontented but well-organized and well-armed citizen soldiers who were for the most part born and bred in the United States of America.

But that's precisely what was playing out before his eyes on the large flat-screen television. It was not the case that Cardinal Levine was unaware that this might, could, or would happen—in fact, he was privy to the planning for it almost since the beginning. But he perceived his role to be passive, not an active member of any conspiracy. He was, after all, a Roman cleric, and it would be unseemly for him to take an active part in any petty internecine strife. That the Church had been so engaged since Constantine was the Emperor of Rome was not lost on him, however, and he took it as his right and his duty to nudge events along a path that was good for his people, good for the Church to which he was devoted, and good for himself.

Still, his mind was racing as he watched events unfold in the nation's capital. He could not help but recall the early days, when he was first approached by David Blinder, a wealthy financier with definite convictions and plans about the course of their country.

Blinder had laid the groundwork for the meeting with his stock in trade: money. He made substantial donations to the Church in New England, noting how he often spent time in rural Vermont and other parts of the area. So when a request for an audience with the archbishop came politely through the appropriate intermediaries, the Cardinal had no choice but to honor it.

He listened intently as Blinder laid out his vision of a New America, an America where the notion of freedom would be tied to the preservation of basic human values, such as respect for life in all its forms, protection of heterosexual marriage, and an enduring exemption of Church wealth from all taxation. Religious leaders would have a strong presence in civil leadership, and the country could once again rightly be called a Christian nation.

To Levine's mind, these were laudable goals, and David Blinder was a forceful advocate. He was also a man of sufficient means, a prodigious capacity for work, and a total absence of conscience. Cardinal Levine sensed in David Blinder a man perfectly suited to the task he had taken on. The Cardinal approved.

"So it is your intention," the prelate recalled telling him, "to do away with the federal government as it now stands." He thought for a moment as he steepled his fingers over his chest. "And it is your desire to propagate the values our Church holds so dear?"

"Yes, Your Eminence," Blinder replied. "And to do so in such a way as to minimize bloodshed and casualties."

The Cardinal listened intently. He really did not care about casualties or bloodshed; these were the stock-in-trade of radical movements everywhere and always had been. What he cared about was his goal. And he saw no reason to equivocate.

"And what kind of assurance can you give me that the prerogatives of the Church will be protected and expanded as you have described?"

David Blinder did not respond right away. He looked at the Primate, the highest-ranking Catholic clergyman in the United States, and took a deep but barely perceptible breath.

"As you know, Your Eminence, these past years have seen a degradation of the prerogatives of the Church. Your priests have been vilified in the press, your dioceses and religious communities have had their finances devastated by lawsuits, and your freedom to preserve your values in your own institutions has been sharply curtailed." He paused for effect. "If it continues in this fashion—and you and I know that it will unless something substantial changes— your organization will be even more sidelined in a few years. Your voice in national affairs will get smaller and smaller."

Levine believed what Blinder was saying was true. Even as the influence of the Church had grown in many quarters, especially with the influx of Hispanic Catholics, her access to the halls of actual power had narrowed. No one seemed to listen: not the members of Congress she helped get elected, nor the Supreme Court, where six out of the nine judges were Roman Catholic. Not even the great universities that the Church had spawned across the continental US. The Church, the sole guardian of truth on this side of eternity, had seen its stature diminish just in Levine's lifetime. It pained him.

"So why are you sharing this information with me?" he asked.

David Blinder leaned forward in his chair and looked the Cardinal straight in the eyes. "Because there are few organizations in the world with the power, the moral authority, and the resources to equal yours," he said. "And because, while we do not expect you to join us in any way, we do want you not to get in our way."

"As you know, Mr. Blinder, the Church does not concern herself with worldly matters except as they impact the morals and salvation of souls," he said automatically. Even he was finding this bland company line less than compelling or even true. What he really wanted was to further the influence and the reach of the Church that had admittedly taken body blows over the past several decades. He wanted to be assured that the Church would benefit from any new political arrangement on the North American continent. But he knew he had to be careful.

"You understand, Mr. Blinder," he said bluntly, "that this conversation is seditious. One phone call to the authorities would create a serious legal situation for you"—he paused and thought for a moment—"and would no doubt be seen as a demonstration of our loyalty to our beloved country."

Blinder did not respond. He was waiting for the Cardinal to get his threats out of the way so they could proceed with the business he came to do.

"But in the event what you are suggesting occurs at some point," the Cardinal continued dryly, "what will change that will impact us?"

Blinder was ready. "There are certain American traditions that made sense when the country was founded, Your Eminence, but that in this time are restrictive. It is our intention to tear down the so-called separation of church and state and allow emerging countries to promote state-sanctioned churches if they so choose. There could possibly be tax support for all Christian churches, as there is in certain European countries, such as Germany . . ."

He paused for a moment because he noticed the Cardinal's eyebrows rise slightly. At that point, David Blinder knew the rest of the conversation was just formality.

"... and there would be a clear distinction between civil law and ecclesiastical law. The former would apply to the general population, but the latter would apply to clerics and priests under the jurisdiction of the Church. It would be illegal to sue a priest or bishop in civil court. All complaints would be directed to Church courts, where they would be governed by canon law."

The Cardinal's eyebrows did not move, but he took a quick if barely perceptible breath at the prospect of restoring to the Church prerogatives it had not had for centuries and never had in North America.

"And what do you want from me?" the Cardinal asked, keeping his voice as even as possible.

"Precisely nothing, Your Eminence. Neither approval nor disapproval, neither criticism nor support." He paused once again for effect. "What we want is your silence."

Cardinal Levine considered this. He was aware of the risk of agreeing to anything with a man like Blinder. Although it was true he could have called the civil authorities and reported this conversation, his agreed-upon silence would enable Blinder to do exactly the same thing: it would allow him to name the archbishop as a co-conspirator. This gave him pause. Of course, there was no real evidence that the conversation was taking place. . . .

"What you are asking for is not nothing," he said candidly.

"No, it is not, Your Eminence. But I assure you that we are willing to pay handsomely for whatever risks you feel you are taking.

"I know the Church's finances have taken a beating in the last decade because of the scandals. These need to be restored. I have a plan for doing exactly that, so that in another seven years the losses will be a distant memory."

Levine knew of Blinder's reputation as a financial wizard and his previous generosity to the Church. He did not doubt for a moment that Blinder was able to deliver what he was promising. It put the eminence in a difficult position: decline and continue to struggle with the financial and civil tensions in which the Church was presently engaged or agree to do nothing and allow that in a few years many of the current stresses would be resolved. What would be better for the Church?

While he feigned thoughtful consideration of these issues, turning his head away from his visitor as if in serious contemplation, the Cardinal knew immediately what he would do. He understood he could not forgo this generous offer. It was his duty to spread the faith, and by all appearances this was a much more secure path to doing that than declining because of quibbles about temporal politics. And while doing nothing may entail some risk, it was minimal.

He looked up at Blinder. "I want to be informed, discreetly, of course, of events as they unfold. Not the details, mind you, but a sense of the timing of it all."

"Of course, Your Eminence," Blinder replied. He sat back in his chair and looked at the Cardinal once again. "Thank you," he said. "I will be in touch as you requested."

David Blinder stood up, thanked the archbishop once again, and let himself out the steel door.

That was the last time Cardinal Levine saw David Blinder in person. However, he had periodic contact with David's brother, George, who frequented the cathedral when he was in town. The two would often have coffee after mass and catch up. The "catching up" contained vague and coded references to events that David and George were presumably planning together. The archbishop knew never to ask specific questions, and George Blinder knew never to provide specific information. It was a perfectly acceptable cover.

But now that the mayhem was unfolding in the nation's capital, Richard Levine could not help but wonder if this was the right path. There was much more bloodshed than he imagined—or that David Blinder had led him to expect—and he felt real pain at the innocent men and women losing their lives or their health in the violent attack on Washington.

He could not help but wonder if the plan would work. But even if it didn't, he lost little and gained considerable equity for his archdiocese, thanks to the financial plan David Blinder had gifted to the Church.

9

The CNN newsroom was in furious motion all morning. None of the news services foresaw an attack on the nation's capital, and the phones had not stopped ringing: land lines and mobile phones; Skype and Twitter and Facebook were all abuzz.

Matthew Robinson, however, was immobile. He was staring at the screens struggling to report on something no one understood. He had listened to a macabre announcement on Fox News that purported to explain events, but his first reaction was that it was a hoax. How could this be happening? How could this many American citizens organize at this level and stay under the radar? He was perplexed.

He watched the Twitter and Facebook feeds scroll across one of the screens. Lots of profanity, shock, and dismay. That would be a polite description, he thought. He took a deep breath.

It was Robinson's job to write the newscast for the anchors. He wasn't the only one who was doing this, but it was his primary responsibility. For the past hour, the anchors had been winging it. They were trying to be "objective," but many of the women and some of the men were having trouble controlling their emotions of shock, worry, and discouragement.

Mary Wilkinson, the primary anchor for the morning news, walked away from her desk, unable to contain her emotions. That move on her part was itself shocking: the anchors at CNN were hardened professional journalists who did not easily show shock or dismay, at least not on screen, at anything they saw. He figured Mary had just cut her time at CNN short.

If ever there were a time to shine, Matthew thought, it is now. He turned to his computer and started writing.

"In an apparent surprise attack on the nation's capital, hundreds of heavily armed, non-uniformed men flooded into Washington, DC, this morning and started shooting. They are presently surrounding the White House. It is believed that President Barack Obama is still inside, although that cannot be confirmed by CNN at this time."

It sounded bland to him, but it sounded accurate.

"The situation is fluid," he continued writing. "Ten minutes ago, helicopters with federal agents appeared in the sky and began shooting the insurgents, who fired back piecemeal. One helicopter was reportedly shot down."

As he was writing, his words were appearing on the teleprompters of the anchors who were reading the news, and he could hear his words spoken as if the anchors were echoing his thoughts. There was usually more lead time between writing and announcing, but nothing about this day was usual.

Matthew kept his eyes on the screens and media feeds.

"US troops appear to be entering the fray, but rebel troops—and these do appear to be rebellious soldiers—are also getting reinforcements.

"There are also reports from Kentucky that Fort Knox has been bombed," he wrote. "Unconfirmed reports indicate that three massive explosions were heard around the federal depository there, and insurgent troops are storming the building."

Matthew's own stress level was rising precipitously. He waved to his colleague to take over and got up and went to the men's room, where he vomited the light breakfast he had eaten a couple of hours before.

eorge Blinder was feeling pretty good about being out of the fray. It was true that he had talked to his brother from time to time about this whole scheme, but when it came down to it, he felt it was too great a risk to take for an uncertain reward. Yes, if it all went as planned it would enrich them by a factor of ten or more, but he was in his seventies, as was his brother, and it was unclear to him why they needed more money than they already had. In addition, long experience had taught him that such schemes seldom go precisely as planned. The potential for chaos and unforeseen consequences was high.

He was congratulating himself for escaping the family compound shortly before the attack began. He had what he believed to be a simple but effective escape plan: arise early, go for his usual morning bike ride, but divert to public transportation heading away from the area of Wichita Falls, Texas, where his family and his brother David's family lived in secluded splendor. He had carefully arranged his finances and other resources he would need in case David Blinder actually decided to go through with the plan . . . as he had clearly done.

George was on a train when news of the attack broke. He was headed northwest to Canada, where he hoped to escape the notice or the clutches of US authorities for as long as it took to build a case that proved he had no part in the devious schemes of his younger brother. He had carefully collected data over the past few years, providing justification for any action on his part that might have been construed as conspiratorial, and he had been putting money away discretely to support his lifestyle no matter how events turned out.

None of this felt like betrayal to George, although he figured David would take it as such. It felt to George like self-preservation, which was a higher value than cooperating with what was at base a fanatical plot. He loved his brother, but George prided himself on being a practical man. While he recognized that David was the risk-taker, George always felt it was his job to keep the massive resources of the Blinder family safe. And his separation from David during this time was critical to that duty.

As the train lumbered toward the northwest, George was following events via a live stream on his iPad. He was so engrossed in what he was watching that he did not notice the train slow to an unscheduled stop.

When he looked up, he saw armed men, some in uniform and some in suits and ties. They headed straight for him.

"Mr. Blinder," said one of the men in a suit, "you will need to come with us."

George Blinder did not move right away. He looked up at the man and was trying to recall the face that was doing the authoritative talking. He knew he had seen it before.

"I mean now, Mr. Blinder."

Blinder started to move, but slowly. He had been feeling fortunate that he was not intercepted before, but he was prepared to deal with the authorities. "Of course," he said politely.

As he stood up, Agent Keith Anderson slapped handcuffs on his wrists. "Officer," he said, turning to the soldier standing just behind him, "take this man into custody."

"Yes, sir," the officer replied. He grabbed Blinder with more force than George was expecting and led him off the train.

"What's the charge?" Blinder asked.

"Treason," replied Anderson icily.

As he was herded off the train, George remembered where he had seen Anderson's face: he was the man who approached him at the bus station earlier that very morning, when he was embarking on the first leg of his journey. He had pretended to be a fan. George shook his head. He should have known the encounter was not so innocent as it appeared. But George was the trusting member of the Blinder siblings. It was his brother David who suspected everyone, manipulated everyone, and trusted no one.

Not even me, he thought.

For all his surprise at being apprehended, George Blinder was surprised by something else, something internal: he felt relief and safety at being in federal custody. He realized in that moment that he had been much more afraid of David than he acknowledged or even recognized. He knew it was his job to remain silent until he contacted his attorney, and he knew he shouldn't do anything out of the ordinary. But every bone in his body wanted to pat Agent Anderson on the shoulder and thank him.

11

The attack on the White House was not going at all as planned. David Blinder could see this from his Situation Room in Texas. He called Aaron McLaren, the man he'd come to think of as his chief of staff.

"What's going on up there, McLaren?" he demanded.

McLaren knew he was in trouble. "The response was much faster and better organized than we anticipated, Mr. Blinder," he said. "They're bringing in reinforcements."

"I can see that, McLaren," Blinder fumed. "Can we get the President?"

"Our forces are bearing down on the White House. The defenses there are thin, as we anticipated, but they are being reinforced by helicopters. Also, it looks like we're being attacked from the rear. Our forces may be pinned down soon."

"What about the MOAB?" Blinder said.

McLaren hesitated for a moment. "We can try, sir," he said simply.

This did not sound like a ringing endorsement to Blinder. "What do you mean, 'we can try'?"

"I mean, if we can get it here we can use it, but we'll lose a lot of our own men in the process. . . ."

"What do you mean, 'if we can get it here'?" Blinder demanded.

"Mr. Blinder, we did not anticipate so many helicopters being so rapidly deployed in the defense. That's not in any manual or procedure. We've taken a lot of losses."

Blinder was silent for a moment as he tried to get his rage under control. He hated incompetence in all its forms, and McLaren was acting like an incompetent.

"You make sure that bomb gets airborne and flattens the White House," he yelled into the phone, "or you'll pay the price for failure."

McLaren clicked off. He had no doubt about what Blinder meant. He was running the maneuvers from a mobile command center just inside the District near the Roosevelt Bridge. He had converted an RV for just this purpose and had spent months placing small wireless webcams strategically throughout the District. He had a bird's-eye view of the battle as it was unfolding, and he did not like what he saw.

Nonetheless, an order was an order. He picked up his mobile phone and pushed a speed-dial number. The phone was answered on the first ring.

"What's the status of the bomb?"

The voice on the other end of the line did not hesitate. "It's ready to go, sir."

McLaren took a deep breath. He had misgivings about destroying the White House. It seemed that would be the point of no return. After that, any leniency in the face of failure would vanish. But this was the course to which he had committed himself, so he put that qualm aside.

His more immediate concern was the presence of those damned helicopters and the overall air superiority of the federal forces. "Okay," he said with less authority than he wanted. "Wheels up."

"Yes, sir," came the terse reply.

One hundred and sixty miles northwest of Washington, DC, a refurbished World War II–era P-51 took off from a deserted airfield near the small town of Westernport, Maryland. It had been outfitted to carry a single piece of ordnance, one of the MOABs similar to the ones used to such good effect in Kentucky.

There was nothing understated about the MOAB. Its force was horrific: the twenty-one-thousand-pound bomb could flatten even a large building in an instant, once it was detonated in the air overhead. Its precision guidance system reflected the latest targeting technology.

The weight of the bomb was a problem, particularly when the insurgents were attempting to target the White House in a stealthy way. They had designed the P-51 to carry this single weapon and had equipped the cockpit with all necessary computer technology. To make room for the bomb, every extraneous piece of equipment had to be removed. This was Aaron McLaren's specialty, and he was proud of what he had been able to accomplish.

He knew the P-51 was up to the task, but it required an element of surprise. The initial plan was to attack the White House first and then proceed with the invasion, but it was determined that the symbolic effect of destroying the White House might alienate large segments of the population to the whole insurgent enterprise. So it was decided to use it only as a last resort.

From where McLaren was sitting, it looked as if the time for a last resort move had come. Bombing the White House would destroy the troops defending it and enable the SC troops to consolidate a line against their attackers from the rear. They would then be joined by reinforcements to create a pincer movement against the US Army. Made sense.

Still, he had misgivings about the ability of the P-51 to get to its destination. It would take about twenty minutes to reach its target. McLaren wondered if that was enough time for the defenders to notice.

He put these thoughts out of his mind. The decision was made, and he was committed to the bombing. He turned his attention to his monitors and started planning for the countermoves he would make once the White House was no more.

12

Across the country, among the windswept peaks of Wyoming, Adam Wilson was contemplating his next move. He had at his disposal a cadre of highly intelligent, well-connected, and accomplished professional men who had pulled out of their elevated positions in academia, business, and government in an attempt to weaken the chain of command as well and sow a sense of uncertainty within the federal bureaucracy.

Since the attack on Washington, they had been busy reconnecting with their colleagues, friends, and contacts in an effort to elevate the sense of danger and emphasize the imminent collapse of the federal government. They did this via an elaborate data network that spanned the globe, making detection difficult. Personally communicated, dire warnings coming from normally cool heads had a disproportionately sobering impact on all who heard them, and these efforts were beginning to make themselves felt, at least from the vantage point of an isolated community in rural Wyoming.

These men had disconnected themselves completely from normal society to go off the grid. They had taken their assets, their families, and their exalted selves to an abandoned mine in rural Wyoming, about a hundred miles west of Casper. There, in a collection of caves and ramshackle buildings, they were able to keep themselves fed, protected from the elements, and faithful to their daily prayer rituals.

This group of devout evangelicals felt a sense of mission that enabled them to place themselves, their families, and their wealth at risk in an effort to reshape the United States into the religious oligarchy for which they longed. To a man, they believed that secular society no longer allowed for the primacy of the Christian worldview, and they were compelled by that view to take whatever steps necessary to redirect the energy and the policies of the country they loved but found wanting.

Wilson regarded all these developments with a mixture of feelings. He openly identified with all of the devout men whom he had engaged in this dramatic enterprise, but only he was privy to the long conversations he'd had with David Blinder over the previous several years. It was during those conversations that Blinder convinced him that the right wing of the evangelical movement was endangered and that, unless major political changes took place, their views, their beliefs, their values were at risk of extinction. Blinder also convinced Wilson that there were sufficient numbers of disgruntled evangelicals to provide him with a viable network.

Wilson was not temperamentally religious. He married into a devout family, however—one with means and very clear expectations. For the most part, he found these unobjectionable. He attended church services weekly and did some perfunctory work on committees where he could be seen and network with other ambitious professional men and women. He was not unsympathetic to the beliefs of his church or his fellow churchgoers, but not once did he consider changing his personal behavior or tactics because of the values of someone else.

Blinder had approached him when Wilson was feeling the first stirrings of boredom and entrapment by the life he chose. He found the church attendance and the singing and the vacuous ramblings of the minister grating on his otherwise sharply developed intellect. He was just beginning to feel resentment about the strictures he had placed on his public persona.

So when he was contacted by David Blinder, he found a whole new reason to not only reenergize his commitment to his religious fellows but also deepen his ties to them. He emerged as a leader, one of the elders of his church and one of the delegates to larger national conventions. He found this new avenue to notoriety stimulating.

And he found Blinder's promise of riches even more beguiling. Wilson was a successful man, but his success required him to work at his duties at Georgetown University, where he taught in the Economics Department. Blinder made it clear to Wilson that, if he cooperated with the plan to take down the federal government, he would no longer need to do any work to sustain his lifestyle. He could do as he pleased.

This was a magical concept to Wilson, whose complete lack of scruples was something he prized. Other men, especially deeply religious men, found making hard decisions daunting. Not Wilson. When George Keenan, a key member of his group, was unable to convince his wife to go along with him, Wilson had no problem ordering his execution and dismemberment, both to punish him and to make his protest an example to the others he had gathered together. And he was skilled at masking his own role in the murder, such that he could feign the same shock and horror that others honestly experienced. He felt pride in his ability to do this.

As far as the bloodshed in the nation's capital, Adam Wilson felt nothing. His major concern was the success of the mission. He had a lot riding on it. At the same time, he had built in trapdoors for himself in the event that things did not work out as planned. He could return to his former life with plausible explanations of his absence and resume his life until another opportunity came along. . Adam Wilson did not lack self-confidence.

But just now he was assessing the odds of success of the mission at hand. He walked over to a table where Aloysius Smitherin had just hung up on one of his contacts.

"How's it going, Al?"

"Good," Smitherin replied. "I think my colleagues back home are getting the message that this is not just a passing thing, that this is the real deal." He smiled, but wanly. Wilson couldn't discern whether he was genuinely happy or if he was having conflicted feelings.

"It will be over soon," Wilson said soothingly. "Let me know if there is anything I can do."

Smitherin nodded. Then he turned to his phone and dialed another number from a list on the table.

Wilson listened intently as he walked slowly away. He could detect no ambivalence in Smitherin's voice on the phone, so he had to assume that Al was probably just getting tired. Momentous events wear people out, he thought.

He checked in with the others before heading back to his own cabin, where he was to call David Blinder and report the group's status. He felt he could give a solid accounting of the work of the men on his team.

13

Captain Dan Weeks was piloting one of the attack helicopters converging on the CIA facility at Langley for its defense. He was strafing the ground, where hundreds of jeans-and-T-shirt-wearing men were firing into the building. He watched disinterestedly as the men he shot fell to the ground. Dead, he hoped.

He was turning for another pass when, out of the corner of his eye, he noticed a nonmilitary plane just enter his horizon. He signaled a break-off to his commander and radioed his base with the sighting. Airspace around the District had been restricted ever since 9/11, and Weeks knew that a lone plane flying at a low rate of speed was probably trouble. He hit the throttle of his Apache AH-64 and headed toward the small plane, which seemed to be picking up speed as he got closer.

He was getting mixed signals from the ground, as they were trying to identify the peculiar object. There was a pause as Weeks worked to shorten the gap between the unknown aircraft and his own, allowing him to use his Stinger missiles. Then suddenly: "Command override," crackled the voice on his radio. "Engage unidentified aircraft."

That's all Dan Weeks had to hear. A second later, he fired two Stingers directly at the lumbering P-51. He recognized the plane as soon as he had closer visual contact. His father flew them in World War II. He saw it for three seconds before it exploded in flames, but that was enough for Captain Weeks to know that he had made the right decision.

The size of the fireball surprised him, and he pulled back hard on the joystick and banked upward and to the south. For a few terrifying seconds, he wasn't sure he could get out of the way of the massive explosion. He pushed his machine up higher both to get away from the explosion and to survey the damage on the ground.

What he saw astonished him. Where the Roosevelt Bridge had stood for decades, now only one broken piece stood on the south side of the Potomac peeking out of the huge cloud of dust and smoke. Roosevelt Island itself was in flames.

Weeks radioed this information to his commanding officer. That old plane was clearly carrying a massive weapon, perhaps a MOAB.

"Your orders are to reengage at CIA headquarters," the radio crackled back.

"Reengaging," was all Dan Weeks had to say. His focus had never been so sharp.

14

The same could not be said of the unfortunate Aaron McLaren, whose converted RV mobile command center was vaporized along with the late Mr. McLaren milliseconds after the plane above him exploded.

David Blinder was looking at the television when the P-51 exploded. He reflexively reached for the phone and dialed McLaren's number. Nothing. He took a deep breath; he realized immediately what had happened. This was an unforeseen and highly unfortunate turn of events, but Blinder was also thinking how he could turn it to his advantage. It did not take him long.

He dialed Bellamy in Georgia.

"Abner," he said when Bellamy answered on the first ring. "We're done in DC. It's up to you and your men now. You have the fate of the new nations in your hands."

"I understand," Bellamy said solemnly. "By morning, the Confederacy will be reborn."

This assured response immediately lifted Blinder's spirits. "I knew I could count on you, Abner."

Blinder then turned to the live feeds from the capital. He had no real way to contact the men on the ground, and in fact he did not want to. They had served their purpose. Perhaps someday they would be recognized as the martyrs of the New Confederacy or the new American arrangement or whatever history would dub this reworking of North America.

He watched as regular US Army troops surrounded and shot or arrested the remaining SC troops in the District. He saw several try to get away, but the Army cordon was tight. They weren't being polite police officers; these people were the enemy who had attacked their country, and they didn't care how many of them they shot or killed.

Such are the wages of armed conflict, Blinder thought to himself. Right now he had to rely on Adam Wilson and Abner Bellamy to carry out the more important part of his plan: to convince state political leaders to do what they wanted to do, declare their independence from the federal bureaucracy in Washington, DC.

There was one loose end that he had to tie up. He called Winslow Parker in Kentucky.

"Report in."

"We're loading the gold as we speak."

Ahh, Blinder thought. While the world was watching the mayhem in the capital, we stole their gold right out from under them and deprived them of a very significant symbol of federal power. He was calculating the impact this symbolic and very real victory would have on the work of convincing the politicians to join the crusade.

"Keep me posted," Blinder said. And he hung up.

15

I t was later said that almost no one slept in America that night. Television coverage did not take its relentless eye off the events in DC and then in Kentucky. The Internet exploded with reactions to the shocking events and reactions to the reactions. The results were surprisingly mixed but, upon reflection, predictable. From the far right: The wages of sin! The wrath of God! Punishment for straying! And there was a subtext: Maybe this isn't a bad thing. From the far left: A cataclysm has struck the US. War on American soil! From the middle: Pray for our country.

Groups of secessionists came out of the closet and paraded their cause in many rural areas of the country. A state of emergency was declared in the capital, and all major cities were on high alert. The President was to address the nation at noon Eastern time.

But it was in select state capitals where the action was hottest. Across the states of the Old South the activity was particularly intense. Pro-secession legislators were persuading, cajoling, and threatening their colleagues to get them to support declarations of secession.

"It is our right, it is our heritage, it is our duty," came the constant refrain from the secessionist members of Bellamy's group. "It is now or never."

The anguish felt by many legislators was real. They loved their state. They loved their country. They loved America. And they could see that this door, long closed, would be open for only a short while. They knew they did not have time to dither. As the night wore on, the prospect of doing the unspeakable came to seem more and more realistic, then more acceptable, and then more likely. Lawmakers were being blown about by a hurricane of escalating rhetoric that few could withstand.

As dawn broke over the low country of Georgia, state legislators in Atlanta were scheduling votes on the issue. Instantaneous communication among states made this feel like the effort was not confined to a single stray geographic area; it took on regional momentum. The fact that similar events were happening in Texas and Oklahoma and along the West Coast added to the momentum and to the sense of inevitability.

Congressional delegations from the Southern states to the federal Congress tried to leave Washington as soon as they could. They did not wish to participate in any efforts to stop what was happening across the South; nor did they wish to contribute to a quorum in their respective august bodies. For many of them, recent events were not a complete surprise. These were men and women who remained loyal to their constituents.

Departure plans were interrupted, however, by the iron-clad lockdown of the District. As US Army troops mopped up the insurgents, no motor traffic or any unofficial, nonmilitary transportation was allowed. All who protested were threatened with being detained; and if they continued to protest, they were arrested. Members of Congress were not exempt.

The governors of states contemplating secession contacted their federal congressmen with instructions to return home at the earliest opportunity. Few were able to comply the day after the initial assault.

In the White House, a grim Barack Obama listened intently to each update. He was surrounded by his closest advisors. After hearing more about what was happening in the state legislatures, he turned to the men and women around him.

"So," he began, with acid in his tone, "what are our options?"

A moment of silence before anyone spoke. Then Joe Biden, who was as traumatized by events as anyone, spoke up. "We can nationalize all state militias," he said. "And we can have them occupy the governors' mansions and the State Assemblies of any state that threatens to secede."

More silence. George Dempsey spoke next. He was not subtle. "You don't think the rebels have planned for that?" he asked accusingly. "We are hearing reports of legislatures across the South and in other parts of the country moving towards votes on secession even now." He paused a moment. "This was carefully planned, and I've never seen anything like it. I've never even thought about anything like it."

Valerie Escapan spoke next. "I say we contact all the attorneys general in all the states and give them the responsibility for preventing secessionist acts." She looked the President squarely in the eye. "They are homegrown politicians; they won't trigger as much animosity, and it won't look so much like the federal government is going to invade individual states." She glanced over at Dempsey. "And the fact is they have a legal and a moral obligation to protect federal interests." She glanced down at the floor for a moment. "And it may give us a little more time."

The President looked around the room. A few heads were nodding. Biden was the first to speak.

"She's got a point," he said simply. "I think this is a good place to begin."

"If the attorneys general are not in custody," interrupted Dempsey. "I think whoever planned this has considered every angle."

The President thought for a while. "That may be, General," he said. "But we have to start somewhere. And I agree with Valerie that a heavy-handed military response now would only work to the insurgents' advantage." He paused for a moment. "Besides, we can always do that."

He turned to Valerie. "Make the calls," he said. "And keep me posted."

cKenzie Phillips, the governor of Georgia, was talking to Hugh
Lewins, the Speaker of the Georgia House of Representatives,
and to Jake McCauley, the lieutenant governor and president
of the Senate, about the upcoming vote on the secession issue. He
was pleased that getting the vote to the floor had gone so easily. It
was 6:30 a.m. the day after the invasion of Washington, DC. The
legislature had been in session all night.

"Hugh," he said. "What are our chances?"

Hugh Lewins thought for a moment. "I think they're good,
Governor," he said. "There are a lot of squawking hotheads, mostly
liberal Democrats, who think this is just outrageous. But I think
most of them aren't from here."

Phillips nodded. He knew the expression "not from here"
meant "not one of us."

"What about the Senate, Jake?" asked Phillips, turning to his
lieutenant governor.

Jake McCauley paused for a moment. A levelheaded man in
his sixties, he had been part of numerous legislative battles. After
some time, he turned to face Phillips head-on. "I think it's going
to be close," he said at length. "Members of my party aren't all
convinced."

Phillips bristled, but silently. He understood that McCauley
was from the other party, as Georgia state law allowed, but that

section of the Georgia constitution and the man sitting in his office were both a pain in the neck. If the lieutenant governor were a good Republican, he would be on the right side.

Outwardly, he gave McCauley a hard look. "I want you to make this happen, Jake," he said in a voice that was low but unmistakably threatening. "And I want you to make it happen today."

McCauley nodded that he understood, and then he got up and walked out of the room.

Phillips turned to Lewins at the moment the heavy mahogany door closed. "What do you think, Hugh?"

"I think our friend from across the aisle has his own ideas."

The Governor thought for a moment. "I think you may be right. We have a plan for that." He looked at Lewins and smiled. "We live in interesting times."

"Yes, we do, Governor," Lewins said. He looked at his watch. "I've got some work to do. I'll be in touch." He got up, shook the Governor's hand, and walked out the door.

McKenzie Phillips was not a violent man. But he was a loyal one, and he had made a promise to his friend Abner Bellamy that he would make the secession vote happen and that the outcome would be in the direction Bellamy wanted. And he was sure he wasn't going to allow some hothead minority voices from the other political party to stand in the way.

For his part, Jake McCauley had no illusions about what was going on in the General Assembly; nor did he doubt for a minute that there was a conspiracy going on around him. He witnessed the strong-arming of his colleagues, and it was clear in his mind that the governor of the state of Georgia had just threatened him. What he wasn't so clear about was precisely what the conspiracy was shooting for. Did they really think they could browbeat the legislature into pulling out of the United States? Did they really believe they had a legal right to do that? The thought seemed preposterous on its face. But, he had to admit, so were the events that had transpired the day before in the nation's capital.

Jake McCauley was not a man who scared easily. Nor was he inexperienced in matters of Georgia politics. He knew that supporting secession from the Union was almost a condition of being part of the political elite in this state—something that politicians paid lip service to but which most of them did not take too seriously. McCauley saw the talk as dangerous and the prospect as ruinous for the citizens of Georgia as well as the citizens of the greater United States.

Instead of going to his office, McCauley headed for the office of Mary McDonald, the minority leader in the Georgia House of Representatives. He found her talking to Jackson Williams, the Republican floor leader of the House.

McCauley and McDonald had known each other for years and agreed on almost all major issues. That was not hard in Georgia, as the longstanding Republican majority in both houses provided the Democrats with clear if largely insignificant voices.

As McCauley was ushered into McDonald's office, he was at first surprised to see Williams there. He and Williams also knew each other, but they rarely collaborated on political matters. They were, after all, from different chambers and different parties. In addition, it was Williams's job to push the governor's agenda through the House, a task that he always appeared to relish.

This morning, however, Jackson Williams wasn't pushing anything. He was pale, and his skin glistened with sweat. Mary McDonald motioned for Jake to take a seat next to Jackson on the couch. She sat on one of the wing chairs facing the two men.

Because of the unexpected presence of Williams, Jake thought it better to wait for Mary to start. Before she did so, however, she reached into her purse and pulled out an odd-looking gadget that Jake had never seen before. She leaned over and plugged the cord into a wall socket. A soft humming noise could be heard throughout the large office.

"It's an anti-bugging machine," she explained to Jake. "It will ensure us a measure of privacy while we talk."

The fact that Mary thought she needed such a device said a lot to Jake. He knew her to be a serious woman who was not prone to exaggeration or paranoia. He nodded.

Williams, on the other hand, had a stronger reaction. He looked at the device as if it would explode; then he looked back at Mary. He started breathing more heavily, and his already moist skin grew clammier. His voice shook.

"How do you know your office is being bugged?" he asked McDonald.

Mary didn't respond right away. She didn't look at either of the men before she answered, and when she did her voice was soft, even nurturing. After a few minutes, she looked directly at Williams. "I don't know that for sure, Jackson," she said. "It's just that things are going on here that are unusual and serious. We need to take extra precautions."

Jackson's breathing moderated a little, and he seemed to be responding to the warmth in his colleague's voice.

Mary began again. "I'd like you to share with Jake what you told me a little while ago."

Jackson looked down at his sweaty, trembling hands. Every partisan rule he had ever followed, every contentious statement he had ever made, every bone in his Republican body fought against what he was about to say.

He looked up at his colleagues, first one and then the other. Then he took a deep breath and began speaking—slowly at first, as he struggled to get his voice under control.

"I met with the Governor a few hours ago. I went to his office to ask for direction in the discussion that the House Speaker had allowed on the floor." He paused for a moment and looked again at his colleagues, as if pleading for their understanding. Mary nodded slightly. Jackson continued. "What he told me shook me to my boots."

Jake leaned slightly in Jackson's direction, both to provide some sign of emotional support and to make sure he heard what Jackson was about to say without distortion.

Jackson continued. "The Governor told me that he was counting on me to push through the vote for secession no matter what and to secure passage of that vote in the affirmative. No matter what."

Mary did not take her eyes off Jackson. He returned her gaze. She nodded slightly once again, and he continued. "Then he told me that Georgia was going to secede even if the vote failed. He said that he was going to issue a declaration of independence for the State of Georgia, no matter what the General Assembly did."

Jackson stopped and took several sharp, deep breaths. "I've never seen Phillips like this. He was angry. He was acting like he owned the legislature and the state. . . ."

"What else did he say to you, Jackson," Mary said gently.

"He said . . . he said . . . he said he would use any means, including violence and open warfare, to support what the Sovereign Citizens began in Washington, DC, yesterday." He paused for another breath. "He did not mention the state militia directly, but his reference to 'open warfare' meant, at least to me, that he was thinking of calling up the militia." His breathing picked up. "He wants to break up the United States, and he's willing to use any means to do it. Why, he wants to be a dictator in Georgia!"

Jake tried to be as comforting as he could in light of Jackson's precarious physical and mental state. "Jackson, how did you respond to him? What did you say?"

Jackson didn't hesitate to answer. "I didn't know what to say. I nodded and left the room. That's what I usually do when I get instructions from the Governor about his agenda. It's my job to just go do whatever he wants done. . . . But this time, I couldn't. I thought what happened yesterday was a terrible, frightening thing. I love my country. I will not participate in breaking up the United States of America." He stared without shaking at his two colleagues. "And I sure as hell won't be part of crowning that traitor a dictator!"

There was silence in the room for several minutes. Jake was absorbing the new dimensions to what had just been a political problem a few moments before. Now it was a legal and possibly a military problem as well. He turned his attention back to Williams.

"You're friends with Attorney General Mercer Willoughby, aren't you?"

"Yes, sir, I am," Williams replied. "We were in law school together. And we've kept up since then. Our families have been friends since he became the attorney general and moved to Atlanta."

"Have you told him about this?"

Jackson paused a moment and thought. He knew the answer to Jake's question, but he wanted to convey his intentions as clearly as possible. "No, I haven't. I've been making my rounds. I wanted to find out where you people were before I contacted him. And I've got to say, members of my party are torn about this. As evil and as ponderous as this sounds, what happened in DC yesterday shook many of them to the core, and a lot of them are seriously considering voting for secession. The fact that it got to the floor at all is unbelievable.

"So I especially wanted to get a sense of where you guys stood before I spoke with him. And I want to know who I can count on if I need support." He paused for a moment. "And it looks as if I am going to need support anywhere I can find it."

Williams let out a long breath. He appeared to be unwinding, to be rising up to his typical, commanding self. "It's looking a lot like this thing will pass," he said in a low voice. "I think we're going to need all the help we can get. And after seeing the Governor's intentions . . . I just need to know if I can count on your support to put a stop to this."

Jake's face did not change expression, but his mind was reeling. He had always thought of Jackson Williams as the Governor's attack dog, willing to do anything for the man and for the party. The notion that Williams might have a mind of his own was a new piece of data for him. He wasn't sure what to make of it. Plus, it wasn't lost on anyone in the room that the attack dog for the Republican administration asking minority Democrats for support was a sign of desperation.

Jake spoke first. "If you're talking about opposing secession, you can certainly count on that. I think it would be suicide for the state and for the country. All that talk and bravado is just so much sentimental hogwash. A lot has happened in the years since the War Between the States, and you and I and everyone in these chambers know it. And most of what has happened has been good for Georgia and good for the country. This secessionist business is lunacy."

Mary interrupted. "But it's well-planned lunacy, Jake," she said softly. "And we need to have more than just a few votes to stop Phillips from doing what he's planning to do."

Jake listened intently and nodded his head. He was sure Mary was right, but politics was his bailiwick. He never saw himself as part of any resistance movement. He was at a loss.

Jackson spoke up. "I'm headed over to talk to Mercer now. Honestly, I don't know where he is in this business, but I'm counting on the fact that he's a thoughtful man who would not risk himself or his family to be part of some fanatic group." He paused a moment and looked away. "But this is going to take more than some arm twisting."

Jake straightened up on the couch, and he looked directly into Williams's eyes. "Look, Jackson, I want you to know how much I appreciate your putting partisan politics on hold and sharing this with us. I assure you I will hold it in absolute confidence as long as I can. I also want to assure you that I will work with you and anybody else who is willing to nip this lunacy in the bud."

Williams nodded. "Thanks, Jake," he said. "I think we're going to need to work very closely on this." Then he nodded to Mary. "Ma'am," he said, and then he left.

17

As dawn was breaking, Valerie Escapan was hanging up with Mercer Willoughby, the attorney general of Georgia. She had spoken to all the Southern AGs throughout the night. It took convincing to alert them to the fact that their states were considering secession. Valerie could tell some were feigning indignation and some were genuinely indignant. Some remained incredulous. But all knew that a call from the White House in the wake of the invasion of the District commanded undivided attention.

Valerie had a sheet of paper in front of her. On it were the names of the eleven men she had spoken with. Next to each was a plus, minus, or question mark reflecting her intuitive assessment of their loyalties. She knew this was not the kind of thing that would fly in a meeting of the National Security Council, but it was something she needed to do to get her emotional and psychological feet on the ground. She trusted her instincts, even if she often had to find data to support them.

She felt good about her conversation with Willoughby. She had met him once at a conference of attorneys general that was held in Washington a few years before. She liked him immediately. He seemed like a bright, thoughtful, no-nonsense kind of guy. Just the kind of person Valerie admired.

It turned out that Willoughby was as shocked as anyone to be informed that there was a larger plot going on and that the attack on the District was just the first step. He thought maybe more military action would follow, but he was astonished to learn that his state, as well as a lot of other states, was seriously considering seceding from the Union. It took a while for him to wrap his mind around this.

"Let me get this straight, Ms. Escapan," he said after she presented him with the situation. "You mean to tell me that legislatures in my state and other states are actually considering withdrawing from the Union and that this attack was basically a signal for that process to start as well as a diversion from the real agenda?"

"That's correct, Mr. Willoughby."

"And this has been transpiring right under the nose of the attorney general of the state, whose office is a hundred feet from the capitol building?"

"I presume so, Mr. Willoughby."

Valerie could hear Willoughby exhaling slowly. He must be trying to catch his breath in the face of breathtaking news, she thought.

"What do you want me to do, Ms. Escapan?"

"I want you to use any legal means at your disposal to invalidate any decree of secession that may arise out of the General Assembly or from the Governor's office," she replied. "If you can, make sure that the Governor does not call up the National Guard, and if he does, make sure that the state militia is under federal control. We will nationalize the militia of any state that elects secession."

There was a long pause on the other end of the phone. "That's a tall order, Ms. Escapan."

"These are demanding times, Mr. Willoughby."

There was a moment of silence on the line.

"I will do whatever I can to help with this, Ms. Escapan," came a subdued response.

"Thank you, Mr. Willoughby," Valerie said before she hung up the phone.

It took Mercer Willoughby some moments to return the phone to its cradle. He was trying to digest what Valerie Escapan had told him, and he found himself a little skeptical. Could this really be happening? Is our country so far gone that fanatics can get close to breaking up the Union? He shook his head and finally returned the phone to its resting place.

Then he turned to look out the window at the burgeoning Georgia sunshine. He loved Georgia. He was born here, went to school here, and worked and lived here. He never wanted to live anywhere else. His wife of seventeen years was also a native Georgian who felt the same way. Both knew that Georgia had become something of a magnet for people looking for work, especially younger people right out of school. It never occurred to either of them not to welcome new people to their state and to make them feel at home. Georgia was a welcoming place. He had trouble fathoming why anyone would want to change that.

As a Southerner, Willoughby also knew about the militaristic undertones of his culture. The War Between the States was a holy legend in this state, which suffered more than most during that war. There was lingering resentment, even after a century and a half had passed. But this is not the Balkans, he thought; this is not a place where ancient enmities impacted life in the present. Like most open-minded people, Willoughby thought people could think what they wanted, but the flourishing of the state, especially in recent decades, was proof enough that old antagonisms were best left behind.

Willoughby had some work to do. He called his assistants and roused them out of bed, instructing them to meet him in his office in forty minutes. In the meantime, he made a list of legal cases to review with an eye toward putting his finger on those powers he could call on to stop this thing from growing.

He thought of the Governor. He had never liked McKenzie Phillips personally and thought he was a vain and power-hungry pol. But he respected the man's intelligence and drive, and he liked the way Phillips worked for the good of the whole state. He had some trouble believing that Phillips would be part of any conspiracy. But that was a rational assessment. In his heart it wasn't hard to imagine at all.

The phone rang and interrupted his thoughts. It was Jackson Williams.

"Mercer," Jackson began. "I need to talk to you."

"I imagine you do," said Willoughby.

"When can we meet?" asked Williams.

"I'll be in my office in twenty minutes," said Willoughby. He figured if Williams was calling him at this hour, he knew what was happening and wanted to do something about it. Willoughby liked Williams, and he figured he was on the right side of the issue.

"I'll be there."

18

Across town, Judith Mayfield was beside herself. She and Abner Bellamy had been lovers for several years, and a big part of their connection was that they were both from Georgia, a state they both loved and longed to return to when they met in the Midwest. They shared an inordinate love of the South, and both had been raised in a web of nostalgia for the Old South, the Confederacy, or at least the antebellum Southern culture, so idealized in the hearts and minds of their extended families. In time they both managed to make it back to Georgia, even though their careers were separate. Abner decided he wanted to be close to the action he knew was about to unfold, and Judith had found employment with a busy medical practice.

Judith was an internist who had considered an academic career at Washington University in St. Louis, where she met Abner, but a year of academia reminded her of how much she hated being in the classroom and how much she loved taking care of people. That experience convinced her once and for all that helping people was her true calling.

That innocent decision had consequences. Where she had been generally supportive of Abner's plans for secession—and she was privy to them—it gradually became clear that considerable bloodshed would be involved. As this awareness dawned on her, her automatic support began to evaporate. She was having trouble tolerating the dissonance between her career of helping people heal and taking care of themselves on the one hand and inflicting wanton carnage on them on the other. The intensity of her response surprised even her.

"I'm not sure I can be part of this, honey," she said to him one evening over dinner at her condo. "I can't stomach violence in almost any form."

At the time Abner shrugged, seeming to dismiss her concerns. She had known him long enough to understand that whatever was of concern to her paled in comparison to what preoccupied him. He may not even have heard her.

Judith and Abner were not officially broken up, but he hadn't called since their last conversation weeks ago. He used to call daily. There was something about the tone of his voice the last time they spoke, when Judith once again expressed ambivalence about violence, that signaled something ominous, something more than passing dissatisfaction. And Judith knew Abner to be a demanding, brook-no-opposition type. It did not surprise her when her phone stopped ringing. She wondered if the relationship was truly over, if Abner was just sulking, or if he just had other things to do.

The longer the hiatus lasted, the more Judith began thinking about her complicity in Abner's plans and the possible legal and ethical issues involved. She went through her email and text messages to determine if there was anything in them that would be actionable from a legal point of view. This was guesswork on her part, since her knowledge of the law was limited, but she thought she should take what precautions she could. And it gave her something to focus on beyond Abner's absence.

That was a few weeks ago. Now she was sitting in her Atlanta condominium staring at the television screen, as she was sure the entire country was doing, feeling aghast at what was transpiring.

How could I have been so blind? How could I have encouraged Abner to get involved in this? She wasn't precisely sure what Abner's role was, but he led her to believe that it was central to efforts at secession. In all fairness to herself, she did not know until the last days of her relationship with him that bloodshed would be involved. It was then that she found herself backing away, inwardly at first, and then directly with Abner.

"I didn't realize you were planning violence," she recalled saying to Abner during one of their last conversations.

"There would be no victory without an armed struggle," Abner had said. "We can't do it without at least the threat of violence."

Judith was quiet for a time. She looked out the window of their bedroom, where the couple lay in familiar, postcoital warmth. Then she turned to look Abner directly in the face.

"Abner, honey," she said softy. "Don't do this. Fight for what you believe in, but don't hurt people. Don't kill them." Abner did not look at her. He turned to look at the wall on the other side of the room, as if he were trying to recall something he misplaced.

"I thought you were on board," he said in a distinctly chilly voice.

"I believe in the cause, Abner, not the methods you're telling me about."

Abner got up, slipped into his shorts, and walked into the bathroom. He mumbled something that Judith could barely make out. She thought part of it was "great deeds demand great sacrifice."

Moments later, he nodded good-bye and walked out of her condo. She had not heard from him since.

Judith Mayfield was not a weak woman. She did not pine for Abner so much as she missed his witty Southern ways. He was charming and funny and could make her laugh at any time. He was bright as hell and knew it, and his confidence affirmed Judith's belief in her own capabilities. In many ways, it was a meeting of equals. In Judith's estimation, that was a rare find in intimate bonding experiences.

She refused to call him. Part of this was tactical: if she did come to the attention of authorities, she could demonstrate that she had had no contact with Abner for weeks prior to the disturbing events that began the day before. Another part of it was simple pride. If he doesn't want to be with me, okay. That's his choice. I will do what I've always done. I will get on with my life.

And getting on with her life in Georgia was so much easier to do than in any other place she had ever been. She loved almost everything about her state: the warmth, the farms, the scenery, the people, and the capital city where she now lived. As she gazed out the window, the resplendent Georgia sunshine contrasted sharply with the dark images flashing across her television screen. She sighed deeply, shook herself into the present, and got ready for work. As far as she could see, Georgia would remain her home for the rest of her life, no matter what.

ercer Willoughby was in his office when Jackson Williams arrived precisely twenty minutes after he hung up from their last conversation. Williams would have come earlier because he figured Willoughby would have been there, but he also knew that Mercer Willoughby was a fastidious man who liked to do things on precise schedules. Plus, Mercer made no secret of the fact that he cherished time when he could arrive in a room and get organized before dealing with troublesome human beings. Today Jackson Williams felt like a troublesome human being.

"Good morning, Mercer," he said politely as he entered his office. He walked past Janice Templeton, Willoughby's secretary, who had arrived even sooner than her boss, so sure was she that he would be in the office early. He walked into Willoughby's office and closed the door.

Mercer nodded and gestured to the seat in front of his desk. If Jackson had felt flustered when he was in Mary McDonald's office, he could see that Mercer was even more agitated. It took a lot to make Mercer nervous—he was by temperament a solid, plodding sort of man who was excruciatingly thorough in all his work. But this morning, he was shuffling paper and twitching in a way Jackson had never before witnessed.

"Are you all right, Mercer?" he asked with genuine concern in his voice.

Mercer did not reply right away. He looked at the ceiling, then off into the distance, then at the floor, and, finally, back at Jackson. Then he looked down at his desk before taking a deep breath, leaning forward, and looking Jackson right in the eyes, holding his gaze in an uncompromising way.

"I need to ask you one question before we talk about anything else, Jackson," Mercer began. "I need to know where you stand with respect to the Governor's agenda."

Jackson didn't respond for a moment. It was a fair question. It was, in fact, the very question he wanted to ask Mercer if Mercer hadn't asked first. It was critical to the meeting they were about to have.

He returned Mercer's hard gaze. "As an indication of where I stand, Mercer, I will tell you that I just met with Mary McDonald and Jake McCauley to get their support in stopping this nonsense before it goes too far."

Mercer took a long breath and leaned back in his chair. He not only understood what Jackson had said; he was clear that Jackson's admission that he had spoken to legislative Democrats was an indication of how firmly he was in the anti-secessionist camp. He was enormously relieved.

Jackson could see that his statement had the desired effect. And he knew from the obvious relief in his friend's demeanor that he and Mercer were on the same side. But he had to hear it for himself.

"And you, sir?" he asked quietly.

Mercer did not hesitate. "I spent some time on the phone this morning with Valerie Escapan and assured her that I would do everything in my power to prevent the United States from losing the state of Georgia. And I intend to live up to my promise."

"In that case," Jackson said, "we have some catching up to do."

"Indeed," replied Mercer.

"Let me tell you about my last meeting with the Governor, Mercer," Jackson said. And he proceeded to bring him up to date.

He also told him he had shared this with McCauley and McDonald.

"Now it seems to me, Mercer, that the Governor is planning on calling up the National Guard to implement his plans. I think that's the first place we should pay attention to."

Mercer nodded. Although Valerie Escapan had told him to take any legal action he could to prevent secession, he knew that any action he might take would stretch the term *legal* a great deal. He looked at his friend with a frown on his face.

"Where we have a leg to stand on is that only the President can call up the National Guard, and those troops have all been trained by the US Army. My concern is . . ."

". . . the State Defense Force," Williams said, finishing his friend's sentence with a sudden glint of recognition on his face. "I hadn't thought of that."

The two looked at each other. The Georgia State Defense Force was a volunteer state agency that reported directly to the governor as commander-in-chief. It was a quasimilitary group that had no allegiance to the US president or to Congress and was not regulated or even mentioned in the federal constitution. The fact was neither Mercer Willoughby nor Jackson Williams knew much about it.

"Who knows about this?" asked Mercer.

Jackson looked at him. "The Governor, and probably Hugh Lewins. Those two are thick as thieves."

The aptness of the analogy was not lost on either of them.

ugh Lewins not only knew about the State Defense Force, he was the intermediary among Governor Phillips, the Sovereign Citizens, Abner Bellamy, and the SDF. It was Abner who first planted the idea of using that force in the actual secession. Under Lewins's direction, it had grown from a constabulary force of about three thousand men to nearly twenty thousand men and women well trained in weapons, crowd management, and assault and defense techniques. Its funding had been buried in the budget for years. It was working in tandem with the Sovereign Citizens. Lewins personally saw to keeping its operations secret.

He was on the phone to Jason Appleby, the commandant of the SDF. "Are your men in place, Jason?"

"Yes, they are, Hugh. We are poised to take over all National Guard facilities and equipment as soon as we get the word from the Governor. After that it will take us one day to mobilize that equipment for defensive action against any aggression by the federal government, whether US military or National Guard."

Lewins could barely contain his delight. After all these years, after all the humiliations at the hands of federal bureaucrats, after all the idle longing for a past that at times didn't even seem real, the time had come.

"Good work, Jason. Keep this line open. The Governor himself will be the one making the call."

After Lewins hung up, he turned his chair to face the glorious Georgia sunshine. For much of his life, he never thought he would live to see this day, the day that Georgia soared as a nation on its own. It was only during the past couple of years that he had gotten involved with Bellamy and through him with the Governor, a man he had always respected but whose allegiances always seemed more political than inspirational.

He picked up the phone to call Bellamy, who answered on the first ring.

"Talk to me," said Abner.

"We're ready, Abner," Lewins said. "Things are moving along in the legislature, but the Governor is determined to secede whether those bills pass or not. I personally think they will: your men have done a masterful job of persuading the weak-kneed members of our party who needed prodding." He chuckled slightly. "Both chambers were in session all night. They don't know they're chasing a mirage."

"Good, good," said Abner. "Let me know as soon as the votes come in. Is the SDF ready?"

"Everything is in place, Abner. This will be a smaller and more focused replay of yesterday, but this time it will have a much clearer objective."

Abner didn't reply to that comment. He was, however, nodding his head.

Lewins paused for a moment and then continued. "I never thought this day would come. I can't tell you how much I appreciate your guidance and direction."

Abner kept nodding. "Keep me posted, Hugh. I'll be here." And he hung up the phone.

Lewins got up and walked over to the large picture window in his office. It was a beautiful Georgia morning, and he wanted to remember this day in every detail. He took a deep breath and then left his office. He was headed to meet the Governor.

When he got to Phillips's office, Phillips was on the phone with the governor of Alabama. He was shouting into the phone.

"What do you mean you don't think you can bring your state along?" he thundered. Lewins had no idea who he was talking to, but he could tell the man or woman on the other end of the line was taking a browbeating.

"You listen to me, Ralph," Phillips said. "You make this happen or all the states on your border will team up to kick your weakling ass out of office and out of your own state. Do you hear me?" He paused, waiting for a response.

Lewins could not hear the other end of the conversation, but he pitied the person on whom Phillips was venting his rage. Lewins thought this was so unlike his boss. Maybe the stress was getting to him. But there was nothing for Lewins to do at the moment, so he sat down within the Governor's line of sight and said nothing.

After a little more haranguing, Phillips put the phone down and turned to Lewins. "That son of a bitch in Alabama doesn't think he can pull this off through the legislature," he fumed. "All the others are in."

Lewins nodded. Then he started to explain why he was in Governor Phillips's office. "I just got off the phone with Appleby," he said. "Everything is set. As soon as they get the word from you, they'll swing into action." He paused a bit. "Today is the day, McKenzie."

Phillips looked back at him with a grotesque half-smile on his face. "Yes, it is, Hugh. Today is the day."

There was silence in the room. Sunshine poured into the large window facing east. The two men looked out onto Capital Square. The thought uttered in their last words bonded them. They both knew they were soldiers now.

ary Applewhite sat at her kitchen table in Waynesville, Missouri, wringing her hands. She was watching the television, something she almost never did during the day, listening to the major news networks struggle to cover the attacks on Washington, DC, and Fort Knox as well as the news coming out of numerous state legislatures, which were considering secession. She could barely believe what she was seeing.

At the same time, her feelings were deeply mixed. She loved her country. When she was young, she was active in all the civic groups she could be a part of: the Girl Scouts, 4-H, the Young Republicans. She was a Presidential Scholar and traveled to Washington right after high school. She voted in every election.

And she was a devout Christian. Raised in an uncompromising Evangelical household, she felt that her faith nurtured and sustained her, both personally in her daily prayer life and devotional practices, such as reading scripture, and socially, as the social life of her entire family centered around frequent and regular involvement in the local Baptist Church. She did not smoke or drink alcohol or dance or engage in any of the activities proscribed by her church. She never had a rebellious stage.

Mary loved her parents even more than she loved her country. Like her, they were model citizens and devout Christians. Her father was an elder in the same church to which she belonged, and her mother was active in all the committees and groups she could possibly manage. Like her, her parents attended services faithfully twice a week, once on Wednesday and once on Sunday. Otherwise, they volunteered their time generously wherever their services were needed.

Prayer and scripture readings were integral parts of their lives. In recent years, being active in political movements became another focus. For many years, Mary listened to her parents lament the degradation of American life and the increasing secularization of America. The day the Supreme Court banned prayer in public schools there was mournful silence all day at the family home on the edge of town. A frequent topic of dinner conversations was a listing of all the abominations perpetrated by government, including allowing abortion, striking down segregation, and so-called equal rights movements. More recently the progress of the gay rights movement sickened every member of the extended family. Other issues, such as climate change, environmental problems, and financial shenanigans just added weight to the already heavy burden of watching their country slide into what they strongly believed to be moral and religious chaos. The end times, her pastor warned.

"Why does this happen, Papa?" she would ask her father as a child around the table. Even at a young age, she could see that he was beleaguered by these events. She said this in part because she genuinely wanted to understand how such things could happen in a Christian country so favored by God and partly to rouse her morose father from what by all indications was a deepening depression over the state of the country he loved. She made little progress with either of these goals.

Over time, her father's mood worsened until it found a set point that enabled him to perform the tasks he ordinarily did, such as work and attend church and show up for meals, but he did these things with a lot less enthusiasm. Somber duty began to replace the joy he once took in living his life.

After he retired, Mason Waverly spent the first few months sleeping, avoiding most social contact, and generally getting through each day as if it were a chore. His wife, Bea, and his children worried about him, including Mary, but all efforts to help the situation were met with downcast eyes, a helpless shrug, and a complete lack of reciprocal dialogue. His silence was a powerful weapon, fatally crippling any efforts to help him.

This somber shadow persisted for several years, sustained by his spending more and more time listening to irate political commentators. He lionized Rush Limbaugh, whom he thought of as a prophet of sorts. His voting became even more conservative. He believed Grover Norquist took a courageous stand when the latter insisted that all true Republicans sign a pledge of no new taxes ever. He believed the members of Westboro Baptist Church were bravely standing up for basic values when they picketed the funerals of gay soldiers killed in action.

For the most part, Mary and her siblings and her mother tolerated these behaviors, thinking with some hope that Mason's engagement in the growing rightward drift of the GOP was preferable to his not getting out of bed in the morning. Plus, these views were not dissimilar from those of most of Mason's extended family. One of Mason's Waverly's brothers was an active member of the emerging Tea Party, and he was instrumental in getting Mason involved. For their part, Mary and her husband, Todd, detested abortion and believed strongly that it should be outlawed. They saw homosexuality as an evil and a choice. They questioned evolution and wondered about the ill effects of the growing federal bureaucracy as much as any of their Republican friends and neighbors. In the town of Waynesville, that included almost everybody.

It was when the Tea Party began to get traction, around the time of the 2008 election, that Mason began to feel he had found not only an ideological home but also a way out of his deepening depression. It was during this time that other family members noticed a change in the man they had come to pity. They began to notice something in Mason that they had not seen for years. Over the course of a few weeks, the man who had been dutifully if life-lessly attending church began to be animated. Instead of getting through the day, the retired contractor woke up enthusiastic in the morning, eager to track the latest political developments and think up ways he could be useful to the cause.

Mason attended every Tea Party rally he could, often driving for miles to find one. He almost always came home refreshed and renewed, a transformed man. He had more energy than anyone had seen in him in years.

"These people understand," he informed his family repeatedly, especially when they were assembled for Sunday dinner, as they did every week. "They understand that the country is on the wrong track. They understand that abandoning religion is at the heart of it. And they understand that the main perpetrator of all this secular-ization is our overstuffed bureaucracy in Washington. They have a plan to change it." He was beaming.

The enthusiasm was contagious. Bea, Mary's mother, perked up, relieved to see her husband be his old energetic self. He was more than energetic; he was energized.

In Mary's view, this began a period of healing for her whole fam-ily. No one looked at Mason Waverly anymore with pity or ques-tions; no one doubted where he stood on issues; no one questioned his loyalty to the cause he had so wholeheartedly embraced. And no one doubted his unwavering commitment to his newly refurbished faith in something he called "small-town America."

The midterm elections of 2010 were a watershed for Mason, confirming God's blessing on the plan. When so many ultraconser-vative Tea Party members unseated ordinary conservative Republi-cans, he was elated. They'll pay attention now, he thought, and he broadcast it to all he knew.

So as Mary sat and watched the wanton destruction of the nation's capital, she felt a sense of inevitability about it all. It was indeed the wages of sin, as her father and her pastor had said. It was bound to happen, she thought, just as they said it would. Something in this situation had to change. And the change had to be drastic. These thoughts did not keep the tears from streaming down her face.

She had taken Ruth and Isaac, her two children, to school as usual. She did this in an effort to sustain a sense of normalcy and because she trusted the religious school they attended to take care of them during the day. It was generally agreed among the parents that keeping to a schedule and keeping a close eye on the children were the best ways to navigate the troubled waters in which the nation found itself. As the Old Testament taught them, sometimes God purges the Earth, and even the just are made to suffer for a time. To them, these events had "God's will" written all over them.

Mary's husband, Todd, also went to work as usual. He too wanted to maintain a regular schedule and keep things normal. In addition, his work as an HVAC contractor meant that, without his assistance, people in the community—his community—would be in uncomfortable or even dangerous situations in their own homes. He didn't want that. So he kissed his wife good-bye in the morning and went about his business as if life were normal.

Of course, life was anything but normal, as Mary could see, her eyes rarely straying from the television in her kitchen.

It was still early. The children had been dropped off at school at 7:00 a.m., in time for their before-school prayers. Todd left about the same time to make his rounds. It was nearing 8:00 a.m.; the President was going to talk at 11:00 a.m.

Mary was mulling over her conflicted feelings when the phone rang. She glanced at the number. It was Todd. He was probably calling to see how she was.

"Hi, honey," came the comforting voice on the other end of the line.

"Oh, Todd," Mary blurted out. What had been tears trickling down her face became a stream. "I can barely stand to watch this."

Todd listened as sympathetically as he could. He was between jobs, and he was hearing the same kind of sentiments from almost everyone he encountered that day. Most people were appreciative of his keeping his appointments, but their feelings were uncharacteristically on ready display.

Todd was torn. Truth be told, he didn't care much about politics or what happened in faraway Washington or Kentucky. He cared about his family in Waynesville, especially his wife and children. He ached to be with Mary today, but they had talked early that morning about how important it was to act normally during this time. They would be shown the way if they needed to change their routine.

He also knew that Mary would never ask him to come home, as she probably wanted him to do. He silently pledged to himself that he would work more quickly throughout the day and get home as soon as he could.

"Todd," said Mary, as she struggled to regain her composure. "Do you think this is God's will?"

After a very slight pause, Todd replied. "No doubt about it, honey," he said. "No doubt about it."

22

Hundreds of miles away, in suburban Birmingham, Alabama, another woman was doing almost the exact same thing. Jessica Cates was sitting at her kitchen table wringing her hands and watching a small television perched on her crowded kitchen counter. Jessica had not taken her twin children to school; she wanted them with her on this day. She wanted to protect them as much as she could. Her husband, an emergency room physician at a local hospital, was still at work on a twelve-hour shift. He was scheduled to be home around 11:00 a.m.

Jessica was not torn by the events in the nation's capital. She was shocked and appalled and enraged by them. She did not believe the politicians in the states considering secession as they brayed on about "taking the country back" and returning to some sort of idealized fantasy of an America where everything was wonderful. She thought the insurgents were criminals and traitors who did not seem to appreciate the implications of their traitorous acts. She was choking with rage, and her fury made breathing hard.

She looked over at Ryan and Melissa, who were watching the television and watching her with almost equal intensity. They were obviously distraught: their young faces were pale, and their voices quivered slightly when they tried to talk or ask a question. Jessica knew this whole business was hard on them. It must have been similar to what she felt during the events of 9/11. Suddenly, the assumption of invulnerability to attack had collapsed. Many people's sense of safety evaporated. Many others found their attitude toward their country shift.

She felt for her children. The country that they had known their whole lives was suddenly under assault, and the outcome was far from certain. What had been a given was now a question. Jessica wanted more than anything else to be available to her children during this time.

"How're you guys doing?" she said sympathetically.

The twins shrugged. They were frightened by what they saw on television, but their fright was worse because their mother was shaky. They didn't know what to think. They were only eight years old, and they were at least as concerned about their mother, who seemed really, really upset, as they were about the scary things that were happening in Washington, which they didn't fully understand. To them it looked like a movie.

A horror movie, perhaps.

Jessica wished with every bone in her body that Maxwell, her husband, were there with his family. She fully understood the demands of being a physician, especially an emergency room doc; she also knew how seriously Maxwell took his responsibilities. Jessica found this devoted part of his personality endearing, and she knew it extended to her and their children. But he had a job to do at the moment, and he was no doubt busy doing it.

It was in the midst of these thoughts that her cell phone rang.

"How you holding up, sweetheart?" came Maxwell's reassuring baritone.

A measure of relief swept over Jessica as she stood up to put some distance between herself and her children for the sake of privacy. "As well as can be expected," she replied. "The kids and I are watching television."

Maxwell was silent for a moment. "I'm a little concerned about a steady diet of that, Jess," he said gently.

"I know, Maxwell," Jessica replied. "But the President is going to be speaking in a little bit, and I think it's important for them to hear him, even if they don't understand a lot of what is going on."

Maxwell wasn't looking for an argument. He hated being away from his family, and he knew he had a couple more hours before he could join them. "I'll be home in a couple hours, Jess. We can talk more then."

Jessica clicked the phone off and returned to the kitchen table. "Did I miss anything?" she asked a little too cheerfully. The ponderousness of the day was getting to her. She wanted some relief.

The twins shook their heads. She realized in that moment that Maxwell was right: watching this wasn't helping anyone.

"Let's turn the TV off for a while," she said, again in an overly cheerful voice that made her children leery. Nonetheless, they glanced at each other and nodded to their mother.

"Let's go into the family room and talk a little." The fact was she did not know what to say, and it was hard to gauge the children's reaction, given their young age. But she had to do something.

The trio trundled into the family room. Jessica stopped at the refrigerator and poured some milk and orange juice, known favorites of her two adorable children. As they all sat on the large sofa, she handed the drinks to Ryan and Melissa.

"Okay," she began. "I know this must all seem a little mysterious to you." She looked at the twins with genuine affection. "So tell me what you are thinking. What do you understand?"

She waited for a response. Ryan spoke first. "Those people who attacked Washington," he started haltingly. "They're bad, right?"

Jessica found herself nodding. "Yes, Ryan. They are bad men who are doing something very, very bad."

Melissa was following this conversation. "I see that," she said. "But what's all that talk about in Georgia? Isn't that where Aunt Anna lives?"

Time for Civics 101. Jessica was unsure just how much the children understood about the political structure of the United States, but she felt a need to provide some kind of explanation. The fact that they lived in a former Confederate state made this a little more complicated. Jessica had always made a point of the twins knowing their state and being proud of it.

But she could barely contain her physical responses. Her stomach churned and she could feel her hands shaking, despite her clasping them together. I can't believe I have to have this conversation, she thought. But she also knew she had to try to help her children understand. She took a deep breath and began slowly.

"The United States, our country, is made up of individual states. Our state is Alabama. When the United States was formed over two hundred years ago, there were a lot of states—thirteen of them— that were like separate countries. They decided to come together to form the United States government." She looked at the faces of her children to determine if they were following her. They seemed to be.

"About a hundred and fifty years ago," she continued, "maybe a little longer, some of the states, including ours, decided they did not want to be a part of the United States anymore. There was a war. It was called the Civil War. It went on for four years." She paused. "It was horrible. The army that wanted to keep the United States together won the war, and the states that wanted to leave had to stay in the United States." She looked at her children again.

Melissa asked, "You mean our state wanted to leave? Why did we have to stay if we wanted to leave?"

Good question, Jessica thought. "It was a little complicated, honey," she said. "The South . . . the states that wanted to leave, allowed people to own slaves. . . ."

Melissa's face displayed her horror. "Slaves? You mean . . . people?" she asked. She looked around for a minute. "They had slaves here?"

Jessica shrugged. "Yes, people, and yes, people in Alabama owned slaves," she replied. "Black people. From Africa."

There was silence in the room. Ryan was looking at his sister with a smirk on his face. "Missy," he said. "People owned slaves for a long, long time."

"How can you own a human being?" Melissa said.

"Ryan is right, Missy," said Jessica. "Slavery was legal for a long time before it was abolished in the 1800s. But in the United States, it took a war to stop it."

"Are we going to have another war?" Melissa asked.

Jessica paused and looked at her two beloved children. "It looks that way, Melissa. It looks that way." Then she couldn't help herself. Tears began to roll down her face.

The twins were caught by surprise. They looked at each other. Ryan spoke first. "Mama, are there going to be soldiers and battles here?" he asked, color draining from his face.

Jessica wasn't sure what to say. It could happen, but she did not want to frighten her children any more than they already were. "I don't know, Ryan," she said softly. "It depends on a lot of things." She tousled his hair. "I hope not."

Hoping did not make Ryan feel any better. "Mama," he said. "What would happen if a war started? What would happen to us?"

Jessica tried to take charge. "If that were to happen—and we don't know that it will happen—there may be some fighting, but it's not likely to happen around here."

"Where *will* it happen?" Ryan interjected.

"I don't know, honey," she replied. "But let's not get ahead of ourselves. If war happens, things will change for a while, but wars don't last forever. And I think there's good reason to think it won't come to that." Jessica glanced over at Melissa, whose face was streaked with tears.

"Mama," she said. "I'm scared."

Jessica placed one arm around each of her children. She pulled them toward her. She couldn't think of anything to say except the obvious. "I am too, sweetie. I am too."

nbeknownst to Mary Appleby and Jessica Cates, each of them had a shared link to the events that were transpiring on television screens across the country. Mary was a member of the same church as Cherie Keenan. Because Cherie, who lived in Rolla, had to leave town in a hurry, Mary had no idea of her whereabouts or what she was doing. She was shocked when Cherie's husband's body was reportedly found dismembered across various venues in Rolla, and she was silently grateful that she lived in a safe, clean satellite community thirty minutes away. She had tried to text Cherie her condolences a couple of times but received no reply. She was sure Cherie had her hands full trying to manage a newly single life with two small children. Mary proceeded to go about her business.

Jessica had been Cherie's college roommate as a freshman at the University of Alabama at Birmingham, and, though their relationship got off to a rocky start—due in large part to Jessica's freewheeling ways and Cherie's traditional attitudes—the two became close friends within the first few months of living together. Since then, they had kept up a long-distance but regular and intimate correspondence.

When Jessica learned of Cherie's husband's murder, she swept into action. She called and left voice messages, emailed and texted her friend, and wrote her a long, handwritten letter expressing her shock and offering her not only her condolences but whatever help and support Cherie might need. Jessica's life in a deeply Southern state did nothing to impede her natural inclination to help her close friend up north.

After days of not hearing from Cherie, Jessica thought about traveling to Rolla to look for her in person. She and Maxwell had talked about it, and he was willing to do what he could to make it happen, given his demanding schedule at the hospital. It was primarily a question of child care, but he thought he could swing that with some timely help from sympathetic friends and neighbors.

Those conversations happened over the course of several days, and by the time Jessica was thinking that such a trip was not only possible but also desirable, pandemonium had broken out in the nation's capital, and her once-proud country was teetering on the brink of disaster. Once the capital was under assault, all thoughts of traveling were shelved.

In fact, Cherie had received the email messages Jessica had sent. She had unburdened herself of her cell phone, as it is an easy thing to track, so she did not get text messages, but she was able to check her email a few times thanks to the technical prowess of Samantha Stranger. She knew that Jessica was being the wonderful friend she had always been, looking out for her in any way she could. Cherie would have—indeed, had—done similar things for Jessica. However, current events were several orders of magnitude more serious than anything the two friends had been through, and now Cherie was hesitant to get Jessica involved.

She longed to talk to Jessica, and she was hoping that she would have an opportunity to do so soon. Just hearing her voice would give Cherie some strength.

And strength was exactly what she needed. After her husband's murder and the events that followed it, Cherie left her two young children with a kind couple who were friends of a former Jesuit professor that Darrin McAlister had known. Ever since she dropped them off, she could not help but believe that they would be better off with someone to whom she was close, and Jessica and her family were her first choice. The thought barely occurred to her at first that Jessica and her family might be jeopardized by such an arrangement if someone traced Cherie's connection to her.

It was a painful dilemma. On the one hand, she was committed to pursuing the path the two government contract workers and she and Darrin had been following. They were in an important position to help quell the uprising. On the other hand, she felt terrible leaving her children in the care of people she didn't know, no matter that Darrin and a priest had vouched for them. She needed a deeper connection, and she wanted her children to be with someone to whom they felt connected, especially since her husband of many years was gone.

Gone but not missed. Cherie was still furious that Daniel had allowed himself to get taken in by a bunch of religious fanatics. She had met Adam Wilson on a few social occasions, and she found him as repugnant a human being as she had encountered. It wasn't that he wasn't civil; in fact, he was entirely too civil, too polished, too manicured for her taste. But Cherie couldn't let her mind wander just now. She needed to take active steps to help herself.

She tried broaching the subject of contacting Jessica with McAlister, as they flew to Texas aboard a private government jet. They were headed for Wichita Falls and the compound of the Blinder brothers.

"Darrin," she said when the two found themselves together in the aft section of the plane and Samantha and Marie were in the forward section. "I know a woman, we've been friends since college. I'd like her to take my children." She paused a moment. She did not want to sound ungrateful for all Darrin had done for her and her family. "I know the Ausbangers are good people. I trust your judgment, and I trust Father Tom's." She paused again. "But I can barely stand the thought that they are with strangers, and I'm sure Jessica would be willing to take them for as long as this takes."

Darrin listened intently. What Cherie was saying was both understandable and complicated. He knew she was speaking from her heart, and he knew enough about her to respect that. There was something about this woman that Darrin trusted. He started trusting her the minute she walked into his office and told him an outrageous story of what her husband was up to, how the two of them fought over it, how Cherie has stabbed her husband in self-defense, and how she felt a powerful need to escape. He helped her. He made the requisite calls, the ones any officer of the law would make in such a circumstance, but the fact was he had little doubt that Cherie was telling the truth then or that she was telling the truth now. She is just a truth-telling person: this belief only grew the more he got to know her.

But how could he possibly help her now? They were in the middle of a war, on their way to Texas, and traveling directly away from Cherie's children.

He didn't know what to say.

"This is a hard one, Cherie," he began slowly. "I understand you want what is best for your children, and right now they have something that's very important to them and to you and to all of us here: anonymity. No one knows who those children are or how they are connected to you."

Darrin paused a bit. In his mind, he was reviewing some of the dangerous situations he and Cherie and Sam and Marie had been in over the past few days. They could have been killed any number of times. And they were all surprised at how closely they were being tracked by methods they did not fully understand and by people they knew little about. Making the circle bigger would endanger other people; Darrin had no doubt about that.

Similar thoughts were taking shape in Cherie's mind. Soon after she had opened her mouth to ask Darrin the question, the idea that getting Jessica involved would endanger her and her family came to full flower in her mind. She shook her head. What was I thinking? Jeopardizing her best friend was absolutely unacceptable. She knew she couldn't do it. She wouldn't do it. Her children were safe. She was putting more miles between herself and them, and that was all to the good.

She turned and looked out the window at the bright blue sky. A steely sense of determination settled over her as she observed herself in her current situation. So much of this was out of her control. So much of it was about things she did not and would not choose. If she were a more religious person, she would be asking God what he was doing with her. As it was, she was sure that was a dead end. Her husband and his murderous compatriots, all good churchgoers, had sealed her decision about religion in her life. His pious "friends" poisoned his mind and then killed him when he did not go along with their insane plans. She would no longer assume that people were good because they were affiliated with a church or proclaimed themselves religious. She was a sensible woman. She knew she was in a difficult position that demanded personal sacrifice on her part and was aware that she might not survive. That thought made her enormously sad, but it did not deter her from her present course of action.

Cherie looked back at Darrin, who was obviously at a loss about what to say. She shook her head again. "Forget about it, Darrin," she said. "I know it's complicated." She glanced down at her hands, clasped tightly on her lap. "I know it's impossible just now." She looked up at him. Her eyes had tears, but they refused to fall. The sense of steely resolve settled into her chest.

Darrin saw the determination in Cherie's face, and he felt the strength of her words radiate from her whole body. He didn't believe he had ever seen her so focused. He leaned back ever so slightly, in part to absorb the strength he was feeling from this hardheaded woman. Her newfound resolve was palpable.

It was at this moment that something strange happened. Not so strange, perhaps, for many adult men, but strange for Darrin McAlister. He felt an intimacy with Cherie that was new to him, but it wasn't just closeness. It was respect and warmth and affection and . . . He had a hard time naming it. Then he found the name: desire. He felt a desire to protect and defend this woman and to help her in any way he could. As a professional matter he had done that already, but up until this moment it was not . . . personal. It was not about Cherie as the unique person she was. Now he knew he would go to any length to help Cherie deal with whatever came her way. He was committed.

Darrin looked into Cherie's eyes but did not know what to say. He leaned over and put his arm around her. This was intended as a gesture of support, but the warmth of Cherie's response surprised him. Cherie allowed his embrace to linger for a moment longer than friendship required. Feelings of relief and warmth tempered her hard feelings of anger and revenge.

Darrin pulled back. "I know this is hard for you, Cherie," he began, but she interrupted him by putting her finger across his lips.

"You needn't say anything, Darrin," Cherie said. "It was a moment of weakness. I understand my duty to my children, my country, and my friends." She gestured with her head toward Darrin and toward the front of the plane, where Samantha and Marie were working, placing them all into that last category. She took his hands in hers and looked him straight in the eye. "Thank you for believing in me, Darrin. If you hadn't, this situation could have turned out much worse."

She let go of Darrin's hands then and leaned back toward the window of the private aircraft. "I can't wait to find these bastards."

Darrin gave a half smile. Events were spiraling out of any control he might have had. He wasn't sure what to make of them. All he was sure of was that he was in the right place at the right time doing the right thing.

He sat back in his seat and looked at Cherie. The half smile melted away and resolved itself into a look of sober affection. I guess I love this woman, he thought.

24

The private government jet began banking for a landing at a small airstrip outside Wichita Falls, Texas, where the Blinder compound was located. Marie LeBrun and Samantha Stranger walked to the back of the plane to bring Cherie and Darrin up to speed about the plan they had been crafting during the trip south.

"Okay," Marie began. "Here is what we are looking at." She nodded to Samantha, who opened her laptop for everyone to see. "After we land, we will meet up with about eighty federal officers from various security services: the Secret Service, ATF, FBI, US Marshals. They have been working to identify ground forces and defenses in the Blinder compound and have been preparing for a ground assault."

She paused and pointed to the aerial map Samantha had brought up on her computer. "The estate itself is enormous, more than eighty thousand acres. But the main buildings are the Blinder residence, which is very large, and the outbuildings that surround it. The residence is twenty-five thousand square feet, and it is thought to be very well defended by troops located in these outbuildings." She pointed to the incongruously tiny picture of the Blinder home on her screen.

"There's a garage that holds dozens of cars; there's a horse barn and stable here. And there are several buildings of unknown uses here and here. We know there are hostiles in each of these buildings protecting the main building." She pointed to each position as she named it.

Samantha joined the presentation. "We know that George Blinder, David's brother, left the compound two days ago. He got on a bus and then on a train. He was apparently headed for Canada or perhaps points beyond. Whatever his destination, he was clearly dissociating himself from his brother's plot, which he appears to have known about in general outline but which he thought up until a few days ago was a pipe dream on his brother's part.

"George was picked up from the train yesterday afternoon. He is presently in federal custody and by all accounts is cooperating." Samantha paused. "Of course, we have to check out every detail of what he's telling us, because it may be that he was planted in this scheme to throw us off track." Samantha sighed heavily. "And these things are hard to corroborate just now."

Marie picked up the narrative. "Our plan is simple: We and the other federal officers are going to enter the compound. We have warrants." She stopped abruptly. "But so did two federal agents who attempted to take David Blinder into custody a few days ago. They have not been heard from." She paused and looked around at the others. "We are going in strong, armed to the hilt, anticipating that those SC troops are not just there for routine security."

All faces around the laptop grimaced at once. They all understood what Marie meant.

The fact is," Marie continued, "we don't know how many hostile troops Blinder has on his compound. We can be sure he has some in these outbuildings, but we also believe he may have many more scattered around his property that he can call upon as needed. And, as we've seen, these people are very well trained, well equipped, and well organized."

"So there are eighty or so of us and maybe hundreds, or more, of them. Is that right?"

"Potentially that's true, Darrin. We just don't know for sure. Agents on the ground are collecting data now. But it's safe to assume that we'll be seriously outnumbered."

A grim silence descended on the airplane. The only sound was the drone of the jet engines.

It was Sam who broke the spell. "But we have some tactical advantages. First of all, while Blinder no doubt is waiting for some kind of action against him, he does not know who or how many or when such an action will occur. Secondly, we have set up technical surveillance to determine any electronic countermeasures he may have installed." She paused for a moment. "And we are taking countermeasures to those."

Cherie didn't know what to think. All of this sounded way out of her league.

"What can we do to help?" she asked, turning to Marie.

Marie cocked her head sideways. Her voice softened from the military tone to a more personal one. "The first thing you can do is not get hurt," she said. "You will not be involved in the assault. That includes you, too," she said, looking straight at Darrin. "We need a command post, and the ATF set one up a couple miles from the Blinder estate. We need you there."

Darrin harrumphed to himself when he heard he would not be part of the assault force. He was an officer of the law, and he felt as an officer and as a man that he should be part of it. He put up his hand to get Marie's attention.

"Don't you think that you're going to need all the help you can get when you storm that place?"

Marie stared hard at Darrin before answering. "We need you at the command post, Darrin," she said in the same soft tone that she used to address Cherie. There was no way she would jeopardize the lives of these two patriots who had already done so much to help their country.

She saw Darrin's quizzical look and decided to continue. "Look," she said more firmly. "Here is the situation: It is clear that this operation had inside information about our systems. We don't know how they got it. We are going to hand over Sam's computer to you two, and you are going to be closely monitoring the situation. You will be in constant contact with us." She gave both Cherie and Darrin hard looks. Then her voice softened. "We know you. We trust you. We do not want to put you in harm's way during the assault." She paused a moment. "Truthfully, we cannot guarantee that you will not be in a dangerous situation at the command post. We are presuming that there won't be bullets flying there. What we really need is for all of our intel to go through you two. Through both of you to ensure that neither one of you is compromised."

Darrin's head tilted back. Now he completely understood what Marie was saying, and Cherie was not far behind. She was just glad to be out of range of bullets and with Darrin McAlister.

"We can do that," he said firmly. Cherie nodded.

The plane touched down at an isolated airstrip fifteen miles from the Blinder compound. The foursome waited motionlessly until the small craft came to a complete stop. Then they turned to each other with a look that served as a seal on their covenant to do battle with the enemy.

25

Back in Washington, the clock was ticking. President Obama knew that he had to address the nation in a few hours and give them some assurance that the ship of state was still afloat. The trouble was that he wasn't sure what the current status was. It was changing by the hour. He would need more information before he could give any kind of solid assurance.

He had spent the early hours of the morning discussing the situation with his advisors. Predictably, the military favored military intervention, the State Department favored negotiations, and the Justice Department favored legal recourse; each area found the arguments of the others unconvincing and downright dangerous. There was no consensus.

The President knew he had an immediate decision to make. He had to tell the American public the truth. And if the truth was confused and the situation was in play with no clear outcome, so be it. There is more power in telling it like it is, he believed, than trying to handhold a nation of adults by downplaying the situation. Parents could decide how to deal with their own children.

At the same time, his single overriding goal was to stanch what threatened to be the imminent dissolution of the Union he had inherited from presidents before him. He had always admired Abraham Lincoln, but he never thought for a moment that he would be in a similar spot.

He turned to Joe Biden, who was sitting on the couch across from the presidential seat in the Oval Office. "What do you think, Joe?"

"I don't know what to think, Mr. President."

Whenever Joe addressed the President by his title, Obama knew he was stumped. He took a deep breath and started again.

"Let me rephrase that," he said. "How much leverage do you think the attorneys general will have to prevent secessionist votes in the states that are holding them?"

Biden thought for a moment. "More than zero," he said, "but it's hard to say how much more. I think it depends on the state. Each one is different with respect to the rights, powers, and obligations of its chief law professional." He paused and gazed at the wall across the room wistfully. "Especially in the South, which appears to be spearheading the secession, the relationship between the executive and the attorney general is usually a little too cozy. Frankly, I think the main thing they can accomplish with this plan is to buy some time by confusing everyone." His eyes twinkled. "We lawyers are good at that."

Mr. Obama smiled inwardly. Count on Joe Biden to crack a joke in the middle of the biggest crisis in modern American history. He appreciated it. He also knew that Joe was most likely correct. He desperately needed time, and he was hoping that the legal situation would entangle the states until the federal government and the various federal branches could identify ways to make sure the secession movement failed.

His phone buzzed, and Anita Decker, his personal secretary, was on the other end. "Mr. President, Chief Justice Roberts is on the line," she said.

"Thank you, Anita." He pronounced the words slowly as he prepared to have a conversation with the head of the other branch of government with whom he was not always on the best of terms. Not that the President and the Chief Justice were not cordial to each other, but they were from opposing parties and were often at loggerheads about important issues. Obama rarely enjoyed interacting with Roberts.

"Mr. Chief Justice," he said after he pushed the appropriate button. "Thank you for making time this morning."

There was a slight pause on the other end of the line. Before Obama could say what he wanted to say to him, Justice Roberts began speaking. "Mr. President, I imagine you are calling to ask for the assistance of the Supreme Court in this present crisis. I want to assure you that I and all the other justices are unanimous in our willingness to do whatever we are able to do to prevent the nation from fragmenting. We have been in session since early this morning, and we believe that there is no legal doubt that any individual secession law passed by any particular state is *ipso facto* unconstitutional." Another pause. "They can't do this, Mr. President."

Barack Obama felt a small wave of relief. He was anticipating a battle of some sort with Roberts, and part of the stress was in not knowing where that conflict would erupt. He exhaled slowly but deeply and silently. He felt a bond with Roberts he had not felt since his first inauguration.

"Thank you, Mr. Chief Justice. I was hoping for your support. I want you to know that we have directed the attorneys general in each state to be the frontline person to counter this . . . whatever this is: a movement, a plot . . . an insurrection. We don't want to use force unless it is absolutely necessary to procure compliance with the constitution."

"How can we help you, Mr. President?"

"You can remain in session to assist and support the attorneys general by hearing any appeals they make to you as quickly as you can." The President paused. As auspicious as the beginning of this conversation was, he had learned to be wary.

"Of course, Mr. President. We are prepared to live here for as long as it takes."

Can't ask for more than that, Mr. Obama thought.

"Thank you, Mr. Roberts. We will be in touch."

After he hung up, Barack Obama felt encouraged. He felt the patriotism in the voice of the Chief Justice and, through him, in all the justices of the Supreme Court of the United States. It gave form and shape and substance to the passion he felt inside to keep the nation united. It gave him strength. It bolstered his determination. He focused now on what he had to do.

And what he had to do was to get tough. Very tough. Every day, every hour this movement lasted gave it a credibility and a force that could become self-sustaining. He could not and would not tolerate that. He did not want to use force, but neither did he wish to foreswear using it in any form.

In any form. That phrase lingered in Obama's mind for a few seconds. He realized that he was thinking only of military force. But there are other kinds of force. He sat back in his chair slightly. His face assumed that maddeningly neutral look it takes on when he is deep in thought. He realized that just a moment before, he felt the need to speak to Americans as the adults they were, not as some kind of interest group that needed to be coddled or spoon-fed. They are not children.

And the United States is, after all, as much their country as his. He was the leader, and it was incumbent upon him to lead. And in this case leading meant marshaling the power that is usually hidden in the vast population of the American citizenry. He might have to call out the military. He had already put it on alert. He would raise the alert if he had to, but more importantly, he wanted the people themselves to speak, to protect the Union. And it occurred to him that the military could be used to protect Americans who would move to protest the breakup of their own country. Americans who would stand against the lunatic fringe that, although well equipped and well prepared and well trained, overlooked massively how much of the country was united under the American ideal, and how many of them will pass that unity on to their children and to their children's children. On and on, for as long as they could peer into the future. The United States is a perpetual union. So said the founding fathers. So said the Supreme Court. So said the blood of a million Americans during the Civil War.

And so will the people say again.

Barack Obama sat up a little straighter as these thoughts came together in his mind. He looked at his advisors around him. He had a couple of hours before he was going live on national television.

"Clear the room," he said quietly.

At first, some of his advisors didn't hear what he said. They looked at each other and at the President with a questioning look.

But Joe Biden heard the President and understood immediately what he was doing. He stood up, and the others followed suit. "Yes, sir," he said simply, and he led a procession out of the Oval Office.

26

On the tarmac outside Wichita Falls, Texas, Samantha Stranger and Marie LeBrun met with and took immediate command of the eighty-three men and women arrayed on the ground before them. Samantha had been in contact with these agents during their flight from Chicago, and everyone was briefed on what was at stake. The agents were dressed in black combat outfits and were checking and rechecking their weapons. They had armed themselves with an impressive arsenal; they had reviewed logistics; they had committed themselves psychologically and emotionally to the fight they knew was coming.

A tall, beefy man walked up to Samantha and Marie.

"Special Agent Riley Schwartz," he said to Marie as he reached out and shook her hand. He did the same with Samantha.

"I want to bring you up to speed quickly," he said. "As you know, we have been preparing since late last night, and our team is as ready as it is possible to be." He paused a moment to collect his thoughts. "There has been no new movement in the Blinder compound since I last spoke to you online. Routine perimeter patrols, two men each hour."

It was then that he spotted Cherie and Darrin. His face darkened ever so slightly.

"They're with us, Agent Schwartz," Sam said. "They are the civilians we told you about. We want them at the command post.

We will be in constant contact with them."

It was impossible to tell if Riley Schwartz approved or disapproved of this arrangement. Either way, he didn't have time to argue. He nodded and waved to another agent, gesturing to the two civilians. Then he continued his briefing.

"We'll talk more on the way. There is no time to waste." He motioned with his head toward a vehicle behind him with the engine running.

Sam and Marie scrambled into the vehicle after a nod to Cherie and Darrin. Darrin took Cherie by the arm and led her to a second vehicle parallel to the first. "Let's go," he said softly, and the pair followed the agent whom Schwartz had assigned to them.

Cherie was silent. She took a deep breath as she and Darrin climbed into the heavy black Suburban. The vehicle began to move as soon as Darrin's second foot left the ground.

The agent in charge of them was a young woman of about thirty. She had taken a seat in the front of the vehicle and turned around to brief Cherie and Darrin.

"We've set up a command post in an abandoned post office. It's been closed for years, but we were able to get utilities up and running. We have communication links with everyone in the field. We also have satellite surveillance of the Blinder estate."

She didn't wait for a response. "We understand that Marie and Samantha want all their communication to go through you. That's going to be a little awkward, but if that's what they need, we'll play it their way. I will be the liaison to help with any technical or other communication problems." She peered at Cherie and recognized her skeptical look. "Under battlefield conditions, our agents tend to use jargon that is not always clear to civilians."

There wasn't a trace of hostility or apprehension in her voice; she was just relating the situation as she saw it.

"By the way," she continued, "my name is Sandy, Sandy Thurmond. I'm with ATF."

Darrin nodded, as did Cherie. They each recited their names.

The command post was only a ten-minute drive away, and they were the only vehicle to approach it. When it stopped, Cherie, Darrin, Sandy, and the driver all jumped out of the SUV. Two other men sitting in the third row exited out the back of the vehicle. They all grabbed their gear, which included weapons and what looked like bulky brief cases.

Sandy led the way to the dingy, cinder-block building with a rusting flagpole that was now the command center. The door was unlocked, and she led the cadre of agents and civilians into a large, brightly lit room with about seven other men and women, all dressed in battle black, scurrying around computer screens and a lot of other exotic equipment.

Cherie stole a glance at Darrin, who looked intrigued, if not impressed. For her part, Cherie felt a mixture of pride at the obvious efficiency of this operation and terror that she was involved in a battle about to take place.

"Jesus," she said softly.

Darrin took his eyes off the equipment for a moment and looked at Cherie straight on. "I think we're going to be okay."

Cherie shrugged. She had no idea how he could be optimistic after what the two of them had been through over the past few days and given what they knew about what was to happen.

"If you say so," she said, a little more sarcastically than she intended. She was trying to find some strength within herself.

As promised, Sandy led Cherie and Darrin to what looked like a computer, except that the screen was much larger than a typical desktop machine. She started explaining the equipment in front of them.

Darrin seemed to be taking it all in. Cherie could barely stand to listen, much less follow what Sandy was saying. She got the overall drift that they were looking at some kind of fancy screen that would track action as it unfolded. She was to wear earphones that would enable her to communicate with Samantha and Marie but still be able to hear and talk to Sandy, who had another pair of earphones that fed her the same communications, and to Darrin, who would be similarly equipped.

Cherie was uneasy about the smoothness of all this. How did they know this was what Samantha and Marie wanted? What did they know about why they were here? She kept thinking about the "real" reason they were there: as trusted links to the battlefield. But Cherie was pretty certain Sandy could control the information they received and sent out. She was feeling slightly less than useful. Or safe.

Darrin, on the other hand, seemed completely engaged. This made sense to Cherie, since Darrin, while technically a civilian, was a law enforcement officer and an ex-Marine. He was in his element.

Even so, it surprised her when she heard him say, "I need a weapon."

Sandy hesitated for less than half a second. "What is your preference, sir?"

"Standard-issue Beretta sidearm with extra clips and whatever kind of automatic rifle you have handy. Also with extra clips."

Sandy motioned to a young man about five feet away and ordered him to bring Darrin what he had requested.

Darrin took the sidearm, checked the magazine, and stuffed it into his waistband. He took the rifle and looked it over. It was a standard-issue M4 carbine. It was close enough to the M-16A4 that he had used in the Marines that he felt reasonably sure he would know how to use it. He checked the stock, the sight, and the magazine. When he looked up, Sandy was handing him three additional magazines for each weapon. He nodded to her, took the additional ammo, and stuffed it into his pockets.

She nodded back. Then she turned to the large screen.

Cherie felt relieved that Sandy did not hesitate about the weapon. Even though she wasn't familiar with military or federal protocol, she thought that if Sandy were somehow on the wrong side of this situation, she would have made an issue about giving Darrin the guns he wanted. Still, she couldn't be sure. Then it occurred to her that maybe Darrin was testing the agents by asking for guns. Not a bad idea.

Cherie was startled out of her reverie when the screen suddenly lit up. Black figures could be seen near the shadowy outline of Suburbans that were arrayed in a wide semicircle.

"Testing, testing," she heard through the earphones. Sandy had just put hers on. She turned to Cherie and motioned for her to do the same. "Roger that," she said.

"Roger that," Cherie said, feeling ridiculous. Then she realized the original voice was Marie's, and the feeling evaporated.

"Cherie, do you hear me?" Marie asked.

"Loud and clear," replied Cherie.

"And can you hear me?" Samantha said.

"Loud and clear."

"Good. We're ready to go. Everything ready there?"

Cherie and Darrin looked at each other and then at Sandy, who glanced across the room. "Ready to go," Sandy said.

"Ready here," said Cherie and Darrin.

"Here we go," said Sam.

27

David Blinder hadn't slept much during the night following the attack on Washington, DC, but he took a nap in his private command room just before dawn. He was so enthusiastic about his plan finally coming to fruition that he didn't feel the need for much sleep. He woke up a couple of hours later feeling good about the prospects for the success of his project to break up the country. In his mind, he was Julius Caesar and the American land mass was Gaul: his for the taking. He could see in his mind through the current turmoil and through the tumult to follow. All of that was incidental to his goal: to enrich himself beyond measure and to establish a permanent oligarchy of like-minded men. Rich, powerful men; takers and builders and masters on the stage of life. He had to take deep breaths to keep himself focused on the present.

He looked around his elaborate command post. He felt secure in his own compound, but the command room was more than that. It gave him a sense of being enveloped in his own power, in his own capability. He breathed in deeply the cool air of the temperature-controlled room. Everything about it was for his purposes and pleasure. He had telephone and backup radio connections to key players; he had secure communication with his own troops and their leaders; and he had visual and audio input from all the major sites where his plans were being played out. He felt the power emanate from his hands as he expertly worked the controls.

True, he lost McLaren in that unfortunate incident over Washington, but by then McLaren's purposes had been fulfilled. In fact, he had already shut down the compromising electronic surveillance on federal agencies that McLaren had set up so expertly for so long prior to the attack, and David felt sure there would be no way to trace it to him.

He looked around the room and smiled. Very few people knew of this room's existence. It was his and his alone. No one but he was allowed access, and the entrance was artfully concealed along an otherwise unremarkable corridor of his sprawling estate. No one in David's family ever questioned where he was; everyone knew that David Blinder was accountable to no one.

David figured at some point there would be an effort to get to him, to take him into custody, as those two unfortunate federal agents had tried to do a few days before. There might even be an assault on his property—the federal government knew no limits when it came to enforcing its will. But nothing about that seemed imminent. David felt sure that if the feds were considering an assault, they would have to proceed through several bureaucratic and strategic steps before they got around to actual implementation. Nevertheless, he believed the attack on Washington, while the feds may not view it as a successful operation, was impressive enough in its scope to get their attention and consolidate their focus. This served his purposes perfectly, as it allowed the important parts of his plan to play out, especially in the state legislatures. Nothing works so well in a situation such as this as deception and mayhem.

He also figured that if an assault came, it would involve a large contingent of US Army troops. The US Army has a policy of using overwhelming force, and that requires time and planning. Blinder thought he had a week at the minimum to maneuver. That was plenty of time. By the time they scheduled an attack, the federal government would be no more.

His sense of security was further cemented by the seven-hundred-man contingent of Sovereign Citizens that Parker had organized and located in strategic places on his sprawling compound. If some rogue federal agency wanted to attack him, this force had enough technical competence to identify it and enough firepower to defeat it handily. Blinder felt as smug as any general could feel about his strategic position.

On that note, David got up from his chair in his sealed chamber and walked to the door. It was nearly time for breakfast, and he wanted to touch base with his wife and with George's wife. They would both be worried about George, who had disappeared without a word. As David opened the door and crossed the threshold, his demeanor changed. His family knew nothing of his role in recent events and were probably as glued to the television as everyone else in the nation. By the time he closed the hidden door and began making his way toward the breakfast room, David Blinder sloughed off his Julius Caesar persona and once again became the essence of the American husband, father, and businessman.

As he walked down the long corridor, David thought about his brother, George. Although David was not so concerned about his own immediate security, he could not help but feel the absence of his brother, who would normally have been present for the breakfast gathering. George's disappearance was a loose end, and David hated few things more than loose ends. He was concerned . . . no, he was flummoxed, irritated even, by George's absence. And in his mind, he could only explain it as a betrayal.

It wasn't as if David hadn't given that possibility some thought. He had from time to time wondered about George's level of commitment to the project the two of them had discussed through the years. George had played a part in it, often serving as a mediator between David and his various constituencies, massaging the appetites of the clergy, for instance, in an effort to neutralize opposition from the right. George also knew as much about the entire project as anyone outside the boundaries of David's mind. That was more than a loose end; it was a vulnerability.

The real problem was personal. David Blinder did not trust many people on the planet, but he trusted George. He knew George, though intelligent, was a follower and not a leader. But he also knew that George had a keen business sense. In many ways, he was the opposite of David: thoughtful and reflective where David was given to action; patient in a way David could scarcely imagine. Over time, David had come to rely on George's quiet intelligence to work through challenging parts of the overall plan. And now he was gone. Without his wife, without David's support. David shook his head, not so much in disbelief—it was, after all, simply a fact—but at the foolhardiness of his older brother's action. He was, for the moment at least, unsure of how to respond to it.

Halfway down the hall, David paused. He was a man of action, and the situation called for action. He turned around and reentered the room he had just left. Breakfast could wait.

He dialed a number he knew by heart. "The target is George Blinder," he said softly into the phone.

If the person on the other end was surprised, there was no hint of it in his voice. There was no hesitation in his response. "Yes, sir."

David put the phone down, closed his eyes for a moment, and then got up from his chair and left the room a second time.

As he walked down the hall, he felt bitterness in his throat, the kind that violated trust engenders, but he reminded himself that this was not the time to lose focus. He allowed himself a small chuckle at the simple elegance of George's plan. Everyone knew that George was in the habit of riding regularly for exercise. No one questioned his early morning bike ride.

David wanted to think about something else, so he began thinking about the key players in the drama that he had masterminded. He thought about Abner Bellamy and felt confident about the states of the old Confederacy. He actually admired Abner for his stamina, his conviction, his intelligence, and his persuasive powers. It was Abner who had engineered the secession movement in the Southern states. He knew Abner to be an ambitious, driven man who held his primary motivations very close. But David always did his homework. He knew about the tragic loss of Abner's father when he was young. He knew about his cynical decision to enter the ministry as a first career. He even knew about his tactical marriage to one of the most celebrated and wealthiest families in St. Louis, and about Judith, Abner's lover. David was nothing if not thorough.

He thought about Adam Wilson, who was another breed of beast. Whereas Abner, for all his drive and ambition and private motivations, was not a bad human being—he actually believed in something—David knew Adam Wilson to be a man utterly devoid of a moral sense and perhaps one of the most profoundly cynical persons David had ever met. Given the breadth of David's acquaintances and his own cynicism, that was a decidedly high bar.

He also knew that Wilson had a murderous and exhibitionistic streak. When he decided to dispatch one of his "trusted" group members, Wilson did not do so discreetly. After having Daniel Keenan killed, he had his body dismembered and spread throughout Keenan's hometown, where he lived and worked. Silly showmanship. David made a mental note to have Wilson done away with after he had served his purposes.

David put these thoughts out of his mind as he walked into the breakfast room, where the house staff was preparing to serve the first meal of the day. As he sat down, he greeted his wife, Mimi, and George's wife, Clarisse, who were the only current inhabitants of the sprawling compound. David had made sure the extended family members, including grandchildren and cousins and various more distant relatives, had been removed to other residences across the country before the action began.

As he walked toward his seat at the large breakfast table, he noticed that someone had brought in a television and placed it on a sideboard so that everyone could view it from the table. David's face darkened.

"I'll not have my breakfast interrupted by that thing," he said, nodding to the television. A house staffer nearby did not have to be told twice; he unplugged the television and removed it from the room. No one else in the room protested.

"Besides," David said soothingly, "we have other things to talk about." He looked at Clarisse. "I'm worried about George." A tear fell out of Clarisse's eye and David reached over and placed his hand on hers.

"We'll find him," he said reassuringly. "He may just have gotten lost, or detained with all that is happening in the country. Who knows?" He looked directly into Clarisse's eyes.

There was silence around the table for a moment. Then Mimi broke in. "Do you really think so, David?" she said. "Do you really think he could have been detained?"

David shrugged. "Stranger things have happened, honey," he said.

Clarisse could not contain her emotions any longer. "I'm so worried!" she cried. "Oh, David, what can we do to find him?"

David paused as he patted Clarisse's hand. "I've already sent some men out searching for him, Clarisse. I think we'll find him before long. And I'm sure that he will contact you or me or both of us as soon as he is able."

Clarisse didn't know what to say. She had a lot of confidence in David. She knew he was the more active one of the pair of Blinder brothers. But she thought she knew George pretty well, and it wasn't like him to go away without saying anything to anyone. Especially her. She had no idea what to think.

David squeezed her hand and turned to Mimi. "You'll stay with Clarisse today?" he asked.

"Of course," Mimi replied.

28

About two miles from the Blinder breakfast table, federal agents were preparing their assault. They assumed that the Blinder estate had state-of-the-art technical equipment, and they assumed it included layers of surveillance to signal them if an opposing force was approaching. A team of young, barely thirtysomething FBI agents had spent most of the previous evening assessing the specific types of surveillance in use and most of the night devising ways around them.

What they found was indeed a sophisticated set of audio and visual surveillance cameras designed to identify any intrusion. They learned that these were heaviest along the main road leading up to a gated entrance and a wide fence, and two narrower access roads along the other side of the large property that were designed for service vehicles. The fence along the front was at least a mile wide, arrayed on either side of a large wrought-iron gate that was electronically controlled.

To attempt an assault from the main road seemed unattractive to both the experienced and the wiz kids on the tech team. That's where the surveillance equipment was concentrated, and presumably that's where the defenses were strongest. The outbuildings were arranged in such a way as to give the defenders an open field of fire if anyone were so foolish as to attempt a direct assault. So even though the front entrance was closer to the main house and to the outbuildings, the decision was made to identify alternative assault points that would not have to go through a twelve-foot-high fence in what would amount to a suicide mission.

Away from the access roads, the surveillance was constant but less concentrated. Cameras and audio monitors were set farther apart but had overlapping sweeping functions. The team could identify no area around the entire estate that was completely free of surveillance.

Agent Schwartz, who was in charge of the overall operation until Sam and Marie arrived, did not like what he heard from his agents.

"Speed is everything here. We'll have to storm the compound quickly," he said to his young lieutenant. "We'll hope that by the time they see us on their monitors, they won't have time to respond effectively."

He decided on two assault teams: one would approach from a largely unencumbered area about fifty feet wide and twenty yards off the west end of the fence; the second would approach from a similar area on the east side. That way, they would not be facing each other directly, lessening the possibility of friendly fire casualties. The spanning cameras on both sides covered an area of about a hundred feet in front of the estate boundary. There was vegetation outside the compound at that point; it was lush but not sturdy: lots of low-lying bushes that federal vehicles could easily drive over without too much disturbance or noise. Schwartz thought that stealth and surprise could be maintained from these attack points.

The advance teams set up their own surveillance equipment. It was no use to make the Blinder cameras go blank; that would be as much a signal of attack as opening fire. Instead, they surreptitiously made videos of the surrounding foliage and landscape and planned to feed these back into the cameras just before the assault on the compound. They did the same with audio surveillance: they made recordings of the ambient sounds around the large estate to feed back into the surveillance system. Fortunately, it was so isolated that the sounds most commonly heard were of birds and small animals in the background.

When the assault teams arrived, Agent Schwartz demanded an update from the tech crew. He wanted to know precisely what measures were in place. The lieutenant in charge of one of the teams described the work that all the advance teams had done.

Schwartz listened with an unrevealing look on his face and did not respond when the young officer finished. After a few seconds of silence, he looked at the young man and said, "You think these will work?"

"Yes, sir," the young man replied without hesitation. Inwardly, Schwartz found the response reassuring. He showed no emotion to the lieutenant.

Instead, he turned to Samantha and Marie to brief them. "Okay. Here's what we've got: we can feed fake data into these cameras; that will give us a fifty-foot-wide entry point on either side of the fence." He paused for a moment. "We're only going to need it for a short time, which is about what we can expect anyway. We need to go in with massive firepower, so that even if the ruse doesn't work, it won't matter that much."

"How many troops have you been able to identify?" asked Marie.

"A few hundred in the outbuildings, including the barn," Schwartz replied. "We have reason to believe there are others scattered throughout the property. Probably five hundred or so. They are bivouacked at what appear to be random points throughout the grounds."

Samantha spoke next. "This is a big estate. What kind of vehicles do they have? What kind of mobility?"

"You mean how fast can they get here?" Schwartz asked.

Sam nodded. "Exactly."

"Pretty damn fast," came Schwartz's reply. "It looks like the outbuildings are heavily reinforced. Once we take those, we'll be in a better position to thwart attacks on our people."

Sam and Marie glanced at each other. "But those reinforced structures are going to make taking those buildings difficult," Marie said.

Schwartz did not reply right away.

"You know those bombs they used in Kentucky and tried to use in Washington?" he said at length.

The two women nodded.

"We have something that's built with the same technology but is more targeted. So even though in absolute terms they are not as powerful, they can easily take out those reinforced structures."

The two women stared at Schwartz for a moment without speaking. "Okay," they said in unison after a moment.

"Plus," he said, "it will strike from this distance." He looked over the heads of the two women to indicate what he was talking about.

Samantha and Marie turned to see a Humvee pulling up behind them with a mounted missile launcher with six tubes.

"We can take out every damn building on the property," he said with obvious pride.

"I don't think we want to do that," Samantha said. "We need information that's inside that house."

"I know. I was just bragging." He smiled the faintest of smiles.

Samantha and Marie split up the agents, each woman serving as a battlefield commander for her group. After they talked to Schwartz, they briefed their agents and began moving toward their respective staging areas. The plan was to lay low until missiles struck the outbuildings. Then the agents were to swarm all the structures, checking for pockets of resistance, set up new staging areas in the remains of the outbuildings, and prepare for reinforcements to arrive from other parts of the sprawling estate. They would have to handle any reinforcements before they could move to an assault on the main house and capture anyone left inside.

Both Sam and Marie had memorized the layout of the compound, as had most of the agents participating. There were three outbuildings of unknown use in addition to the large garage. One of these buildings appeared to be a barn. Sam opened her computer to have direct access to the satellite telemetry, which showed heat signatures in those buildings: closely grouped bands of men, presumably Sovereign Citizen troops, arrayed in various positions. Some were obviously sleeping, while some were just as obviously standing guard. Some were armed. Some were lying close to their weapons. All told, it looked like two hundred and fifty hostiles in the outbuildings, and another hundred in the garage. It was clear to Samantha that those buildings had to be dealt with as a priority in the assault.

She looked over at the missile system Schwartz had ordered to be brought up. She could not think of a reason not to use the missiles to destroy the buildings and to signal the beginning of the assault. It was an all-weather weapon that could stay out of range of the surveillance equipment and out of visual range. Once it started firing, the weapons system could target the buildings in rapid succession, or so Sam hoped.

Marie was assembling her team on the other side of the compound. She and her agents made their way through underbrush to a site similar to the one found on the west side of the fence. Their mission was to make sure no one fled the outbuildings to meet up with reinforcements and to keep other troops from reaching them if possible.

Schwartz did not say exactly what kind of damage the ordnance would do. Presumably it was impressive, but it was unclear to Samantha and Marie if it would demolish the buildings completely or just make defense untenable. They prepared for the worst.

29

Dawn was breaking in Texas, and the men inside the compound were restless. Even though Blinder had told them that an attack was not likely, Winslow Parker was not so sure, and he had instructed his staff to make sure there were no lapses in preparedness.

Chip Wolbert, the on-site commander, took Parker's caution to heart. Wolbert knew that lack of preparation or, worse, a surprise attack could be disastrous for his men. While they had a significant contingent of men on the property, the numbers were not so high as he would have liked. He was a military man, and he understood that the Sovereign Citizens had other priorities. He was proud of what his army had accomplished in Washington and in Kentucky. He was not about to let his superiors or his men down.

Wolbert felt the loss of Aaron McLaren more than most. McLaren was a technological genius with few peers. Wolbert had a huge interest in the technology of warfare, and he and McLaren had worked together in building the technological aspects of the Blinder estate defenses. In addition, Wolbert knew that it was McLaren who devised the system of covert surveillance within the federal government—a system that by all accounts was never detected. And the system that McLaren built for the family compound gave Wolbert some extra peace of mind about their prospects for defending the property, if the situation ever came to that. They had the latest tech backup.

One of the advancements that McLaren implemented on the estate was recognition of thermal imaging sweeps. It was McLaren who discovered that such intrusions raised the ambient temperature in a given building a barely perceptible amount: .002 degrees with an unusual but identifiable pattern of alpha waves. He had installed a device to detect this in each of the outbuildings where the Sovereign Citizen troops were staying.

So Wolbert knew that the estate was being surveilled regularly and that it started several days before the attack on DC. It was this fact that led him to question David Blinder's reassurances about the time it would take to arrange an attack. It was not definitive, but it suggested that the Blinder estate was on the feds' radar. Literally. At the same time, Wolbert could not be certain of what it really meant. For all he knew, the feds could be surveilling the whole nation. As soon as it was discovered that the machine was registering readings he informed Mr. Blinder about it. David Blinder did not seem concerned.

Wolbert knew enough about the billionaire not to question his judgment or insist that something had meaning when he wasn't entirely sure what the meaning was himself. Still, the readings concerned him. He worked out a schedule and sent men out to reconnoiter at random intervals. So far, no one reported anything unusual. These men patrolled the perimeter of the estate, but especially the areas around the main buildings. Wolbert also kept his men on heightened alert, just in case Mr. Blinder was wrong. Of course, he did not tell Mr. Blinder that he did this.

But he did report it to Major Parker, who thought it was the wisest course of action.

As he was thinking about the heat signatures, two men came off their patrol and walked up to him at his small desk in the corner of the barn.

"Captain Wolbert," said the taller one, saluting him. "Nothing to report. Nothing unusual."

Wolbert nodded but didn't say anything. He didn't know why, but he wasn't reassured. He just had a feeling.

"Get some rest, gentlemen," he said at last. He was appreciative of the discipline of his men. And proud of it. He knew that they would brief with the next patrol and bring them up to date. War is a lot of waiting around, he thought bitterly, echoing something his father had told him a long time ago.

30

Cherie Keenan had a hard time believing that any of the agents she was surrounded by were traitors. Agent Thurmond was nothing but helpful. When she thought there was something that Cherie heard or saw on the monitor that she might not understand, Thurmond offered a simple explanation. She encouraged questions and gave concise answers. She seemed to Cherie to be one of the good guys. Definitely one of the good guys.

Darrin hadn't spoken much since he had requested a weapon. He kept the pistol in his belt and the rifle on the table a few inches from his right hand. It seemed to Cherie that he was staring at the screen without blinking. Maybe he's in some kind of trance, she thought.

She turned to watch the other agents working exotic equipment. She had no idea war was so complicated or so reliant on technology. It all made it seem like a video game or something her children would do to entertain themselves. It also seemed vulnerable to attack. She shuddered as she thought about it.

With Thurmond's help, Cherie felt she was able to understand generally what was happening, and all the agents, though stoic, seemed to harbor a kind of unspoken optimism about the mission. This seemed a little odd to Cherie, who understood that the agents in the field were seriously outnumbered.

She was feeling anxious about all this activity and the coming assault. She turned to Darrin and tapped him on the shoulder.

"How's this going for you?" she whispered. "I mean, does this all seem okay?"

Darrin took his eyes off his monitor for only a moment to glance at Cherie. "I think it's going okay," he said in a low voice. "I think those missiles will even up the odds nicely if they work as advertised." He glanced at Cherie again and winked.

Given the circumstances, Cherie found that usually charming gesture devoid of grace. To her the thought of blowing up buildings with people in them bordered on the unreal. It felt obscene to kill people . . . unless, of course, they were trying to kill you in return. This thought gave her pause, but it did not fit her peaceable nature. She recognized that soldiers or federal agents took this sort of thing in stride; it was, after all, their life. But it was a world she was not familiar with and one she did not want to cozy up to in any way.

Still, duty was duty. If saving Marie and Samantha and Darrin, if saving the United States of America required this kind of action, she could not bring herself to oppose it. But her heart sank at the potential human cost. A tear of unbelieving fear rolled down her cheek.

For his part, Darrin was trying to be attentive to Cherie while not losing track of the activity in the field. He glanced at her, then back at the screen, then back at her, then back at the screen. He felt a conflict between sincerely wanting to be available for Cherie and being mesmerized by the activity in the field. He had not felt this engaged since he left the marines twenty years before. He loved the feeling.

Cherie felt Darrin's struggle and smiled at it, but inwardly. It seemed like such a guy thing. Don't miss the action. She turned back to watch the other agents, and it was at that moment that she felt something was not quite right.

On the other side of the room, a young man in an FBI jacket had bent over toward the floor, obscuring Cherie's view of him. He didn't stand up right away. She almost got up to see if he needed help, but before she could move, he not only straightened up but raised himself to his full height. He had a gun in his hand.

Cherie sank her fingers into Darrin's leg next to hers, the closest contact point to her body. Darrin looked over and saw the man with a gun. Without thinking, he reached for the rifle that was two inches away from his right hand.

The young man raised his pistol and checked the sight. He held it at a forty-five-degree angle toward the ceiling. Then he put it in his holster.

Cherie and Darrin both let out a sigh of relief. Cherie was comforted to know Darrin was so quick—he had his rifle in his hands within seconds—but she also recognized that she completely misread a situation in a room full of weapons and agents who knew how to use them. She shuddered at the enormity of what she was involved in and turned to glance at Darrin before she fixed her eyes on the screen in front of her. I need to stay focused, she thought.

gent Schwartz was not a novice agent. He had been with the military for years. He understood that fighting was an unpredictable business. He was a firm believer in being prepared, but he also understood that armies usually fought new wars with last-war technology and tactics. The human species was wondrously imaginative when it came to developing new ways to make mayhem.

So he didn't feel entirely settled, even as he saw his plans and preparations come to life in the fields outside the Blinder estate. In his head he checked and double-checked everything. He ran every detail of the plan by the two women who had flown in from Chicago to take charge. He didn't mind that; there was plenty of risk to go around in this bizarre situation.

He radioed Marie, who, along with her agents, had taken up positions on the eastern side of the wide fence that served as the entrance to the estate. He motioned for Samantha, who was standing near him, to come closer. Dawn was breaking.

"Are you ready?" he whispered into his radio.

"Yes, we are ready." There was a pause. "One more thing," Marie whispered back. "We've spotted scouts along the perimeter of the estate. Two men walked along for several hundred yards." Another pause. "I am thinking there are sentries all along the perimeter of the estate."

Schwartz nodded and looked at Samantha to make sure she understood what Marie was saying. He turned and motioned to a lieutenant behind him who had also heard the message. The young lieutenant knew exactly what to do. He went off to search for scout teams.

"That makes fewer men in the buildings," Schwartz said into the radio. He turned and looked at Samantha. "But be sure you take out those troops before approaching the buildings."

Sam nodded.

"Will do," Marie replied.

Schwartz raised his head to survey the preparations one more time. He gazed around in a complete circle. Then his gaze fell on Samantha, who was staring intently at him.

"Ready?" he said quietly.

"Ready."

"Ready?" he repeated into his microphone.

"Ready."

"On my signal, we will launch the missiles. Two for each building. Once they hit, proceed to the outbuildings and kill or capture any remaining troops. Fortify whatever is left of the structure and prepare for a counterassault from the other SC troops who will no doubt come to help."

"Got it," said Marie. Sam nodded.

Schwartz took a deep breath. "Here we go."

32

Barack Obama sat in the empty Oval Office staring across his desk at the portrait of himself on the far wall. At the moment, he did not feel much like the most powerful man on earth. He did, however, feel a sense of potency in his clear-eyed decision. His hands were flat against the smooth surface of the Resolute desk.

His senses were on high alert. He noted the absence of human noise in the room and the various electronic sounds in the background. He could even hear the voices of nature outside his bulletproof window. His vision was sharp and his mind clear. His teeth were clenched, and his jaw was set against the tide of rebellion across important areas of the nation.

He was focused on the plan of action that had just occurred to him several moments before, when his office was filled with advisors and their respective entourages of assistants, secretaries, gofers, and related votaries.

As he saw it, the action in the state legislatures in the South and in other parts of the country was the greatest threat the nation had faced since 1861, when his predecessor and hero, Abraham Lincoln, sat in this same building. At that time, the geographic lines were clearly drawn, and war, which had been threatening to break out for years and had been quietly lying in wait in the background, was gaining momentum.

That part was not so different from now, he reflected. But then, the South was one large aggregate of a nation. And even though the principles of those states were not so solid as those that created the Union in the first place, they looked like, acted like, and even felt like one separate nation.

This time, the states of the South, while considering confederation, were more oriented toward disbanding. It wasn't one country against another, as in 1861. Now, Texas was talking to Oklahoma; California was in talks with Oregon and Washington. Mr. Obama's eyes flared when he beheld in his mind the elaborate evil behind this massive plot. They flared again at the fact that this had been brewing *sub rosa* for years and almost no one in the government was aware of it.

He was sure that what he was facing was decisively different from that which his haloed predecessor had faced, and it called for a different response. While Mr. Obama disagreed with the Confederate agenda of those days, he knew the states were fighting for their culture, as abhorrent as it was to him and to many people in the North and as incomprehensible as it is to the vast majority of Americans now.

But the people Obama was facing now weren't fighting for culture. They were fighting for greed and self-aggrandizement. It made him sick. Whatever the ultimate fate of the United States, he was unable to allow it to be manipulated by moneyed and fanatical interests who merely wanted to further their monetary and fanatical goals. The United States stands for more than that, he thought grimly.

War in this day and age was of a different order than what Lincoln commanded. And Mr. Obama was not at all sure how it would work out. He knew a couple of things: One was that this battle was for the soul of the nation. That is not so different from 1861. Another was that this battle was not his alone but belonged to the American people. And he believed in the American people, no matter how wayward he often found their political representatives. But it was his job to lead, and this meant calling on the resources of the American people, which he believed to be endless. His job was to marshal that strength, to form a bulwark of protection against the moneyed and fanatical groups that coalesced to threaten the Union that those brave men two and a half centuries earlier had, with much blood and treasure and uncertainty, knit together.

Mr. Obama believed in his heart that the vast majority of Americans stood with him against this abomination, and he intended to lead that vast majority to give voice and power to their most basic and cherished values.

To that end, he was composing a speech. He had three hours before he would address the American people. That's plenty of time, he thought. This wasn't the time for refined, grandiloquent language; this was the time for the plain and simple truth. The powerful truth. And the potent truth was that no one owns the United States: not him, not the Blinder brothers, not the Sovereign Citizens. The country belongs to all Americans, and if the American people wanted to preserve the Union, they would have to take a stand to protect it.

Obama recognized that although he saw the show of force as a peacekeeping measure, it would not in all likelihood play out that way on the ground. Some people might—probably would—get hurt. Some might—probably would—die. But sacrifice is not unknown to the American people. They have been called to it before, and they will be called to it again. It was his job to do the calling.

He knew that working through the attorneys general of the states was at best a stop-gap measure that may give him some more time. He needed something larger and more decisive. It was his intention to call upon the American people to assemble around the state capitals of the dissident states and let it be known to their legislators what every decent citizen in the United States knows: that you cannot destroy the Union, that you cannot destroy the United States of American by violence and subterfuge.

He had to bring his staff up to date, so he pushed the intercom button on his phone.

"Anita, tell everyone to come back in."

He waited quietly as his advisors filed in and resumed their places around the Great Seal of the United States woven into the carpet that decorated the floor in front of his desk. He waited for everyone to get seated.

"Ladies and gentlemen, as you know, I will be addressing the nation in a few hours. I intend to explain this situation to them in simple, clear, and unmistakable terms. I also intend to ask them to make their presence felt in any state capital that is considering secession. Their physical presence. If they can't travel, they can call or email or text. But mostly I want them to go and surround their state legislatures in vast numbers and let their wishes be known to those whose values were perverted by money, greed, or unadulterated self-interest."

No one spoke, and the President did not ask for a response. He looked around the room. Silence.

"We can offer brave citizens protection either by federal marshals, the US Army, or nationalized state militias. They will assemble around the crowds to protect them from any assault by any force that impedes their right to peaceably assemble in the nation's interest."

He turned to Eric Holder, who was sitting on his left. "Eric, I want you to draw up a statement that can be distributed to our citizens explaining clearly and simply what their demands are from their local governance authorities. I want it to include a statement of what the consequences will be for those authorities if they refuse."

Eric looked at the President. "And what are the consequences, Mr. President?" he asked without a trace of irony in his voice.

"At the very least, trial for treason," the President replied. "Perhaps by a military court, as these actions are connected to armed military action against the United States government."

Holder nodded. "I'll have it on your desk in thirty minutes, Mr. President."

The President then turned to Joe Biden. "Joe, I want you to go over to Congress and tell them they will be in session until this crisis is past. I don't want any of those Southern delegates or the delegates of any state considering secession to leave the Capitol. Or the chamber, for that matter.

"And I want you to let them know clearly that if they do not embrace a repudiation of these movements they will also face trial for treason, sedition, and consorting with the enemy."

Joe nodded wordlessly.

Finally, he turned to the head of the joint chiefs. "General Dempsey, do you understand what I am asking of the military?"

"Yes, sir, I think I do."

"Can you do it?"

"Yes, sir, we can."

Obama's gaze fell on General Dempsey for a moment. "After your heroic response to the assault on the capital yesterday, General, I believe you."

Mr. Obama sat back in his chair. "I want to be informed of every significant detail as these events play out." He paused for a moment, then looked each person in the eye. "Okay, ladies and gentlemen, we have work to do. Let's do it."

Once again, Joe Biden was the first to respond. He stood up and gestured for the others to follow him.

Once again, Barack Obama was alone in the Oval Office. He took up a pen and started writing his speech to the nation. Despite facility with computers and word processors, the President thought that writing with a hand instrument provided time for thought and reflection as the ideas coalesced in his mind.

He was deep into his work when his phone buzzed.

"Mr. President," Anita said. "Max Grabel is on the line."

"Put him through."

"Mr. President," Max said. "I wanted to bring you up to date personally on what our agents have been doing and what they are about to do."

"Go, Max."

"As we speak, about eighty federal agents are preparing an assault on the estate of David and George Blinder. We believe that these men, particularly David Blinder, are the ones who stitched together the dissident groups in the country to coordinate yesterday's attack." He paused. "We also believe they are even now orchestrating events in key state legislatures to bring about secession."

"What is the situation on the ground, Max?" the President asked. "How big is the estate and how heavily is it defended?"

"The estate includes about eighty thousand acres in the heart of Texas," Max replied. "It is defended by about eight hundred Sovereign Citizen troops."

"Same group as yesterday's attack."

"Same group. Also the same group that stole the gold from Fort Knox."

"What do you need from me, Max?" the President asked.

Max paused. "We have a warrant to enter the property. In fact, we've had it for several days. Two days ago, two agents went to the Blinder estate to serve it." A pause. "They have not been heard from since."

Mr. Obama did not respond right away. People will probably get killed, he thought. He said a quick prayer for those agents.

"You didn't say you needed more people."

"I don't think we do, just now, Mr. President. We have some of our best agents on the scene with more on the way, and they are very well equipped."

"That's fine, Max. But I want backup for those agents."

"I think it would be a mistake to wait, Mr. President."

Mr. Obama thought for a moment. "Sheppard Air Force Base is right there. All of our forces are on high alert. We can get you air support in a matter of minutes."

"Let me check with the agents on the ground, sir."

"In the meantime, I'll alert Sheppard."

Max clicked off and punched Schwartz's number. He explained what the President was offering.

"We can use all the help we can get, Max. Especially when the SC reinforcements arrive. Helicopters, if you can spare them."

"Okay," said Max. He clicked off and redialed the President's number.

"It's a go, Mr. President. The agent in charge there says he could use helicopter support."

"You got it, Max."

The President had just hung up with General Dempsey, who was already putting a plan into action.

"Let me know if you need anything else, Max," the President added.

"Will do, sir. One more thing: I want to be sure that you know about this, and that you know that our evidence is solid and becoming more so every hour. Since the attack ended yesterday and the Army took over, we have been pouring all of our resources into identifying the major players in this insurrection."

The President sighed. Where would the United States be without good men like Grabel?

"Anything else?"

"No, sir, I'll keep you posted as events unfold."

"Use my direct line, Max."

"Thank you, Mr. President."

"Thank you, Max," the President replied.

33

About six hundred miles west of Washington, another agent was talking to Major General Jeremy Spader, the commanding general of the Fort Knox Army facility. Special Agent Matthew Spalding of the FBI and General Spader were reviewing how it happened that one of the most closely guarded buildings in the world collapsed and its precious contents carried off in a matter of minutes. Neither was happy, but the General was enraged.

"It was the MOABs," said Spalding.

The commanding general was not in the mood for overly simplified explanations or for pointing fingers. He wanted data, hard data about how the facility was compromised so effectively.

"Anybody can get a bomb," he said tartly. "I don't think that was by itself critical."

Spalding did not disagree. The fact was that he was at a loss to explain how a facility with almost thirty thousand Army troops within a mile could be compromised so quickly. Still, the use of MOABs figured prominently in his mind, as did the element of surprise.

"We could probably have dealt with a single MOAB," he said in a conciliatory tone of voice. He wasn't trying to alienate the General; he was looking for answers himself. "But there were at least two and perhaps three. It completely destroyed the building."

"You are not thinking broadly enough, Agent Spalding," General Spader said. "These people not only flattened the building—any moron with enough firepower can do that—but they knew exactly how to enter the vaults belowground and collect the gold. They knew who to threaten, who to kill, and who they needed to keep alive for access." He paused and looked out the window of his large office at the ruins of the depository. He shook his head. "There were traitors in the mix."

Spalding did not dispute that. He knew that the FBI was getting some intel about a compromised computer network that may have been used to penetrate defenses of key government agencies. But he didn't have enough hard data for Spader. "We're looking into that," he said to the irate General sitting across the conference table from him.

He decided to take another tack. "We are repositioning our satellite surveillance to track the intruders," he said. "It turns out they are very skilled at stealing Army material and then hiding it quickly. We're scanning for it now."

"And just how do you intend to find it?" demanded the General.

"We can track the amounts of gold in the aggregate. Unless they divide it up into leaden shoe boxes, we believe we will locate it within a matter of hours." He looked at the General. "It took some time to reposition the satellite," he said with just a hint of apology in his voice.

The General looked at the agent squarely. "When you find it and get a lead on the men who did this, let me know. I want those bastards, and I want to be the one who brings them to justice. One way or the other."

Agent Spalding nodded. He hoped the FBI would find the gold soon, as he had no doubt that Spader meant exactly what he said.

Spalding walked out of the office and called Stanley Schindler, the head of the FBI and Spalding's boss, on his mobile. Schindler was coordinating the FBI response to the terrorist attack personally. He had a contact person on-site at every venue where events were unfolding. Or spiraling out of control, depending upon one's perspective, Spalding thought darkly.

"Spader wants in on recovery of the gold," he said, describing one version of the conversation.

"I'm sure he'd love to kill those bastards personally," came Schindler's reply. "We'll see about that, but for now keep him in the loop."

"Update on satellite surveillance?" Spalding asked.

"We have a bead on three separate caches of gold," Schindler replied. "They are all within a hundred and fifty miles of your location, and they are all going in separate directions." He paused a moment. "We're in the process of setting up roadblocks, but far enough ahead of them so as not to draw attention to ourselves. We will implement them simultaneously and quickly once I give the order."

"What about Spader?"

"Keep him up to date and stay open to input from him. We may need his help; he's got lots of personnel. But keep the communication between you and him personal and discreet. We're not one hundred percent sure the bugs they've had in our systems are down."

"Understood," Spalding said. He clicked off.

Spalding walked back into Spader's office without knocking. "Just spoke to the director," he said. "He concurs that you will be in the loop, so we'll keep you apprised of the situation." He then described what Schindler had told him about the gold caches, their movements, and the roadblocks.

Spalding wasn't sure about what changed in the General's demeanor. It wasn't his ice block of a face, because there was no external shift in his facial features. But he felt something. After a moment, he decided it was focus. The General now had a direction in which to proceed.

"I want in on this," he reminded the agent unnecessarily.

Spalding looked slightly askance at the General. "We want you in on it, General," he said. "We need all the help we can get."

The General stood up and walked around his desk to a large map of the Fort Knox part of Kentucky. "Do you know where they are precisely?"

"It's on the move, but that information will be coming in momentarily in real time."

The General picked up his phone. "Get my adjutant in here," he said firmly.

Adjutant General Walker Nicholson was at the door in under a minute. "Sir," he said simply.

"Nicholson, Spalding; Spalding, Nicholson," the General said by way of introduction. "We're going to fry these bastards," he said to both men.

Neither doubted him.

34

Winslow Parker was feeling pretty good about the attack on Fort Knox. He was not a sociopath, and he felt genuine remorse for the lives lost and the bodies injured during the assault on the federal depository. But this mission was so critical to the overall success of the battle, he couldn't help weighing the larger picture. This was war, after all, and in war people die. Sometimes needlessly. He was especially pleased that there were so few casualties among his men: a few wounds, but no one on his side was killed. He was grateful for that.

As with most of the operations in which Parker had been involved, this one came off with mathematical precision. The gold was loaded and was driven off-site within an hour. About fifteen miles from what was left of the depository, it was divided into equal parts in three unmarked civilian trucks. And now each of those trucks was en route to a secure facility in the Blue Ridge Mountains. One had a fairly direct path, but the others had circuitous ones that they used to evade detection. Parker wasn't overly concerned with being discovered. He had done similar things before, and he could smell success when it was upon him. The feds couldn't respond quickly enough. The underground bunker where the gold was to be stored had been ready for weeks. It had taken months to build, and it was as secure a facility as could be devised. Deep underground, it had no telltale building on top of it the way the Fort Knox facility had. No one would know it was there.

Parker was riding in what looked like an old American-made jeep ahead of the trucks that had the most direct route. He was anxious to get to the site as soon as possible, both to coordinate the delivery of the gold and to remove himself from surface activity, where it was possible, if not likely, that someone or some satellite could spot him either deliberately or by accident. He figured he had another couple of hours before he and his crew would arrive in that part of Tennessee.

In the meantime, he had been on the phone with the commander at the Blinder estate. While Parker felt confident in himself and in those activities in which he was directly involved—he did not lack self-esteem—he was always tenuous about the commands of others.

It's not that Chip Wolbert wasn't a competent fellow. Parker had picked him because he was a cut above the competition for the second-choicest command in this whole operation: protecting the Blinder estate. Parker knew that David Blinder was the only person who was privy to all aspects of the overall operation, and he had to be protected no matter what. But the fact was that the assault on Washington had taken many more troops than Parker had originally thought, and the men he selected for the protection of the Texas property, while among the most competent and well trained in the Sovereign Citizens corps, were few in number. They were well equipped, however, and Parker had confidence that they could handle any danger coming their way.

Parker also knew that David Blinder was a great deal more sanguine about the likelihood of an assault on his home. It was obvious that Blinder had little respect for the flexibility of the US military. While in general terms Parker agreed with Blinder, he preferred to cover all his bases.

He had last checked in with Wolbert about an hour ago. He presumed if he heard nothing from him in between their scheduled reports that everything was all right. He required Wolbert to check in every two hours.

Still, Parker was antsy. He was on the passenger side of the front seat of the jeep, which was being driven by a young man, a local, whom he had selected specifically for this task. He liked the kid. He reminded Parker of himself at that age: focused, hard, willing to do whatever needed to be done to further the mission. Parker respected that in him.

The kid was content to be silent. He had not spoken since they had picked up their consignment of gold from the distribution point after the initial assault. That was fine with Parker. He wasn't in the mood for conversation. Still, once the battle was joined, as it was now, he had some trouble containing his anxiety.

"How long do you estimate it will be before we get there?" he asked the young man.

"Under two hours, sir."

Parker took a deep breath. In his mind, he worked over the details of the plan, how it was conceived, why it was conceived, all the details as they were anticipated and as they actually happened. He could not identify a single flaw in his analysis. This worried him.

He swung around in his seat to make sure the trucks were still behind them at a close distance. Of course, they were, so he turned to face forward again. I bet this kid thinks I'm a batty old man, he thought. Maybe I am.

Parker picked up his cell and called the men in charge of the other trucks. "Any problems?" Neither reported any difficulties. It all seemed to be going according to plan. It all seemed to be working perfectly.

What am I missing?

35

It was clear to General Spader what Parker was missing. As the satellite imagery came online, he immediately recognized the enemy's plan. He could even envision the general location where the three trucks would converge. He pictured an area just east of Chattanooga. He was so confident of this he ordered two companies of his men to head in that direction by air to be available if and when he needed them. He also ordered nearby Army units to proceed in that direction.

Government haters often underestimate the professionalism of all government. It was clear to the General that whoever did this counted on a feckless response from whatever government agency had jurisdiction. This made General Spader chuckle internally. It was not a chuckle of mirth; it was recognition of how fatal a mistake he hoped it would be in this circumstance.

What such people never seem to grasp is how high the bar is set for military and civilian workers in the US military structure. General Spader had at his disposal more trained intellectual and physical talent than any professional football team, any academic department, or any corporate headquarters on the planet. And the fact that all that talent was in a system over which he had nearly regal control made him both proud and focused. He would marshal that talent to crush the enemy.

The General's office was suddenly transformed into a whirlwind of activity. He did not bark orders; he did not have to. He spoke orders that he knew were fulfilled as soon as practicable after the words exited his mouth.

Agent Spalding watched in something akin to awe. Being a high-level FBI agent, he was not unfamiliar with institutional discipline, but watching the General in action was impressive even by the rigorous standards of the Bureau. And through it all, Spalding understood each order and how that order fit into the larger picture.

As he saw it, the General was providing backup for the agents manning the roadblocks. He was instinctively doing what Director Schindler wanted him to do. And not just in the rear of those formations, but all along the incoming roadways for several miles. What the drivers of those trucks did not know was that they would soon be driving into a funnel at the end of which there would be no possibility of escape. Not forward, not backward, not sideways. Nowhere.

The troops the General had sent to Chattanooga, the area he believed was the likely intended destination of those trucks, were being helicoptered in using RAH-66 Comanche helicopters, the stealthy ones used to such good effect in taking down Osama bin Laden. By the time they got close, the destination would be pinpointed, and the troops would land far enough away from their target so as not to be noticed. Also en route, those men were briefed on exactly what to do when they got there: secure the ground, control all incoming and outgoing communication, and await his signal.

Spalding had a problem with none of this. He was always proud of being part of the FBI, but now that pride extended itself to include working with the kind of top-notch talent he witnessed at this moment. He relayed all these events to Schindler in Washington.

"Good work, Spalding," his boss said. "Keep me up to date."

"Will do, sir," Spalding replied, knowing full well that the credit was not his. His part was to "liaise," as military jargon described it: to serve as a mediator between the resources of the Bureau and the US Army now swinging into action. He had every intention of making sure that whatever credit there was would be shared by all these brave and talented men and women.

36

Outside Wichita Falls, dawn had broken, and the tension among the agents was palpable. Agent Schwartz listened carefully to the radio on the epaulet of his uniform as his agents checked in. He was absolutely immobile. When the last agent signaled that she was ready, he turned and made eye contact with the agent controlling the missile launcher. He took a short breath and nodded once.

The firing of the missiles made surprisingly little noise, in sharp contrast to the sounds that followed milliseconds later when six missiles exploded into the outbuildings of the Blinder estate. Those explosions rocked the ground at his feet.

"Move, move, move," he shouted into the mike. In his hands he was carrying a standard-issue M4 carbine. He had multiple clips attached to his belt. He moved forward from his position to get a sense of the damage done to the buildings. He could hear gunfire in front of him.

Schwartz raised his binoculars, as if they would allow him to see through the haze of the explosions. He turned his head to make sure the missile tubes were being reloaded in case they were needed, and he squatted to watch and listen to whatever telltale sounds of battle he could hear.

There wasn't much. There was some screaming, no doubt people writhing in pain. Probably not his agents. There was an occasional crack of small-arms fire that sounded like the report of a carbine just like the one in his hand. He leaned forward.

It was then that he noticed lights going on in the main house of the Blinder estate. He picked up his binoculars again and registered that lights were turning on throughout the enormous mansion. He also noticed movement inside, near the windows. He was pretty sure he saw the outlines of men with automatic weapons on the move.

"Hostiles inside main house," he said into his mike.

Silence.

In Schwartz's mind, those men, if they were SC troops, were probably trying to get a handle on the situation. They could also be waiting for reinforcements they knew were on the property. But they were no doubt looking for people to shoot at.

"Armed hostiles in the main house," he said again, this time in a louder voice. "Sam, Marie, report in."

His radio crackled for a maddening moment. "This is Samantha. I see them." A moment later: "This is Marie, copy that."

Schwartz considered firing missiles into the main house, but he knew that would risk killing David Blinder, and his orders were to take him alive. Still, in battle, casualties happen. "Only fire at the main house if someone inside is firing at you," he barked into his mike.

He did not have a lot of time to think. His radio crackled again and he heard the sound of motor vehicles racing toward the largely demolished outbuildings. Damn, he thought. He wasn't sure his agents had time to get there to assess the damage or use what remained of them as cover.

To his right, Agent Schwartz saw the red lines of laser sights crisscrossing the field toward where his agents were in place. He heard more gunfire—his agents picking off the snipers, he hoped and assumed.

More SC troops were streaming in from behind the burned outbuildings. He was tracking them through his binoculars as well as the smoke allowed. Some were looking for casualties among the ruins; some were setting up a new perimeter. Damn professional men, he thought with a touch of admiration. "Reinforcements coming in fast," he barked into his shoulder mike.

The SC troops were taking up positions on the far side of the Blinder mansion and racing to the same ruins that the federal agents were trying to use as cover. The sound of gunfire intensified as the two opposing sides fought for the same ground.

Schwartz turned to the missile vehicle and hand-motioned the controller not to fire again at the same buildings. Firing again would have killed as many of his men as the enemy. The operator stood down, and the missiles were armed, ready, and useless.

Schwartz surveyed the battlefield. He figured the SC troops would try to outflank his men. It was just a matter of when. Bingo! He saw slower-moving personnel carriers carefully moving away from the center of battle in an effort to find an opening. Damn, damn, damn.

"Personnel carriers on east and west sides," he spit into his mike. He looked back at the missile launcher to recalibrate the targets just before it burst into flames.

The blaze from the launcher lit up the early Texas morning and gave everyone on the other side a bird's-eye view of where the attackers were coming from. Live fire started pouring from the personnel carriers and from the main house. Agents who were not on the ground got there fast.

"Where the hell did that come from?" Schwartz said, hitting the ground hard. He was too shocked to incorporate this new data. In the few seconds it took him to realize that the SC troops had targetable missiles, Schwartz heard another explosion in front of him. It was only after he had gotten used to that noise that he heard the soft whoop-whoop of the stealth helicopters Grabel had obtained for them.

"Agent Schwartz," crackled his mike. "This is Squadron Leader Moberly Shaftner at your service."

That was close. Schwartz could see that the copters were targeting the SC personnel carriers to great effect. He could also see his agents fanning sideways to discourage the attempt at flanking their positions.

So far so good, he allowed himself to think.

Right after that thought, he saw another missile heading for the helicopter. He tried to radio Shaftner, but he could see that the pilot was taking evasive action. In one coordinated movement, he dodged the incoming missile and fired one back at the launcher. Schwartz watched as the ground-to-air missile exploded uselessly in the air and the air-to-ground missile hit its target square on.

He heard another helicopter behind him. He turned to see a Sikorsky H-92 transport ship landing behind him. About two dozen US Army troops poured out. The lieutenant in charge found Schwartz within minutes and saluted.

"How can we help, sir?"

"There are a lot more troops where those came from. They were trying a flanking maneuver when the gunships showed up. I think they've changed their minds, but just to be sure, split your men between the east and west sides and protect my agents' flanks."

The young man saluted and did not ask a single question. He turned and barked orders at his men to take up positions on the eastern and western flanks of the black-suited agents. The lieutenant then went to greet another two dozen troops arriving on a second Sikorsky.

Schwartz continued to hear the gunships pounding the positions of the enemy. He had deeply mixed feelings about this. He was grateful beyond words to have the support of the military, but he also respected the defenders of the estate. They were, after all, Americans as well. And even though they were following a different flag for the moment, they were his fellow citizens, and it pained him to know they were being mowed down.

But such is war, he reminded himself, as he prepared for the final assault on the Blinder mansion.

ack at the command post, Darrin and Cherie watched these developments with alternating feelings of shock, horror, relief, and dismay.

"Where are those missiles coming from?" demanded Darrin.

Agent Thurmond did not take her gaze off the monitor. "From a launcher positioned about a mile back from the main house," she said evenly. A moment later: "It's gone now." She continued to stare at the screen. "There may be more." She was working to identify remaining targets for the helicopter gunships.

Neither Darrin nor Cherie had heard anything from Marie or Samantha for some long minutes. They did not want to initiate any contact so as not to impair their attention to their work on the ground, but they were feeling less than useful.

Cherie looked down and realized she was squeezing Darrin's hand. She must have been doing this since her overreaction to the agent checking his weapon minutes before. Mildly embarrassed, she gave Darrin's hand a small squeeze and removed her own from his lap.

Sandy Thurmond was speaking what sounded like gibberish into her mouthpiece and had her eyes glued to the large monitor in front of her. Her face betrayed no emotion.

Cherie tried to guess her age. She had her pegged at early thirties at most. Her heart welled with appreciation of the talent, discipline, and dedication of this young woman, a feeling that she easily extended to every agent in the room.

She glanced around the large space. Every single agent was engrossed in the task in front of him or her. The atmosphere in the room was tense but engaged, earnest. These men and women were united in a single task. They seemed to speak only when necessary, and they were mostly silent.

All at once, everyone froze in place. Cherie looked over at Darrin, who had noticed the change.

"Okay," said Agent Thurmond. "We're down to the main house."

Cherie looked back at her monitor. Then her earpiece crackled.

"Cherie, this is Marie. We're halfway there. Few casualties. How're you doing?"

Cherie was flustered that Marie would take the time to check in with her for no reason, and she didn't want to keep her. "Everything's fine here. Are you okay?"

"Yeah. We're getting ready to approach the main house."

Cherie looked at Darrin, who was listening in on the same conversation. He was nodding.

"Keep safe," said Cherie with her eyes on Darrin. She felt stupid for saying it, but it was precisely what she wanted to say.

Then the activity in the room ramped up again as the agents went back to their jobs, focused and on task. For the first time since she left Wichita, Cherie Keenan felt safe. She put her hand back over Darrin's and squeezed gently. Safe is good, she thought.

38

As attorney general, Mercer Willoughby had had some dealings with the State Defense Force in Georgia before. He considered it a motley group of largely older men who liked to play soldier and who kept the light of freedom, by which they meant secession, alive in the hearts of their like-minded contemporaries. But Mercer knew they had access to weapons and depots ordinarily used by the National Guard.

He also knew that Hugh Lewins was a member. He regarded Lewins as a dangerous man, all the more so because he had built his life on deception. In Willoughby's mind, this put him beneath contempt.

So long as Lewins is free to move around, Willoughby thought, he is a danger and an unknown quantity. He gazed up from his desk and considered his options. I could have him detained, he thought, but then he wondered about the loyalties of the officers he would choose to detain him. And then he wondered about what possible grounds he could use to detain such a high-ranking state official. If Mercer Willoughby were a less focused or a younger man, he would have been befuddled.

But befuddlement was not his style. Mercer calmly thought through the options. He considered the sergeant-at-arms of the Georgia state legislature, but he was a man Mercer knew only casually, and Willoughby had a sense that the sergeant was in on the subversion. No, Mercer thought, it would have to be a federal official.

He picked up his cell phone and found the Atlanta office of the FBI in his contacts list. As he pushed the button, he got up from his desk and left his office. He recalled what McAuley had told him about Mary McDonald's office being bugged. He couldn't be sure his wasn't. He stepped out into the Georgia sunshine and waited to be connected.

He told the receptionist who he was, and he insisted on speaking with the agent in charge. She put him through.

"Agent Withers," came the deep baritone of the agent in charge.

"Agent Withers," Mercer began. "I have to speak with you about what's going on in the legislature this morning. I have reason to believe that what is happening may only be a diversion from the actual agenda of the Governor and his . . . his . . . " He wanted to say "cronies," but that sounded vaguely unprofessional. "His supporters," he said after a moment's hesitation. "I am especially concerned about a man by the name of Hugh Lewins, who is the Speaker of the House."

"How can I help you, Mr. Willoughby?"

"I believe that Lewins is planning to use the Georgia State Defense Force to back up secession whether it passes the legislature or not." He paused at the enormity of what he was saying. Mercer Willoughby was above all a careful man, and he felt as though he were hurling accusations that were as much reflections of fear as of sober analysis. But he did not see an alternative.

He continued. "What I would like you to do is to detain Mr. Lewins so that he cannot actuate this plan or any other seditious action that he might be contemplating."

Withers paused a moment before responding. "Do you have evidence of this, Mr. Willoughby?"

"No," Mercer replied candidly. "But I have evidence that Mr. Lewins is spearheading the secession movement in the legislature.

And that, I believe, is seditious in itself."

Withers nodded silently on his end of the phone. "Do you know where Lewins is now?"

"I presume he is either in his office or in the offices of other legislators whom he is in the process of strong-arming."

Withers glanced at his watch. "I'll send men over right away, Mr. Willoughby. They should get there within a half an hour."

"Time is of the essence."

"I understand."

Willoughby hung up, hoping that thirty minutes would not be too late.

He thought for a moment and then dialed Jackson Williams's number. "Jackson," he began. "I just got off the phone with Agent Withers at the FBI. I explained our concerns about Lewins. They're sending some men now to talk to him. They'll be there in thirty minutes."

"What do you want me to do, Mercer?"

"I want you to make sure that Lewins doesn't leave the capitol before they come."

"I'll see what I can do, Mercer."

"Good. Keep me posted."

39

Hugh Lewins hardly felt threatened. He was a little surprised some-one had not confronted him with his treasonous behavior, but he knew he had the support of most of his colleagues, the security structure of the capitol, and, of course, the enthusiastic support of the State Defense Force. As he went from office to office to discuss the legislation before the House, he knew that troops of the defense force were en route to the capitol itself. Ostensibly, they were there to keep order. But Lewins knew they were there to execute the resolution of secession or the Governor's edict, whichever it took to free the state of Georgia.

Whether it passes or not, he thought darkly. He was nearly certain that his chamber would pass the bill, but he felt reassured knowing the Governor would ignore the House action even if it failed and would declare secession by executive decree, pointing to the developments in the surrounding states and to the momentum across the country. He had said as much. But Lewins liked to cover all his bases, and he wanted the support of his legislative body.

There was no small amount of pride in this. Lewins regarded himself and his abilities as higher than those of almost all the other politicians with whom he dealt. He even regarded the Governor as a second-rate intelligence. But people had their uses, and McKenzie Phillips was willing to bully people to get his way and seldom felt constrained by the law of the land or any other law. Phillips wanted what Phillips wanted: it was that simple. And because of that, McKenzie Phillips was a gem in Lewins's mind. A useful and perhaps temporary gem, but a gem nonetheless.

Lewins was walking to the House chamber to see if there were any representatives there when his cell phone rang. It was Jackson Williams, the floor leader in the House, the man he was counting on to help him push the Governor's agenda through.

"Lewins," he said, as if he didn't know who was calling.

"Hugh," Williams said. "Could you swing by my office? I need to touch base with you about some of the holdouts."

Lewins thought he heard an odd tone in Williams's voice. He wasn't sure what it was. "Sure, Jackson. I'll be there in ten minutes." He clicked off his phone.

Jackson Williams was nervous. He and Lewins worked closely together all the time, shepherding legislation through the House. It wasn't so unusual for him to ask Lewins to come by or for him to visit Lewins's office. What was unusual was lying to him outright. He was having some trouble keeping his voice steady.

Lewins went about his business, checking the House chamber and, finding no one there, calling on the next House member on his list. In the back of his mind, however, he couldn't shake the notion that Jackson Williams was up to something. It was his tone of voice: a slight nervousness that was not at all characteristic of Williams.

As Lewins left the office after a brief visit to another House member, he picked up his cell phone.

"Where are you?" he asked. He was speaking to Jason Appleby, head of the State Defense Force.

"About three miles out."

"Hurry it up. We may have trouble."

Lewins stopped by a water fountain in the corridor and took a long drink. He was giving himself time to think. He regarded his instincts as excellent sources of information, rarely fallible, and the bad feeling he had about his short conversation with Jackson Williams kept growing. He ran through the options in his mind. Could Williams have gone over to the other side? Could he have been in contact with federal authorities or with the holdout Democrats in the chamber?

Lewins decided not to risk a confrontation. He headed for the Governor's office and walked past his secretary without a word, closing the Governor's door behind him.

"McKenzie," he said to the mildly surprised Governor. "I think everything is set up and ready to go. The vote will be this afternoon. I'm going off campus to check on our other preparations."

Phillips thought he knew what Lewins meant and smiled a small conspiratorial smile. He nodded in apparent approval. Lewins had no idea how Phillips took his innocuous comment.

Lewins walked out of the office as breezily as he had walked in and headed toward the parking lot. As he moved, he found his speed increasing. The uncomfortable feeling he had was now snowballing in his mind and in his body. I have to get out of here.

He found his car in its reserved spot, got in, and started the engine. Out of the corner of his eye, he noticed a black SUV with dark windows, apparently a government vehicle, enter the parking lot. As he eased out of his parking spot, he kept glancing at the black SUV, noting where it parked. By the time he got to the gate and was ready to put his card into the slot to raise the arm, he was watching two men in dark suits getting out of the vehicle. The feds! He recognized them immediately. No one dresses like that, drives a vehicle like that, or puts on pretentious airs like agents of the Federal Bureau of Investigation. He pushed his card into the slot, the arm raised up, and he drove quietly away.

That was close.

Lewins drove in the direction he believed troops of the State Defense Force were heading toward him. What had been a sense of uncertainty, a vague fear, a suspicious instinct had turned to anger. That son of a bitch Williams. I'll kill him, he thought.

Even better: I'll have him killed.

That idea brought the slightest smile to his face.

It was in the next few seconds that Lewins made a decision. All of a sudden, he realized that it didn't matter what the legislature did. What mattered was force. While he hoped and believed that the Georgia state legislature would vote to secede from the Union, he also recognized that this move would mean nothing without force to back it up. And he was in charge of that force. No matter that the defense force was nominally responsible to the governor, it was Lewins who had built up the force into a viable military unit and who had handled all the negotiations and preparations. They knew him. He had Jason Appleby in the palm of his hand, and it was Appleby to whom he was heading right now. I'll take command of the military action. When the legislature acts and Phillips signs the bill of secession, it will be me who takes over. I won't need the legislature then; nor will I need that half-witted Phillips, who, while admittedly useful for a time, is on the verge of outliving that usefulness.

The smile on his face widened.

Hugh Lewins drove until he saw a convoy of military vehicles heading straight toward him. He rolled down his widow and pulled up next to one.

"Where's Appleby?" he shouted to the driver of the first vehicle in the convoy.

The driver did not hesitate. "He's in the Humvee just behind me, sir."

"Pull over here." He drove to the next Humvee and saw Appleby sitting in the passenger side of the oversize military vehicle. He waved at him to pull over.

Appleby gestured for his driver to stop. Beyond the Humvee, Lewins could see another ten or so personnel vehicles, along with a menacing-looking vehicle with a turret and a stubby gun jutting out. Lewins recognized it as a BTR-4, a personnel carrier with a large gun mounted on the top. It was not a tank, exactly, but in urban environments it was just as useful. He breathed in deeply the smell of metal and gunpowder and felt the power that goes with military strength.

He pulled his car over to the other side of the road, got out, and walked up to Appleby's Humvee. "I'm going with you."

Jason Appleby complied. He had been taking orders from Hugh Lewins for months. It did not occur to him to contravene or even dispute an order from him. Lewins scrambled into the backseat. "Let's go." The procession began moving again.

ack in the capitol, Mercer Willoughby was talking to the FBI agents. He had just gotten off the phone with Williams, who informed him about what transpired. Yes, he told Mercer, he had called Lewins, who said he would be in his office in ten minutes. He did not show up. After fifteen minutes, Williams could not take the anxiety and went looking for him. He heard from the Governor's secretary that he had left the building, secure in the belief that the vote in the afternoon would go his way.

Damn, Willoughby thought. "Damn," he said to the agents. "He left."

There was a disappointed silence in the room for several moments. Then one of the agents spoke. "Agent Withers told us to take any action to circumvent any movement to secession," he said. He turned to Willoughby. "What would you recommend?"

Mercer Willoughby thought for a moment. He knew this vote was unconstitutional on its face and treasonous in its intent. He knew also that the Governor supported it. He took a deep breath. "I think there is only one thing we can do, gentlemen," he said softly. "I think you need to detain the Governor."

The two agents looked at each other, as if their joint brain was digesting this directive. They were not opposed to detaining the Governor, but they were practical men. "Okay," said the first to speak. "We can do that." The second man glanced at the first and then looked at Willoughby. "I think we'll need backup," he said simply. He pulled out his mobile phone and punched a speed-dial number. He murmured into the small device.

In the meantime, Jackson Williams had entered the room. "I'm sorry, Mercer," he said, but Willoughby cut him off.

"No need to apologize. Plans have changed." Mercer looked at the two men and then back at Jackson.

"The state constitution provides that if the governor is no longer able to perform the duties of his office, the lieutenant governor steps in and becomes governor. Fortunately, that would be Jake McAuley." He called to his secretary. "Get the lieutenant governor over here."

Willoughby's secretary did as she was told. As she did so, the second agent said, "Help is on the way."

Jake McAuley showed up within three minutes. He had been sitting in his office trying to figure out ways to stop the insane juggernaut that was gathering steam all around him. He was thinking how it threatened to sweep away all in its path: the United States, the good fortune of his beloved Georgia, all the politicians who vote for it, and the peace and tranquility of people across the land. He was not happy. So when Willoughby's secretary called, he did not hesitate a minute.

During that short interval, Willoughby picked up his desk phone and punched a speed-dial number.

"Madame Chief Justice, I am here with several FBI agents. We request that you join us immediately." Willoughby knew that the justices were not in session and were working in their respective offices, no doubt wondering about their future and the future of their state.

Precisely five minutes after Jake McAuley entered the room, Amelia Reinhardt, the chief justice of the Georgia Supreme Court, entered Willoughby's office.

Willoughby introduced the FBI agents to the recent arrivals and got down to business. "We need to stop the Governor from doing what he's doing," he said to the four officials arrayed before him.

Justice Reinhardt and Jack McAuley each nodded slowly.

"How?" Jake asked.

Willoughby hesitated for just a moment before responding. He looked squarely at Justice Reinhardt as he spoke. "What McKenzie Phillips is promoting is treasonous and seditious. He is violating his oath and fomenting rebellion. He is engaging in criminal conduct and is therefore not fit for office."

A ponderous silence filled the room.

Willoughby turned to face McAuley. "As lieutenant governor, you are the next in line." He gestured to the FBI agents. "These men will take him into custody."

Willoughby turned to Justice Reinhardt. "Do you concur, Madame Chief Justice?"

More silence. Justice Reinhardt's head was bowed slightly, and her eyes were focused on something no one else in the room could see. She was thinking, and Willoughby knew from long experience not to interrupt that process.

Slowly, Amelia Reinhardt raised her eyes to face Willoughby. "Given the circumstances, Mr. Attorney General, I don't see that you have an alternative."

Willoughby was visibly relieved. He let out a long stream of air and nodded. "Okay, then. We are agreed."

"When?" said the stunned McAuley.

"Now," replied Mercer calmly.

Jake McAuley swallowed hard. He was a solid man, but he always saw himself as a man of peace, not confrontation. He could not imagine that McKenzie Phillips would go quietly. He had no immediate plans for being governor, especially in his red home state. He just wanted to contribute to the general welfare. In many ways, it surprised him that he ended up in politics.

Willoughby interrupted these thoughts. "It's up to you to stop this insanity, Jake. There is no other option."

The five officials looked at each other gravely and nodded. Silently, they left the office of the attorney general and walked to the office of the governor.

McKenzie Phillips looked up from his desk when the five entered but did not look surprised until he saw Amelia Reinhardt. Then his breathing got shallower and his face reddened slightly. He looked up from his desk and swiveled in his chair to face the visitors directly. "Good morning, Amelia," he said in what Willoughby thought was an exaggerated Southern drawl. "What can I do for you this fine morning?" He kept his eyes on the chief justice.

Willoughby did not wait for her to respond.

"Mr. Phillips," he began solemnly, "we are here to remove you from office."

Phillips looked Willoughby directly in the eye. "You know full well you have no grounds for removing me from office."

"In fact, I do," replied Willoughby, nodding to the chief justice. He turned to the FBI agents.

The first agent stepped up to the Governor's desk. "Mr. Phillips," he said, "you are under arrest for treason and sedition under the United States Constitution. You have the right to remain silent. Anything you say—"

Phillips waved him off. "I'm familiar with Miranda."

For a single moment, the five men and one woman waited in silence. Then the second agent walked around Phillips's desk. "Please stand up, sir."

Phillips did not move. "I'll bury you for this," he growled at Willoughby. Then, after a tense, long pause, he shook his head and stood up.

The agent clamped handcuffs on the Governor. "During the time of your indisposition, the lieutenant governor will assume your duties," Willoughby said. He turned to Reinhardt. "Madame Chief Justice."

Amelia Reinhardt picked up a Bible that was sitting on Phillips's desk. "Mr. McAuley," she said evenly, "please place your left hand on the Bible and raise your right hand."

Jake moved forward hesitatingly. The small muscles in his face were twitching, and he was losing color in his cheeks. His breathing also grew shallower. He did as he was told.

"Please, repeat after me." Justice Reinhardt proceeded to administer the oath of office to the new governor of the state of Georgia.

"Congratulations, Governor," she said stiffly when they were finished. She shook McAuley's hand.

An FBI agent was standing on each side of McKenzie Phillips, whose face was turning an ever-deeper shade of red, reflecting the rage that was building in his mind. "You will regret this sooner than you know," he said to Willoughby, although his eyes were locked on McAuley.

The FBI agents escorted Phillips out the door. They were headed toward their vehicle.

Willoughby turned to McAuley. "Jake, I figure you have about an hour to diffuse this thing."

McAuley nodded. Then he took a deep breath, walked around the desk, and sat in what had just been McKenzie Phillips's chair. He looked up at his attorney general. "Okay."

Willoughby turned to the chief justice. "Thank you, Amelia." The two shook hands.

"Let me know if there is anything else I can do to help, Mercer," Amelia said softy. "I'll be in my office." Then she added, almost as an afterthought, "You did the right thing here."

The small group broke up. Willoughby left the Governor's office and walked back to his own. He sat at his desk and let out a sigh of relief. He could not recall as challenging a situation as this in his entire career. In his entire life, really.

Jack McAuley sat down at his new desk and allowed himself a few moments to recover from the shock of the previous ten minutes. Then he picked up his—the governor's—phone and called his now former secretary. "Amy, I want you to come to the Governor's office immediately." He hung up and busied himself with clearing off the desk of the chief executive of the state of Georgia, careful to inspect every piece of paper he picked up. He did not dispose of anything.

Meanwhile, Mercer Willoughby tried to relax for a few minutes in his office. He turned to look out the window, as he often did for the solace he found in the abundant Georgia sunshine. He closed his eyes for a moment. When he opened them, what he saw shook him to the bottom of his soul.

s the FBI agents were putting McKenzie Phillips in their SUV, other agents were pulling up to the capitol. One agent got out to confer with the first two. Everything seemed in order.

Another person, however, was watching from a block and a half away. Hugh Lewins had taken a pair of binoculars and began sweeping the capitol building site as soon as conditions allowed. He caught sight of the handcuffed Phillips being bundled into the black SUV, the same one that had arrived just as he was leaving the building.

"Stop here," he said to the driver of his Humvee. The driver complied and signaled the personnel carrier in front of him to do the same. The long line of military vehicles came to a slow stop.

I'll be damned, Lewins thought. They actually got him. He was running rapidly through his options. He knew immediately that Jake McAuley was now in charge; this was not a good sign. He had mixed feelings about Phillips's departure: on the one hand, he had planned to replace him anyway. On the other hand, he was counting on Phillips to declare secession right after the vote this afternoon, no matter how the vote went. He knew that McAuley wouldn't do it. In fact, he was figuring that McAuley would do everything in his power to derail the vote itself. He paused in disgust.

Mercer Willoughby has to be involved in this, he thought. Somewhat absentmindedly, he began devising a kill list. But he had more pressing matters to attend to. He picked up his binoculars to make sure the FBI agents had gone. When he saw them drive away, he turned to Appleby sitting in the seat in front of him.

"Let's move. Position your men around the capitol building. And don't let anyone in or out without my personal approval."

As usual, Appleby did not question his orders. He picked up a radio and began giving orders to his subordinates. Surrounding the capitol had been the plan all along, so no one was surprised by these developments. Only Lewins knew that Phillips had been detained and replaced.

A procession of military vehicles slowly but steadily began moving around the perimeter of the capitol. Willoughby could almost feel the noose tightening around his neck as he watched from his office window. He picked up the phone and called Withers.

It took Agent Withers a few minutes to get on the line, and each second seemed endless. Willoughby's vision narrowed. He could not keep his eyes off the military vehicles. He counted ten of them.

"Agent Withers," came the familiar voice on the phone.

Willoughby blurted out what he was seeing. Then he held his breath.

"Son of a bitch," said Withers in a measured tone. Both men fell silent.

Finally, Withers spoke. "Look: you stay on the phone and let me know if any direct action against the capitol or its employees is taken by these people. I'll contact the US Army at Fort McPherson and make them aware of this situation." He paused a moment. "This confirms what our agents who just left there saw when they were driving away." Willoughby could hear Withers taking a deep breath. "We will have ample military units there within an hour to handle this situation."

Willoughby did not know what to say. He thought he should feel reassured but in fact he didn't. An hour seemed like a long time.

He couldn't take his eyes off the slow-moving vehicles arraying themselves around the building in which he found himself.

"I'll call you back in a few minutes," Withers said. The phone went silent.

As Willoughby watched, he saw that the vehicles had come to a stop. Troops began jumping off the personnel carriers. "Troops" because they were wearing standard-issue Army fatigues. Each was armed with some kind of assault weapon. No one was smiling.

Willoughby looked on in disbelief. He had always thought of the State Defense Force as a collection of older guys who played at being soldiers. As he looked out his window, he saw that most of the troops had gray or graying hair, confirming his suspicion about their age. But the guns they were carrying gave them an aura of authority despite the color of their hair. Willoughby's feelings of disbelief and apprehension deepened.

Should I go out there and ask them what they're doing here? I am the chief law enforcement officer in the state. This appears to be an illegal act. With his ear still to the dead desk phone, he reached over and dialed Amelia's number.

"Are you seeing this?"

"It's hard not to see."

Mercer thought for a moment. "I'm going to gather every security person I can find in this building, and then I'm going to go out and ask these people what they are doing here," he said.

The chief justice did not respond right away. Mercer was glad she was a thoughtful person, he just wished she could be a faster thoughtful person.

"I think that's dangerous, Mercer."

"Sitting here watching people aim guns at us doesn't exactly feel safe."

More thinking from the other end of the line. Mercer took that as assent.

"I'll contact you as soon as I return," he said, then hung up.

All I wanted to be was a lawyer, Mercer thought as he walked into the anteroom of his office where his secretary was. "Gather up all the security personnel you can find and have them here in five minutes." Then he walked back into his office and speed-dialed McAuley. "Governor, I am gathering all available security personnel on campus, and I intend to go out and confront those men who are surrounding the building."

McAuley could not have been more surprised. "What men . . . ," he started to say, but as he did so he turned and looked out the window. "Good God!"

We hope so, Mercer thought, suppressing a fleeting doubt about the goodness of the deity. He could picture exactly what McAuley had done. "Those men. They are members of the Georgia State Defense Force, and I believe Hugh Lewins is directing them to do precisely what they are doing. I think they are here to lend military backing to the secession that he and Phillips had been planning. They are here to take over the government of Georgia."

bner Bellamy could not take his eyes off the television or his ear away from the telephone. His mood had reached a stable pitch of exuberance the likes of which he had only experienced momentarily prior to this day.

He had been on the phone with his supporters all morning long, encouraging them, soothing their fears, and promoting the view of a new order on the North American continent, one that placed their state and their interests at the center of the action. No more rapacious federal bureaucracy; no more subservience to the "greater good"; no more arbitrary rules from afar; no more bondage. Just freedom: freedom to shape the state of Georgia into whatever Georgians want. And he could tell by his constant phone conversations that his supporters wanted exactly the kind of freedom he wanted. Abner wanted Georgia to be the first to declare its independence. It had suffered the most during the War Between the States a century and a half ago, and it was important to him and to the state that it lead the way in the current struggle.

Abner had great respect for McKenzie Phillips and his team, especially Hugh Lewins, whom he knew well. In Abner's mind, it was a toss-up between the two political giants as to who was more ambitious and more supportive of Abner's agenda. Good soldiers, both of them.

When he got the call from Lewins about Phillips's arrest, he was stunned.

"What do you mean, he's been arrested?" he demanded, feeling the euphoria resolving itself into a kind of steely focus.

"The FBI loaded him into a vehicle and carted him off about twenty minutes ago. McAuley's in charge."

McAuley, McAuley, Abner thought. He was trying to place him. "You mean that Democrat, the lieutenant governor?"

"The same. And you know he is not on our team. He will not play ball."

Lewins proceeded to update Abner about the status. He told him that troops of the State Defense Force were surrounding the capitol and were prepared to move on his command. He also told him that he would be in contact with House members to make sure the resolution would pass. And he would demand assurances that it would pass over a possible veto from the ad hoc governor.

This gave Abner pause. He had always respected the solid front that the high officials in the Georgia legislature had presented. Phillips and Lewins had been brilliant in orchestrating the legislature to move in the direction to which Abner had guided them. Now there was a hitch. And it seemed like a big hitch: McAuley was no partner in this enterprise.

"Who's third in line?" Abner asked Lewins.

Lewins almost smiled. "Why, I am."

"So if something were to happen to Mr. McAuley, you would be the governor?"

"Yes, sir."

Abner stood up and walked around his living room. "Do you think you could make that happen? You know, amidst all the turmoil and everything?"

Silence on the other end of the phone. Then, in a lowered voice, "Yes, sir, I believe I can."

"Then I believe we will be in the clear. And the plan can move forward as intended."

After hanging up, Abner walked out onto his balcony, from which he could see the capitol in the distance. It's our building, he assured himself. We are simply taking possession of what is rightfully ours. He pulled out his cell phone and began calling other Georgia legislators just to give them his support and encouragement.

Lewins, on the other hand, had a specific target. He waited as the remaining troops disembarked from the personnel carriers and took up positions around the capitol. They had been briefed on what to expect and what to do. They were good at following orders.

He pulled out his binoculars and scanned the troop formations. Solid citizens all, he noted with pride.

Inside the capitol, twenty-three security personnel were crowding into Mercer Willoughby's office. Jake McAuley was there as well. He and Mercer were discussing strategy.

"It's too dangerous to go outside," Jake was saying to Mercer. "Let's build a defense structure that will give the Army troops time to get here."

"And not give these people a chance to state their real intentions?" Mercer said in disgust.

Jake looked at him askance. "You think there is something unclear about their intentions?" He nodded in the direction of the window.

He turned to the head of capitol security. "Kurt, what kinds of weapons do we have?"

Kurt Meaney did not hesitate. "We have a pretty good array of assault weapons as well as some shoulder-mounted RPGs," he replied. "We also have lots of ammunition, handguns, and stun guns." He was nothing if not thorough.

"And how many entrances are there to the building?" he asked.

"Four," came the reply. "Three on the main level, and one into the basement."

"Okay," Jake said. "Arm your men with everything they can carry. Divide them up and assign one group to each entrance." He looked Kurt straight in the eye. "You will be in charge and report directly to me." He paused for a moment. "Don't let anyone out of the building without my express permission."

"Yes, sir." Kurt saluted and ordered his men to follow him.

Jake turned to Willoughby. "I think this is a better plan, Mercer. And I think it's safer for you."

Willoughby did not protest. He was thinking that maybe all the excitement had gotten to him. He knew in his heart that McAuley was right. He was tired of the confrontation and wanted it all to be over.

He nodded to McAuley. "What do you want me to do, Governor?"

"I want you to stay alive and stay near a phone for when the US Army or the FBI calls."

"Yes, sir."

43

The fact that they were surrounded by armed troops was not lost on the members of either houses of the legislature. Most of them had no idea who the troops were, why they were there, or what they intended. The tension in the room thickened the atmosphere, and some of the members were visibly shaken.

Of course, Abner's men knew exactly what was going on, and they proceeded to spin the presence of the troops in the most positive light.

Clarence Hardy took the podium in the House. He was a member of Abner's original group of twenty-two hand-selected men who had spearheaded the secession movement, unbeknownst to the other legislators. He had been in the State House for two decades.

"Ladies and gentlemen, we have been informed that units of the State Defense Force of the great state of Georgia have assembled outside our building to protect us and to maintain order in the case of public discord." He raised his head solemnly and surveyed the sea of eyes that were all trained on him.

"I move that we take the vote now and not wait until the two o'clock scheduled time," he continued. "As many of you have noted, now is the time, this is the place, and we are the people who can change the course of Georgia history. We can rise to the stature of our natural place in the order of the New South. We can take our rightful place in charge of our destiny."

He surveyed his colleagues once more before continuing. "What we are about to do requires courage, sobriety, and wisdom. We have talked and talked; now has come the time for action." His voice rose in volume and intensity. "Do we wish to continue to be under the thumb of federal bureaucracy in Washington, DC, or do we want to take our destiny into our own hands and carve our own future? Do we want to be slaves or do we want to be free men?" He paused for just a moment. "Those are the choices we face today. Those are the choices that are ours to make.

"Therefore, I move that we vote on the resolution for secession immediately and announce to the world our true desires."

Since Lewins was not present to moderate the rules, Hardy did it himself. "Do I hear a second for the motion to be voted upon?"

For a moment, no one moved. There wasn't a sound in the chamber. Then a gaunt, white-haired man with a thick Georgia accent rose and said in a halting voice, "I second the motion."

"All in favor?" bellowed Hardy.

"Aye," thundered the crowd, as if finally allowed to speak.

"All opposed?"

"Nay," said a few dozen defeated voices.

"The motion is passed! The vote will proceed immediately."

Tradition and antique protocol dictated that each legislator's name be recited, his or her vote voiced, and the tally recorded by hand. One by one, the names of the 180 House members were read aloud. Time slowed down.

Forty-two minutes later, Hardy rose to announce the results of the vote. "Those in favor of the resolution: 91; those opposed: 89." He looked up from the tally. "The resolution is approved!"

The chamber was quiet. The traditional applause led by the legislative victors did not ring out. Instead, a feeling of dark solemnity settled over the assembled officials. The enormity of what they had done and the closeness of the vote hovered over the heads of all present.

Hardy forged ahead. "We will now send the results of this vote to the Senate chamber." He collected the papers in front of him, stepped down from the podium, and walked to his desk.

Jackson Williams looked across the aisle at Mary McDonald, who was shaking her head in apparent disbelief. Williams turned back and looked down at the top of his desk for a moment. He was sure that Hardy would go to the Senate chamber personally to deliver the results and bully them into taking a similar vote as soon as possible.

Williams slowly stood up amid the low conversational buzz that had started around him. He clapped his hands twice to get everyone's attention. "I formally protest this illegal vote," he shouted, hoping that his position as a faithful partisan would carry some weight in what he regarded as a group of people seduced by illusory power. "And I call on all my fellow legislators to renounce it or face the consequences of treason."

Jackson Williams stood motionless in the midst of the silence that suddenly enveloped him. Finally, the elderly man who had seconded the original motion stood up. "You're too late, Williams," he said with as much volume as he could muster. "The vote has been taken. It is our right, it is our duty, and it is our decision." He glared at Williams and peered across the aisle, whence most of the nay votes originated. "It's over."

"If that is the case," Williams said, "I hereby renounce my membership in the Republican Party and resign my office in this illegal body." He glanced over at Mary McDonald, turned, and walked out of the room.

After several moments of silence, the legislators who voted nay each began to stand up. Each announced his or her name, protest, and resignation. They filed out of the room in one continuous line until all of their desks in the chamber were empty.

The remaining members observed the departure with varying responses: some openly contemptuous, some neutral, some anxious.

Several were shaking their heads. The silent question foremost on many people's minds was strikingly similar: What have we done?

And the second was: What happens now?

44

The latter was precisely the question in Hardy's mind. He had left the House chamber and was en route to the Senate chamber with a copy of the resolution and the written tally of votes in his hand. What he wanted to happen now was for the Senate to follow his lead and vote affirmatively on the resolution he was holding. He had every reason to believe he would get his wish.

At the same time, there were other reasons for his haste. The principal one was that, despite his assurances to the House about the intentions of the State Defense Force outside their windows, he really had no idea why they were there. He assumed that they were there to enforce secession somehow, but he wasn't high enough in the food chain to be privy to their specific directives.

He thought of passing by the Governor's office on his way to the Senate, but he decided against it. With every step he took, anxiety and a sense of urgency gnawed at his confidence. *I've got to get this done.*

When he finally reached his destination, Clarence Hardy walked into the Senate chamber to find only a few senators sitting at their desks chatting. He noticed that Jake McAuley, the presider of the Senate, was not among them. He wondered where everyone had gone. It wasn't quite eleven, and the Senate was usually in session. He walked up to the small cadre of men who were chatting around a desk.

"Where is everybody?"

The three men standing together each looked at him with some degree of incredulity. Finally, the man closest to him spoke. "Haven't you heard? The Governor's been arrested for treason."

At first Hardy didn't register what the man said. He had never considered that the plan he and the others had been working on for so long would not happen or that something so major would derail it. The landscape of his internal world shifted.

"What?"

The senator recognized the befuddled look on Hardy's face, so he took a breath and began again, more slowly this time. "A little while ago, Mercer Willoughby, the AG, along with Amelia Reinhardt, the chief justice, walked into Phillips's office with two FBI agents, who took him into custody." He paused to make sure Hardy was following him. "Jake McAuley was immediately sworn in as the new or at least interim governor by Reinhardt. Phillips was taken to the FBI building downtown."

Clarence Hardy felt light-headed. His pulse quickened and he could feel his face flush. Suddenly aware that he shouldn't show his shock, he took a couple of steps back, forced himself to take a deep breath, and turned away from the group for a minute.

As he focused on his breathing, he felt his body settle down and return to something like normal. He turned back to the men.

"So, what happens now?"

The same man responded. "We have no idea, Clarence. We were just talking about that." As the man spoke, Hardy looked at the other senators in the room. He recognized that they were all Republican colleagues. He did not know precisely what to do, but he believed it was better to forge ahead rather than retreat.

"Look," he said to all three of them, "the House just passed the resolution for secession. It was a little closer than we thought it would be, but it passed." He looked each of the men squarely in the face. "There was a lot of eagerness to get this done, so we moved up the time." He thought maybe they were wondering why it was already done when it was well known that the vote was slated for 2:00 p.m.

The faces of his senatorial colleagues were all grim. "Clarence," said the ersatz spokesperson for the group, "the vote doesn't matter. McAuley will never sign the resolution. It will be a futile gesture." He looked at Hardy, who did not seem to be comprehending what he was told. "Do you understand?"

Hardy was too angry and confused to reply. "I need to get some air." He turned and walked out of the room.

Good luck with that, thought the three men standing in the Senate chamber.

Hardy walked toward the nearest building entrance. He was in such turmoil he had forgotten about the troops arrayed outside. He turned the corner before the exit and was stopped in his tracks by a uniformed security guard carrying an assault rifle.

"I'm sorry, sir. No one is to leave or enter the building until further notice."

"On whose orders?"

"The Governor's."

The Governor? He means McAuley. He looked up at the guard. "I have important business to take care of that requires that I leave the building at once."

"I'm sorry, Mr. Hardy," replied the guard. "You will need a written exemption from the Governor for that."

Hardy considered pushing himself past the several guards behind the door, but he could not help noticing all the hardware. In addition to his service revolver, each man had an assault rifle at the ready. There were other weapons lying on a table to the side of the door. "This is an outrage!" he shouted. "I—"

No one spoke. Hands tightened around weapons, a subtle move that was not at all lost on Clarence Hardy.

"I will take it up with the Governor immediately." He turned on his heel and stomped off.

Once around the corner and out of view of the guards, Clarence slowed his steps. He had to think about his next move.

He quickly decided a call to Abner was in order. He leaned against the large windowsill along the corridor, his back to the troops lined up outside, and pulled out his cell phone. Abner's line went straight to voicemail. I'm sure I'm not the only person Abner's talking to, he thought reasonably. He left a short message for Abner to call him back and clicked off his phone.

He sat on the sill for several moments pondering what to do. There was no sense returning to the Senate chamber; they had clearly lost their nerve. He could return to the House chamber, but he figured very few members would be left there. He stood up and decided to go to his office, where he could think about how to approach Jake McAuley.

45

President Obama had just gotten off the phone with Max Grabel, who was updating the President about the assault on the Blinder compound, when Valerie Escapan opened the door to the Oval Office and stuck her head in.

"It's Mercer Willoughby, Mr. President. The attorney general of the state of Georgia. He insisted on speaking with you directly. He says it's urgent."

"Put him through"

"Mr. President," said Willoughby when the President came on the line. "I think it's important for you to know what's been happening here in Georgia."

"Go on."

Willoughby took the President step-by-step through the events of the previous twelve hours, leaving nothing out. "So I think, Mr. President, that we may have forestalled an actual declaration of secession, but I am not sure what those troops are doing outside. They've made no move yet, and we have asked for the assistance of the US Army. They should be arriving momentarily. But I am pretty sure those troops are here to carry out Phillips's original plan to secede and put some muscle behind it."

Good Lord, thought the President. Please don't let this turn into some godforsaken civil war. "Are you safe, Mr. Willoughby?"

"I believe so, sir. We have barricaded all entrances with heavily armed guards. But from the looks of it, if the defense force decides to move against us, we won't be able to hold out long."

Mr. Obama glanced at his watch. It was almost eleven. One hour until his address to the nation. "I will do what I can from here to expedite the Army's arrival. Keep me posted if anything changes."

"Thank you, Mr. President."

Mercer Willoughby put the phone down. It seemed a little over the top to call the White House, but he wanted to make sure that the President had the most current information in what no doubt was the most serious constitutional crisis since 1861.

The President, meanwhile, punched the intercom for Anita. "Get General Dempsey on the line."

The General was available within forty seconds. "Yes, Mr. President."

Obama briefed Dempsey on what Willoughby had told him.

"I am aware that our troops have been requested by the FBI in Atlanta. I will check on their specific progress and get back to you within a couple minutes."

Less than two minutes later, the General was back on the phone.

"Our troops will be arriving within eight minutes," he told the President.

"Thank you, General." He called Valerie and told her to call Willoughby back and tell him about the time frame.

The President then pushed back from his desk. The text of his speech was in front of him, and he wondered if he had covered all his bases. The situation was both layered and fluid. What was true one hour may not be true the next. It was critical that his speech capture the moment he gives it, even in the midst of rapidly shifting events.

The phone rang again. Obama had given Anita a short list of people from whom he would take calls that morning, including key federal personnel and all the attorneys general in afflicted states, so he assumed it was someone on the list. Of course it was.

Stanley Schindler got right to the point. "Mr. President, the assault on David Blinder's compound in Texas has begun."

"Feed it into the Situation Room," said the President.

"Yes, sir."

Mr. Obama disconnected the call but held onto the handset. This is it, he thought. He speed-dialed the first number of his phone. "Michelle, how are the kids?"

Pause on the other end of the line. "They're fine, Barack," Michelle Obama said softly. "They are going a little stir-crazy down here." She automatically looked at the windowless wall surrounding her and the two girls. "And they're not alone," she teased gently.

"Meet me in the Situation Room in five minutes."

"Gladly."

Mr. Obama replaced the phone on the receiver and turned to Anita. "I'm going down to the Situation Room to follow developments. Michelle will join me there."

The First Couple's walk to the Situation Room was urgent for both husband and wife. Both walked swiftly, with their respective Secret Service details working to keep up. At the door of the Situation Room, they embraced for the first time in hours.

"I'm glad you're here," Mr. Obama said.

"Me too."

The agents held back out of respect for simple intimacy. When the lead agent felt it was over, he opened the door for the couple. "Mr. President," he said. He nodded to Mrs. Obama. "Madame."

The President strode into the room, where his national security team had assembled. The walls were ablaze with screens recording activity on the ground and in the air. Most were in color; some were in black-and-white. The President scanned them as he took his seat at the head of the table. Michelle took a seat along the wall. She was just glad to be with her husband; she knew not to interrupt him.

46

By the time the President and his team got settled, federal agents outside Wichita Falls, Texas, were surrounding the Blinder mansion, supported by US Army troops provided by nearby bases. Helicopter gunships were hovering above them. The crackle of gunfire could be heard in the distance, but the area around the main house was quiet for the moment. The distant fire was becoming more sporadic by the minute.

Marie and Samantha met with Schwartz to assess the situation. They were standing behind the remains of a masonry structure that had been one of the outbuildings on the property. No one knew if the troops inside the building would start firing or not. Federal guns were aimed at the windows from a respectable and safe distance.

There were still a lot of unknowns. They knew there were Sovereign Citizen troops inside the residence, but they had no idea how many. Even though no gunfire was coming from the house at the moment, they figured, given what they had seen so far, that the troops inside still had considerable firepower.

Marie and Sam and Schwartz knew everyone wanted Blinder alive. That ruled out an all-out assault on the residence as they had done during the initial wave.

Schwartz spoke up. "There's always the old-fashioned method."

He pulled out his megaphone and raised it to his mouth. He stood up from behind the shelter of the masonry wall.

"Mr. Blinder," he bellowed. "Your home is surrounded by federal agents. Your troops have been defeated. We are caring for the wounded as best we can. We want you and all the others with you to come out of the house with your hands in the air. We want whatever troops you have inside to put down their arms. We wish to avoid further bloodshed."

David Blinder was enraged. He had been watching the mayhem around him for the past few hours, and he had no illusions about how the battle had gone. He didn't expect an assault so soon. Plus, he had been assured by Winslow Parker and all of his other men that the SC troops could manage any assault on the estate. He watched as his men blew up the missile launcher that was used to such devastating effect on the outbuildings. He was encouraged for a moment.

But then the helicopters came and rained down havoc on his men and on their equipment. He had no idea how many federal troops were trespassing on his property or how they got there so quickly, but he was sure it was a fraction of the number of SC troops he had protecting him before they arrived. They will all pay dearly, he muttered to himself.

It did not occur to David Blinder that he had lost, but he recognized the moment when a tactical retreat became necessary. And he was rarely if ever at a loss for Plan B. Several scenarios quickly ran through his mind. He could herd himself and some faithful troops into his secret control room; he could order a strong counterattack and hope that the feds wanted him alive. Or he could simply vanish. He had a way out: labyrinthine, high-tech tunnels hidden in a wall in his control room would enable him to vanish in a few minutes. It would take the feds hours to figure out how he did it or where he might be.

David Blinder had no desire to go out in a blaze of glory or ignominy. This temporary setback was a tough pill to swallow, but he prided himself on facing reality. He never doubted his capacity to adapt.

As his emotions settled down and his mind cleared, he determined that disappearing for the present was the wisest option. He had made contingency plans long ago for exile, if it came to that. In the meantime, he wanted more than anything to see how political events were playing across the country and see if he could continue to influence them. He was sure he could; he just needed more time.

What do I have to lose? he thought. Even if the entire plot fails, the United States is still governed by a legal system I can manipulate. Let the courts try to prosecute me. I'll have them tied up for years, and—who knows?—I might die in my sleep before the legal issues are resolved.

So with the sounds of gunfire and explosions abated, he gathered Mimi, his wife, and Clarisse, George's wife, along with the house staff in one room and the fifty or so SC troops in another. He addressed the terrified women first.

"For some insane reason, the federal government has decided I am guilty of being a part of what happened in Washington yesterday." He looked at his wife and the wife of his brother with sad eyes. "I thought we would be safe here, but it appears that the federal bureaucracy cannot tolerate the thought that we would live in freedom. So I have decided to surrender. I cannot bear the thought that the people closest to me would be hurt. It would be intolerable." He looked at Mimi. "I will not risk your being hurt." He looked at Clarisse. "Or you, Clarisse."

He went to each woman and took her hand, hugged her, and kissed her gently. Then he turned to both of them and said, "I have some things to do. In ten minutes, I want you to do as they are demanding: walk out the front door with your hands up. Go even if I am not there."

He turned to the house staff, most of whom were crying. "Take care of these women."

Mimi and Clarisse, both pale and trembling, nodded slowly.

Taking his leave of the women, Blinder walked into the room filled with his troops and closed the door. He looked around. He thought briefly of masking his feeling about their performance, but it was hard to disguise his disappointment at the failure of their organization to protect him and his family, and he did not want to.

"I put great store by the professional training you men received. It was my expectation that you would be able to protect our interests as well as my family." He glared around at the attentive troops. "You have failed. Right now, federal troops are in front of my house after gunning down most of your fellows. And right now, they are demanding that we surrender." He glared some more.

"You have one chance to redeem yourselves. My family is going to walk out the front door in a few minutes. They are going to surrender." He paused for a moment. "There will be a narrow window when the feds won't be sure what is happening, and you will have the high ground." Blinder's eyes were aglow. "I want you to kill as many of those invaders as you can." He strutted across the room, raised his head slightly, and then lowered it to peer into the eyes of the men surrounding him. "Reclaim your honor."

He turned, walked out of the room, and went directly to his secret command center. There he opened a panel on the inside wall and entered a series of numbers. A small panel opened along the far wall. He entered it and turned to set a timer inside the room that would begin the sequence that would result in the complete obliteration of any information in the chamber.

As he worked he was silently congratulating himself for installing these features in the control room. When he had them built, he thought it may have been a waste of money, but his brother George had advised him to build them just in case. David rationalized this by thinking that the explosives would destroy evidence after his plan was complete. And as far as the tunnel went, he knew about the best-laid plans of mice and men. Now he had to use it in the most extreme and unpalatable circumstance conceivable. As relieved as he was to have these features in place, the bitterness in his throat began rising again.

He pushed a button to seal the door to the tunnel. As soon as it closed behind him, the tunnel was filled with enough light to see clearly. He stepped onto the small trainlike vehicle that would transport him to safety and away from the clutches of the federal agents. He knew what he had to do. After taking one last deep breath in his home, he stepped aboard the train and activated it. Within a few minutes, he was traveling rapidly away from his estate, deep underground where no sound could be detected.

After about a minute, he thought he heard the command room explode, but he couldn't really be sure. The noise of the train, while not loud, echoed softly throughout the narrow tunnel. He pictured the devastated control room, which only yesterday felt like the center of his universe. The bitterness in his throat did not subside.

Meanwhile, the stunned SC troops looked at each other. They were loyal men and they felt shame at the failure of their compatriots. They all had friends and some had relatives in the battle that had apparently just ended. No one knew who was dead or who was alive, and they had no way to find out. There was bitterness all around.

"We heard the feds too," said one junior officer. "It would be suicide to try to kill them."

No one responded right away. Everyone was lost in thought.

Then another young man spoke up. "I agree. I think we lost this battle. It hurts like hell, but there's no sense dying for nothing."

No one contradicted him. At the same time, giving up without a fight felt shameful to most of those present. "We can live to fight another day," said the junior officer.

The men started looking up at each other, moving from face to face, trying to gauge the sense of the whole. Long deep breaths; heavy silence. One by one, the men started putting their weapons on the floor. "Let's get out of here," one of them said.

Clarisse, Mimi, and the house staff walked toward the front door. They paused there and Mimi turned to face the others. Her hands were trembling, and the small muscles in her face were twitching. I need David to be with me, she thought. But she knew he would not be. It was in her husband's nature to give orders that were obeyed, not to be available at critical moments such as this. The births of their children flashed through her mind: another important event at which David was not in attendance. She turned back around, nodded to Clarisse, and opened the door.

A strange silence descended upon the property. The noise of the helicopters above, so distinct just a moment ago, now seemed oddly dulled. The two wives and their staff raised their hands and walked slowly out the door.

The agents were clustered about fifty yards back from the front entrance. Their guns remained trained on the house and on the people walking out the door. They, too, felt the silence.

"Walk toward me," Agent Schwartz said loudly into the megaphone.

The procession shifted course slightly.

When the troupe finally got near Schwartz, agents approached from either side with handcuffs. "These are for everyone's protection," a young agent said apologetically.

They had gathered the half dozen people in a circle and begun leading them to waiting vehicles when the front door of the mansion opened again.

The agents tensed. Those who had lowered their weapons raised them again. Those who had not, tightened their grip.

SC troops began the same sad procession the house staff completed just a few minutes before. There were no visible weapons, but the agents were still hyperalert. No one trusted what he or she was watching. Most of the agents were crouched behind the masonry remains of the outbuildings or their vehicles.

The SC troops were still coming out the front door when a muffled but distinct explosion was heard from inside the house. Many of the federal agents and the SC troops hit the ground.

Sam and Marie had the same reaction. But just as quickly, they got up and moved to surround the surrendering troops. They wanted to get inside the house, and they did not want to waste any more time. Each led a contingent of agents to either side of the weaponless men arrayed across the front of the residence. When the SC troops who were still in the house heard the explosion, they ran toward the front door.

What had been an orderly surrender all of a sudden seemed precarious. Some of the SC troops on the ground were getting up, but they had all forgotten to raise their hands. They were just standing there, defenseless in the morning sun surrounded by black-suited federal agents. The world felt surreal, and the explosion added to the unreality.

Agents surrounded the SC troops and made sure each one was unarmed. They rounded them up in a circle and handcuffed them and then asked if any were injured.

The young soldier who had spoken up inside the house whispered to the soldier next to him, "That son of a bitch would have killed us all."

The other man, still in a bit of shock, nodded. The same thought was on the minds of nearly all the SC troops.

Samantha overheard this conversation and began looking around quickly, going from face to face. She had never met David Blinder, but she had seen his picture often enough to recognize him. She scanned the faces of the SC troops, then she turned and scrutinized the house staff.

Finally, she walked up to Mimi Blinder. "Where is your husband?"

"I have no idea," Mimi replied honestly.

Samantha sensed that she was telling the truth. She motioned for Marie to join her.

"Blinder's not here."

"I had the same sinking feeling," Marie said. "Let's get in that house."

The two women walked swiftly up to the front door. There were no more troops coming out. They walked in tentatively with pistols drawn, uncertain what to expect. What they saw were beautiful rooms with discarded weapons lying around carelessly. Abandoned weapons.

They held up their pistols and went room to room, but it soon became apparent that the mansion was so large and so unknown to them that the task required more people. Samantha radioed Schwartz.

"Blinder didn't come out. We're searching the residence. Request more agents."

"You got it."

Within minutes, three additional agents joined the two women. They communicated through hand signals, directing each to take a section of the house.

While this was standard operating procedure, it took only a few minutes for the realization to sink in that David Blinder had somehow managed to exit the building. Nonetheless, they continued their dutiful sweep of the building.

In the meantime, three buses pulled up, and the fifty SC men were loaded onto them. The two wives were escorted to an armored SUV. A shuttle pulled up for the house staff. The buses headed for a nearby Army base, while the SUV headed toward the local FBI headquarters.

"Where are you taking us?" Mimi asked casually, as if they were out for a day excursion.

"To headquarters," the agent replied.

Mimi's demeanor did not change. She registered the destination as if it were the most normal thing in the world to surrender to federal agents who had attacked their home with military weapons and taken them into custody.

"Oh."

If Mrs. Blinder seemed cool about the whole affair, the young SC troops who had been protecting Blinder did not. They felt ashamed and angered by the defeat of their fellow soldiers, but they felt betrayed by David Blinder, who obviously did not give a damn about their lives or the lives of anyone else. Many of them had idealized Blinder and believed in his cause enough to take up arms, but many others had simply been swayed by his enticements. To a man, they were angry and felt hoodwinked and insulted.

The fact that Blinder would have sacrificed his men's lives for the sake of making a point weighed on each of them. When the bus pulled into the Army base, most of them relaxed just a little. They knew they were an insurgent army, but they were also inducted into a service that had a high level of discipline and rigor. The Army base felt like home.

After a few minutes, a staff sergeant approached with a clipboard and a pen and a recorder discretely hidden within his uniform.

"Anyone want to tell me how you got here?" he asked with more congeniality than the situation warranted. His question was friendly, almost as if he were talking to his own men. This was not lost on the SC troops. They started talking.

As they were processed, the general outline of the Sovereign Citizen military became clear, and important details began to be filled in. The young recruits gave up Winslow Parker's name as well as the names of his subordinates. They admitted they received information on a need-to-know basis, however, so beyond the general structure of the organization and the names of a few key leaders, they could not share a lot of other details.

But what was very clear throughout this processing was that David Blinder was at the heart of the rebellion. The SC troops knew that Blinder's orders superseded all others, they knew that Parker took his orders from Blinder, and they knew that it was Blinder who betrayed them.

Federal prosecutors moved in and took their statements and depositions.

47

Winslow Parker was the first to be aware of the roadblocks. He had sent some men on motorcycles to reconnoiter ahead of the convoy, and they radioed back to him that there were long lines of traffic about twenty miles ahead of Parker's position.

Damn, he thought. But military maneuvers seldom went as planned, and his mind automatically went into contingency planning mode.

"Slow down and get ready to turn right off this road," he instructed his young driver.

The driver did as he was told. Within a few minutes, he spotted a well-camouflaged turnoff. He glanced over at Parker, who nodded.

The turnoff road was barely more than a dirt track through some soybean fields. The tops of the plants came up to the jeep's window, so they provided some coverage. Not enough for Parker's taste, however.

"There's a fork in the road about a mile ahead," he said to the driver, gazing through his binoculars. "Bear to the left." He thought he saw some trees in the distance. They might provide additional cover.

It was at that point, however, that he heard the faint buzz of surveillance drones scanning the ground around them. He raised his binoculars toward the sky. He counted three drones. "Shit."

Parker gestured with his hand and the convoy slowly came to a halt. He got out of the car and signaled for the occupants of the other vehicles to do the same.

When the thirty men of his convoy were gathered together, Parker nodded toward the drone and began. "In case some of you don't know what those are, they are surveillance drones designed to scan large ground areas. They have high-resolution cameras that can spot a moth on a soybean." He paused to let this information sink in. "They are used primarily by the US armed forces to assist in search missions." He paused again. "What that means is that they are looking for us. Now I want each driver to put space between yourself and the vehicle in front of you. They may have seen our vehicles, but there is no way they can be sure it's us."

The young men looked at Parker and waited for his command. They did not have to wait long.

"Here is the plan," Parker began slowly. "There is a copse of trees about a mile and a half off to the left. We are going to make our way there slowly and unload these trucks and bury as much of the gold as we can in that area. I am familiar with this general area. I'll be able to identify where we do that." He looked at the faces of the young men arrayed in front of him. "We need to do this as quickly and as quietly and as carefully as possible. Let's get started. I'll direct you as to where we should dig when we get there."

The troops returned to their vehicles and did as they were ordered. The first vehicle started driving slowly down the dirt track. A hundred yards later came the second vehicle, and a hundred yards after that came the next. Each vehicle proceeded in the same way until the procession lengthened and all of the vehicles arrived at the copse of trees, which was about a half mile in diameter.

Parker selected a spot almost exactly in the center of the trees to begin digging. He assigned six men to dig a hole at least six feet deep, three feet wide, and forty feet across. The men formed a line to pass the gold bars to that point. They began loading the gold into the ditch as soon as the diggers reached the six feet mark.

About an hour into their work, the SC troops heard the whoop-whoop of helicopters hovering above them.

Parker contemplated his options. The trees were dense, but they did not give complete coverage. He figured that the enemy had heat signature equipment that would reveal the presence of his men. It was also possible—and even likely, as he thought about it—that they were using gold detection equipment. A combination of a group of men and a lot of gold would, in the minds of the searchers, seal the connection. He figured he had one option and that was to take a stand and fight off any attack.

He ordered a couple of men to get out of the line and set up the Stinger missiles they had stored in case of emergency. Then he split up the remainder of his men: half would keep digging and loading, and the other half would grab their weapons for an attack on the machines in the air.

As the men unpacked the weapons, he could hear the helicopters lift upward. They are watching us closely, he realized. It confirmed in his mind that they had the latest technology.

The first team to get a Stinger up and running raised it and fired. The helicopter deployed its countermeasures, and the weapon exploded uselessly in the air.

An aggressive response followed immediately. A second heli-copter, an Apache AH-64, swooped down and began strafing the ground from just above tree level, scattering the SC troops and destroying several of the vehicles. A half dozen men were struck while still holding gold bars in their hands. The others hit the ground and tried to protect themselves as best they could among the foliage and the trees.

Parker was hit in the ankle. He let out a small scream and hit the ground hard. "Everybody, man your weapons!" The remaining troops crouched toward the vehicles where the weapons were stored. The relentless hail of bullets from the sky made this a risky move, however, and most of them lay with their arms above their heads. Praying probably, Parker thought.

The bullets did not stop for several minutes. A realization began to birth itself in Parker's mind. This is revenge, he thought. They're not trying to just stop us. They are trying to kill us. He pulled his Beretta from his holster and wriggled himself up on one knee, despite the searing pain in his ankle. He began firing at the Apache and at a larger helicopter, which he recognized was a troop carrier. He was going to go down fighting.

He got his wish within moments. A half dozen 23 mm rounds tore through his body. What was left of Winslow Parker was splayed across the side of the jeep he had arrived in at this desolate spot.

There were no other shots coming from the troops on the ground. There was only silence. The helicopters circled around the field a few times, and then the personnel carrier landed and a dozen regular army troops disembarked with guns raised.

Contrary to what the late Winslow Parker thought, the US Army troops were not under orders to exact revenge. They were under orders to tolerate no resistance. So when a wounded SC grunt reached for his weapon when he heard Army troops approaching, his life was ended immediately. Others who surrendered were rounded up and treated in a makeshift field hospital.

It did not take long for the American troops to find the hole half-filled with gold. They searched what was left of the vehicles and gathered up the remaining gold bars. After the lieutenant got a nod from his sergeant, he radioed General Spader, who was monitoring the action from a control room at Fort Knox. "This shipment is all accounted for, sir."

"Good work, Lieutenant."

48

Hugh Lewins decided he did not give a damn about the legislative process. He had muscle on his side, and he intended to use it. He was familiar with the security forces in the state capitol, and he was certain they were no match for the forces he was commanding at the moment.

But he also understood that he had only a brief window of time in which to act. God only knew what the leaders in the now Democrat-led administration had in mind.

He got out of his Humvee and surveyed the troops surrounding the capitol. He wanted to strike a balance between strength and caution. He did not want to alienate everyone in the building, most of whom, he was convinced, were on his side. He ordered his troops to concentrate on the three entrances on the main level of the building.

"We are going to enter the capitol," he said into his radio. "I want Platoons 3, 6, and 9 to break formation and assemble in front of those entrances. I want Platoon 5 to man the entrance to the lower level. Everyone else, stay where you are and make sure no one leaves the building. Shoot only if you have to, and only shoot to wound if you have a choice." After all, he thought, these were all Georgians. They all loved their state. They did not want to cause death or injury unnecessarily.

"Move," he commanded. The formations began to shift, and the platoons began edging toward the assigned entrances.

"Mr. Lewins!" cried a junior officer. He was pointing to the sky above the capitol, where helicopter gunships were hovering.

Lewins was confused for a moment. Why didn't I hear them? He reached for a pair of binoculars and looked more closely. He realized they were stealth copters; he only heard them now if he listened very closely. Once he understood this, he also understood that they were probably not alone. He turned around to see US Army units taking positions behind his men. Damn.

He was trapped. Or rather, he thought, his men were trapped. If they undertook an assault now, they would be mowed down by the Army troops behind them. If they tried to leave, he was uncertain of the response. He turned toward the incoming troops and began walking toward them, away from his Humvee and his men.

"Who's in charge here?" he asked the first troops he came to. Their guns were leveled at his men and at him as he approached.

"Major Sheridan."

"Take me to him."

The young soldiers radioed the request up the line. After a few moments, he nodded. "Come with me, sir."

Lewins followed the young man to a Humvee with official markings. He figured it was the command vehicle.

A tall, lean man stepped out of the vehicle.

"Major Sheridan?"

"Yes?"

"I'm Hugh Lewins, the Speaker of the House for the Georgia Congress. I've been trying to dissuade these men from doing something foolhardy, but they wouldn't listen. Thank God you've come in time."

Major Hank Sheridan was pretty sure he had not heard such a bald-faced lie in his entire life. And, being a career military man, that was a high bar. He regarded Hugh Lewins for a long moment.

"Corporal," he said to the young man standing just behind him without taking his eyes off Lewins. "Take this man into custody."

Lewins raised his head in disdain. "What? I'm here to help you! I'm on your side."

Sheridan looked at Lewins with undisguised contempt. "You may make whatever case you want at your trial for treason, sir." He turned and got back into the vehicle.

Lewins closed his eyes in defeat. He opened them to see soldiers moving toward him with restraints, which they no doubt intended to use on him. He felt the blood drain from his face, and the blood in the rest of his body seemed to turn cold. Time slowed down. He looked up at the blue Georgia sky for a moment and then pulled out a small revolver from his pocket and put a bullet in his head.

The SDF troops nearest to where Lewins had walked away heard the shot and froze in place. They raised their weapons and aimed them at the Army troops who were still arriving in significant numbers. For a few tense minutes, both sides seemed ready to open fire. No one moved.

A voice came over a loudspeaker. "To the men surrounding the capitol building, put down your weapons immediately and walk slowly to the east side of the building. Put your hands in the air."

The SDF troops looked at each other. They knew they were outnumbered and outgunned. They weren't sure if they were leaderless or not, but Hugh Lewins was nowhere to be seen. None of them saw much chance in engaging a superior force. One by one, they lay down their weapons and walked slowly and dejectedly toward the waiting Army troops on the east side of the capitol.

49

The events in Georgia riveted the nation. Not only the general population but also the political elites of the other states watched, especially those neighboring states in the South, but also California and Texas, where the secession movements seemed to have a similar sense of inevitability.

Edwin Regis, governor of Texas, was especially attentive. He had been in contact with Tad Grover, his counterpart in Oklahoma, to discuss combining the two states to reestablish the Republic of Texas. He had also been in contact with David Blinder, who was encouraging him to move quickly. But he had not been able to reach Binder for several hours, and he sensed that something was amiss.

In addition, Melinda Meyers, the attorney general of Texas, was in constant contact with key legislators. It was clear to Regis that she was trying to dissuade them from taking the action that both Regis and Blinder had desired. At first, Regis thought of this as an irritant, but as the time in which he didn't hear from Blinder lengthened, he grew more cautious.

It is sometimes said of politicians that their reflexes are most akin to snakes: they move slowly and silently, watch, and move slowly once again, constantly monitoring conditions around them. Edwin Regis was doing precisely that. It was his natural element, but it was disconcerting, even for him. He was beginning to wonder if the Grand Plan might not succeed.

He began to think that, if Georgia failed to secede, the odds that others would succeed decreased substantially. He decided that waiting for another state to take the first step was the wisest course of action. He couldn't take his eyes off Georgia.

The suicide of Hugh Lewins was flashed across the country within minutes of its happening. Once the shot was heard outside the capitol, reporters and broadcasters swarmed in that direction. Even though the armed soldiers kept them away from the command post, no one had an interest in hiding the truth. Major Sheridan ordered his press secretary to brief the media soon after it happened. He figured that neither the Army nor the state of Georgia nor the US government had any interest in restraining the media. Let them see what happens to traitors.

No one heard the message quite so clearly as Edwin Regis. His reptilian instincts kicked into high gear as he considered his options.

He called Blinder's private number one more time. A recording said that the number was no longer in service. How could that be? He was beginning to feel alone in the middle of a huge sea not entirely of his own creation.

He called a local state office in Wichita Falls and asked them to check on the Blinder estate. The bureaucrat who answered the phone said that he didn't have to.

"Haven't you heard? The feds invaded the Blinder estate hours ago. The word is that David Blinder is in federal custody. I'm not sure if he is or not. It hasn't been confirmed by the federal agents. But they made one hell of a racket around here."

Jesus, Regis thought. And I didn't know this? He thanked the man and hung up.

Now what? If David Blinder, who was the brains and the money behind this whole scheme, was in custody, what were the odds of the rebellion succeeding? If he wasn't, what was his next move? If the feds wouldn't confirm the arrest, that meant they didn't have him. Damn! Damn! Damn! But Regis recognized that he was now dealing with a situation that was much trickier and more precarious than he thought it ever would be.

Regis decided to call in the opposition. For practical purposes, that meant Meyers. He buzzed his secretary and asked her to ask Meyers to come to his office.

"Yes, sir."

Regis wrung his hands, looked out the window, and wondered about the outcome in Georgia. He had thought—assumed, really—that the Georgia effort would succeed. He had great confidence in McKenzie Phillips, and he knew that Abner Bellamy had the biggest stake in the state. It was his home; it had suffered more than most states in the first Civil War; and Abner wanted it desperately to be the seat of the New Confederacy. It should have succeeded.

Now everything seemed up in the air, and Regis needed to play both sides.

Fortunately, he had done almost all of his arm-twisting by proxy and kept his active role in the secession movement invisible to most of the players. It was this skill that had served him so well in his ascendance to the governorship of his state and which, he was sure, would help him with even higher office, no matter the political structure.

But that was a thought for another time. Right now, he had to determine to forge ahead with the Republic of Texas or cut his losses and stand up for the country of which he was currently a citizen.

He was distracted from those thoughts by another. Where was Melinda Meyers? He was about to pick up the phone and ask his secretary when the intercom buzzed. "Ms. Meyers is here to see you, sir."

"Show her in."

Melinda Meyers, six feet tall, thin, attractive, entered his office with her typically self-assured manner that played to all her strengths. She reached Regis's desk in a few graceful steps, held out her hand, and said simply: "Mr. Regis, what can I do for you?"

As Edwin Regis shook her manicured hand, he could smell the smug tone in her voice. He always resented his AG. She was too smart by half, seemed unflappable, had an imposing presence, and seldom said an unkind or an unnecessary word. Everyone liked and respected her. And she was uncanny in her ability and willingness to say what she meant and to call a situation by its real name. He was not looking forward to this conversation.

A new thought occurred to him: she was undoubtedly more up-to-date on the unfolding situation than he was. His resentment was not diminishing.

"Ms. Meyers, I have heard that the legislature has been considering following in Georgia's footsteps."

Melinda Meyers did not move. The expression on her face did not change.

"And it appears that the federal government has shut down that particular movement in Georgia, even though, I must say, the people's house there passed a resolution for secession."

Still nothing from Meyers.

"So what I want to know from you, as the attorney general of this state, is . . . is . . . is this: Is this legal? Is it possible? As the top law enforcement official, I am asking for your professional opinion."

"It is neither legal nor desirable, Mr. Regis."

"Not desirable?"

"That is correct. If we attempt to secede, it will trigger a major response from the federal authorities. Look what is happening in Georgia. Also, you may or may not know that federal agents surrounded David Blinder's estate this morning and attempted to take him into custody."

Why does everyone know this but me?

Meyers gestured to the television across from the Governor's desk. "And you know that federal troops surrounded the State Defense Force that was trying to muscle the Georgia legislature into seceding. Secession is clearly illegal, and there is nothing to be gained by bringing destruction down upon our state. Therefore, as your attorney general, I strongly advise against it."

Regis thought for a moment. He wasn't actually thinking; he was weighing what Meyers was telling him and feeling his way through the consequences. He always put great store by his instincts. And he had a distinct feeling that she was correct.

"Was what the feds did in Wichita Falls legal?"

"Absolutely. They had warrants and they had probable cause to believe that David Blinder played a significant role in recent events." She paused for just a moment. "And there was an issue about two federal agents who disappeared on that estate two days before, to say nothing of the mayhem in Washington."

Regis nodded, not so much in agreement but in registering what his AG had said. "I see. So what do we do now?"

"Nothing. As you may know," Melinda said with a touch of irony, "some legislators have been talking about secession and reestablishing the old Republic of Texas that seems so dear to the hearts of some of our less-well-informed citizens. However, I think it wise that those ideas never see the light of day in Austin."

Regis had thought of asking the AG where her sympathies lay, but the answer was clear.

"Thank you, Melinda. As always, I appreciate your candor, and I will take your remarks under advisement."

"Thank you, sir." She stood up and started to walk out of the room. Before she reached the door, however, she turned and looked back at Regis, whom she felt was in some kind of turmoil.

"The people don't pay me to give political advice, Edwin, so this is more or less off the record." She stared at his face for a moment. "But this might be a good time to assure the citizens of Texas and the government in Washington that Texas will play a leading role in preserving the federal government."

Then she turned and walked out of the room.

Edwin Regis reeled internally from Meyers's comment. The thought that Texas would come out for the federal government and cut the secession movement off at the knees was something he could barely fathom or stomach. Still, he thought, if the secession plan was not going to work, it would not hurt his prospects in Texas or beyond to stand up on the national stage to support the inevitable.

But was it inevitable? Could these developments just reflect setbacks rather than failure? He wasn't sure, so he decided that for now, he would just give events time to play themselves out. He was by nature a patient man.

Where was David Blinder?

50

That question was also on the top of the federal agents' minds in Texas. Samantha Stranger and Marie LeBrun were walking through the Blinder residence. More agents had arrived and were inspecting the house with latex gloves, cameras, and all the other tools of the forensic trade. Samantha and Marie were wandering the rooms, trying to get a sense of the place. A sense of the spirit of the place. Of David Blinder. They were trying to understand how he could have escaped.

It did not take long to discover the hidden doorway to the command center in a back hall. Technicians had already begun work on opening the door, stripping away the wallpaper and molding that masked the presence of the entryway, when the two women approached. Marie put her hand on the steel door that had muffled the explosion they had heard earlier. It was still warm. She figured that behind the door were the remains of David Blinder's command center.

As the technicians worked, they examined the very low tolerances around the edges of the entryway. Marie could tell they were impressed with the fine craftsmanship that went into that part of the house.

But fine craftsmanship was not limited to the heretofore secret passageway. It typified the entire mansion, which was done in traditional elegant style: high ceilings, columns, and heavy woodwork around openings of doors and windows, all of which was accented by beautifully designed furniture. David Blinder was a man of taste. A man who had grown accustomed to the finest of everything. Everywhere Samantha and Marie looked, the impressions of money and power and control dominated. It gradually became clear to the two women that David Blinder was not a man to leave anything to chance. Of course he had an escape plan, one that no one, probably not even his wife, knew about.

Marie turned to Samantha. "We need to find out what's behind that door."

Sam didn't argue. She knew the agenda. But the other agents were on it, so they continued wandering around the mansion. They knew that even well-organized explosions leave behind information that can be found by a trained observer and a careful investigator. Sam and Marie qualified on both counts. So did many of the agents working on the doorway.

The possibility of additional explosives and booby traps within and around the command center were a concern for everyone in the building. The tolerances were so small around the doorway that a camera could not be inserted, so they had no visual on the inside. Marie doubted that a camera would be much help anyway. All it would show would no doubt be a pile of rubble. The agents also learned that the entire room was wrapped with some kind of metallic coating that defeated the efforts of infrared penetration. So far, the team had had zero success in entering the room.

"There's always the old-fashioned way," Marie said, nodding toward an agent bringing up a drill.

Sam turned to watch the young agent set up a high-speed drill and connect it to a stand and to an electric outlet. He nodded to the two women watching him. "This should work."

Sam and Marie looked on as the drill warmed up to its highest speeds. Metallic shrieks pierced the air, and they had to cover their ears to avoid pain. They noticed that the operating agent was wearing earplugs.

They walked away to preserve their hearing.

"It could be hours before we gain entry to that room," Sam said.

Just as she said that, they heard a muffled explosion. The technicians had used the drill to insert small explosive devices at critical points in the door structure. The command center was wide open.

Marie looked at Sam. "I guess not," she said.

They followed the technicians into the room after donning gas masks. As predicted, the former command center was a pile of rubble. Shredded plastic, twisted wires, blown-out computer screens, melted telephones: the chaos of the command room was in stark contrast to the state of the rest of the house. The agents shook their heads.

"It's going to take some time to go through this," Marie said.

Sam nodded. Instinctively, she began scanning the floor, walls, and ceiling for hints about an escape route. The floor was difficult to see, given the debris strewn through the room, but the walls and ceiling were less obstructed. Sam began running her hands along the wall. There was one area where the wall covering had melted, revealing what look to be another steel door. She waved the technician over.

"Does that look like another entrance to you?"

The technician walked over and felt the hard metal. "Could be."

He stripped away some of the wall covering, revealing hinges that were built flush with the wall. He shook his head in admiration. "This guy knew what he was doing."

The drill was brought over and new charges set around what appeared to be the perimeter of the doorway. Within ten minutes, what had been a steel door was lying on the floor of the control room atop another pile of debris.

When the smoke cleared, the agents peered into what they expected to be a tunnel. Instead, what the saw was a collapsed pile of rock, cement, and dirt obscuring the path of what had once no doubt been a tunnel. They could see metal tracks sticking out a couple of inches.

"Shit!" everyone said at once.

51

Samantha and Marie were bone tired and filled with divergent feelings: glad about the success of the day's operation; sad about the losses they suffered and inflicted; angry at the need for the entire enterprise; and uncertain about the status of the plan of rebellion overall. They had been so focused on their small part of the counterattack that they were not in the loop about the situation in the rest of the country.

They both knew they needed rest. They walked out of the residence to find Agent Schwartz. He was talking to several agents who had helped round up the remaining SC troops. He looked up as they approached.

"Good work, Agent Schwartz," Marie said. "This went as well as could reasonably be expected."

Schwartz's face was grim. "It's never good to lose good men," he said tersely.

"No, it's not," Marie agreed. "But losing them in victory is better than losing them in defeat."

Schwartz did a tiny shrug as if only barely convinced. To him, it all felt like needless tragedy.

"We need to get some rest," Marie said. "Where can we crash?"

"We've commandeered a hotel a couple miles from here," Schwartz replied. "It's been vetted and swept for bugs and weapons and all the usual nastiness. You can set up there." He motioned for someone behind the women to come closer.

"Agent Williams will take you there," he said.

Sam and Marie looked at each other with relief. They glanced back at Schwartz. "Thank you," they both said.

"Thank you," Schwartz replied. "If we hadn't had your intel, this could not have happened as quickly as it did."

The women nodded and turned to follow Agent Williams to a waiting vehicle.

As they drove in silence, both Marie and Sam were wondering about the status of the rebellion, which is how they came to think of it. That would have to wait. Then they looked at each other. "Darrin and Cherie!" they both said.

In the heat of battle, they had forgotten that they left their two civilian partners at the command center.

"Agent Williams," Sam said, "could you drive by the command center? We have some business there."

"Yes, ma'am," the agent replied. She flipped on her blinker to take a right, away from the direction of the hotel. Within a few minutes, they pulled up to the command center and walked inside.

The inside of the command was still abuzz with energy: men and women working and walking back and forth, lots of computer screens flashing information, and there, near the center of the action, sat Darrin and Cherie.

Samantha and Marie started walking toward them. Cherie, who was facing the entrance, spotted them first. She jumped up with a shriek and ran to the women and threw her arms around both of them. Darrin, who was unsure what was happening at first, followed suit—minus the shriek. He was glad and relieved to see the two women in person and alive.

"It is so great to see you," Cherie said once the hugging subsided. Darrin nodded in assent.

"Same here," said Sam.

"Listen," Marie said. "We're going to a nearby hotel to get some rest. Would you like to come along?"

Darrin and Cherie nodded gratefully. "Absolutely," said Darrin. The command center was a professional but intense place, and they both wanted out.

"Let's go, then," Sam said, and the foursome walked toward the door.

Sandy Thurmond caught up with them just before they reached the door. She signaled for them to stop.

Cherie turned and looked at her, vaguely apprehensive that she might prevent them from leaving.

"Sam and Marie," Thurmond began. "I want to thank you for being with us. It was a challenging day. Good luck to you."

Sam and Marie nodded in response.

"Thank you for taking good care of our friends," Marie said. "It meant a lot to us."

"You are more than welcome." Sandy shook four pairs of hands and looked at the group one last time.

"Be well," she said. And she turned and walked back to her post.

52

The President had forty minutes before his speech to the nation. He was alone in his office working on it, revising and refining his text.

The situation continued to evolve, and his last update was ten minutes earlier. He knew the Army had surrounded SC troops in Atlanta, and he knew that Hugh Lewins, who it now appeared was very involved in the secessionist scheme in Georgia, had shot and killed himself rather than face arrest. But a lot of things were still up in the air. While Georgia may turn out to be a victory for the Union, as Mr. Obama began to think of it, there was still considerable activity going on in the remaining states. He had spoken briefly to several of the attorneys general, but some of them remained aloof. Everyone, it seemed, was watching Georgia.

In order to counter this, we need the people to speak, the President thought. Citizens of the United States are free to criticize the government; they are free to express their opinion; and they are free to fight for that freedom. Even if they don't agree. Mr. Obama understood that the genius of America lay in its diversity and in the freedoms cherished by its citizens.

And that's what he intended to talk about. He gathered his handwritten speech.

My fellow Americans, he read. *Over the past thirty-six hours, we have experienced a terrorist attack on our nation's capital, a homegrown terrorist attack that was not based in some far-off country but was born right here in the United States. It was devised and implemented by different groups of discontented citizens who came to believe that legal and political processes were insufficient to attain their goals.*

That attack was repelled by our civilian and military forces.

But the goal of the armed gangs that flooded into the nation's capital and started shooting was not to take over the country, but to cause mayhem. In the wake of that turmoil, it was their wish that a carefully orchestrated plan to compel individual states to secede from the Union would have time to work.

In a separate attack, Fort Knox was invaded, and the insurgents loaded America's gold onto trucks and carried it away.

That plan is being thwarted by our forces as I speak.

In Atlanta this morning, one house of the legislature took a vote on secession. It passed by a couple votes. The plan was to bring in truckloads of armed men to force the other house and the governor to support it. Fortunately—and once again, through the rapid and professional response of the US military—those armed men are now in custody.

I remind every citizen who is considering being a part of this plan that such actions are contrary to law and will not be tolerated. While I do not relish the idea of taking arms against our fellow citizens, I assure each of you that I will fight this evil plan with every resource at our disposal. And, as exemplified by our response to recent events, our resources are considerable.

To every local politician who is considering voting for secession: be advised that such a vote is treasonous, and you will be held accountable for any such action. To any state that is considering secession: be advised that what you are considering is illegal and has been judged so repeatedly by the Supreme Court and by the national legislature. This government will not tolerate any such move. We will continue to use all means available to us to prevent the dissolution of the United States of America.

There is nothing so powerful as a united citizenry. Nothing so strong as the voice of the people. Therefore, I ask every American who is able, to make his or her voice heard. Write, email, or text your representatives in

Congress and in your state legislatures. If you are able, go to your state capital. Go in great numbers. Go and tell the legislators by your presence that the United States, conceived in liberty and dedicated to the proposition that all men are created equal, cannot be made to vanish from the earth by a small but well-funded group of fanatics. Tell them until they hear you.

We have arms, and we will use them if necessary. But our first use of arms will be to protect citizens that show up in their state capitals to protect the heritage of the American people. I have been assured by senior military staff that we have the resources to protect the citizens who do this, and I assure you we will do so.

We will stop this insanity together.

Mr. Obama sat back in his chair and considered his position. This is a gamble. But it is the right gamble.

He picked up the phone to tell Anita to make copies of his notes and then gather his advisors together. He needed to wait but a few minutes.

Mr. Obama passed around the copies of his notes. "I believe this says everything I want to say. This is not the time for speechifying; it is a time for absolute clarity."

Heads bobbed around the room as they scanned the text. Within a few minutes, everyone was up to speed.

"Anything to add?" Mr. Obama said.

Silence and a few wordless shrugs.

"Okay, then," he said. "We're on in thirty minutes."

53

Thirty minutes seemed like an eternity to Abner, who was nearly delirious with rage at the events in Atlanta. He could barely believe the news as it came to him over the phone and on his television and computer. His line of communication to David Blinder was not working, and his colleagues, the men he had trained for this very day, were not picking up.

He shook his head at the cowardice of the state government leaders he believed he could count on. And he knew that, if this effort failed, it would just be a matter of time before the feds pieced together the puzzle and came knocking on his door with handcuffs.

He even tried to call Judith, his erstwhile lover to whom he had not spoken in weeks. No answer. He did not leave a message.

Crazy ideas swept through his mind. He looked at his watch to see if he had enough time to get to Washington to kill the President before he went on live television. He considered arming himself and going down to the Georgia capitol himself to start shooting those duplicitous bastards. He thought of killing himself.

But he knew he was being irrational. The rage and betrayal he felt inside were feelings he had not experienced since childhood, when his mother gave him up to relatives after his father was murdered. When she abandoned the task she was given to raise him.

In some ways, this was even worse. At least then he had relatives on whom to rely. Now he was watching as his handpicked associates abandoned the cause to which they had committed themselves. Even his lover had abandoned him. He was alone.

Or had they? It's true they were not answering their mobile phones, but that could be because they feared tracking by the all-powerful resources of the federal government. Abner looked back at the television. The news anchor had just said something about the governor of Texas making an announcement. Maybe this wasn't the end. Maybe it was time for him to rally his men in person. Then he would have a better sense of what was going on. If he could see them, he could assess what side they were on and the lengths to which they would go to follow through on the plan.

Abner didn't bother turning off the television. He reached for the keys to his car, checked the apartment quickly, and walked out the door. He took the elevator down six stories to the basement garage, where his black BMW sat ready for service. He got in, pushed the ignition button, and drove calmly out of the subterranean garage.

It wasn't a long drive to the capitol. In fact, he could see it in the distance from the balcony of his condo. As he drove, he deliberately monitored his breathing, taking deep breaths in an effort to calm down. By the time the capitol loomed ahead of him, his breathing had normalized. He was ready.

Abner saw the US Army units surrounding the capitol. Fortunately, he knew there was an underground passageway connecting the capitol with several of the surrounding office buildings. He parked his car on the street and entered the Twin Towers office building unopposed. It was the newest structure on the campus; he headed straight for the lower level.

When Abner reached the door that led directly to the tunnel, he noticed that it was guarded by an older man in uniform, probably a retiree, who was sitting at a desk reading a book. I guess people don't use this much, he thought with some relief. He nodded in the direction of the guard, who didn't even bother to look up, and walked through the unlocked door.

As he moved along the half-mile tunnel, Abner began to feel a sense of empowerment. Being on the ground interacting with people was far preferable to managing events from the comfort of his condo, even if it was only a few miles away. He felt a rush of excitement as he anticipated changing the course of events, which he believed with all his heart he could do.

As he neared the entrance to the capitol itself, Abner slowed his pace. He knew Phillips was not there, and Lewins was dead. Jake McAuley was now the governor, but he was a Democratic governor in a Republican state, so the fact that he was in that particular chair was an issue more than it was a problem. Abner had his own cadre of legislators.

He had arranged for four influential congressmen to serve as point people in the plan, two from each chamber. He headed first to the office of Jeremy Whitcomb, the principal in the House. It was, after all, the House that actually passed the resolution. Let's start with success, Abner thought.

He made his way to Whitcomb's office and let himself into the antechamber. Denise, Whitcomb's secretary, nodded and pointed with her head to Jeremy's office. Abner entered the congressman's office without knocking.

Jeremy Whitcomb was leaning on one knee on a window seat looking out at the US military formations surrounding the capitol. When he heard the door, he didn't bother to turn around. He figured it was Abner.

"It doesn't look good, Abner," Jeremy said after a few moments with a heaviness in his voice that Abner had never heard before. "After all this time . . ." He shook his head and turned slowly around to face Abner.

"Get away from that window, Jeremy. It will just sap your spirits." He motioned for him to have a seat on the couch, as if he were hosting the congressman instead of the other way around.

Whitcomb followed Abner's direction and sat down. On his way to the couch, he deftly picked up a crystal decanter and two glasses and set them soundlessly on the coffee table between himself and Abner. He poured two glasses of Kentucky bourbon and handed Abner a glass.

"To the South," he said humorlessly, raising his glass. He and Abner clinked their glasses.

The two men sat in silence for a few moments, vaguely listening to the sounds of military machinery outside but otherwise focused on their immediate predicament.

Then Jeremy looked Abner squarely in the face. "What do we do now, Abner?"

Abner paused for just a moment before responding. Then, putting his glass on the table, he said, "First of all, it's important to know what we don't do. And what we don't do is throw in the towel. Not now, not when we are so close."

Jeremy didn't say anything. He just looked at Abner.

"Now is the time to make sure we don't lose our stride, the time to build on the resolution the people's chamber passed this morning."

Jeremy Whitcomb did not disagree with what Abner was saying, but he had no earthly idea what the next move could possibly be.

The two men sat and sipped their whiskey as if they had all afternoon to wile away. Then Abner picked up his cell phone and speed-dialed Adam Wilson, who was monitoring events from his Wyoming redoubt.

"What the hell is happening in Atlanta?" Wilson said by way of greeting.

"The US Army, that's what's happening. We've got to act fast."

Wilson, whose eye rarely strayed from self-interest, waited for a moment before taking the bait. "What do you want me to do, Abner?" he asked in a mildly more considerate tone.

"I want you to pull all the weight you can in Georgia to send up a huge pro-Confederate demonstration the likes of which has not been seen since 1865."

Wilson considered this. It was easily something within his capability to do: he had lots of contacts in the South, and his little group magnified the sphere of influence by a factor of ten or twenty. "When?"

"As soon as you damn well can. Today. As soon as possible. I want to give these Army troops something to do besides babysit the state legislature."

Wilson did not take to being spoken to in such a tone, but he let it go for now. He was sure that Abner Bellamy, for all his gifts, was no match for his own brilliance, contacts, and persuasive powers. In the end he would show that little Southerner how things really work.

"I'll have it up and running in a few hours," he said with just a touch of subservience in his voice. Wilson always thought Southerners loved the illusion of being in control. He was willing to play this game a little longer.

"Thank you, Adam."

Wilson put his phone back into his pocket and turned to a small group of men at a nearby table. "Who has contacts in Georgia? We need to get a demonstration up and running today. Now!"

The men looked at Wilson without flinching. Just another task they felt easily able to manage. "We'll have thousands by close of business," said one. The others all nodded in agreement.

"Good," said Wilson. "Let's do it. The sooner the better."

In Whitcomb's office, Abner and Jeremy continued sipping Southern bourbon while contemplating this next stage.

"Abner," said Whitcomb, "what do you expect to get from a demonstration? Do you think those boys out there will allow one?"

"Freedom means freedom for everybody, Jeremy." He took another sip of bourbon. "It's un-American to stop a peaceful protest." Another sip. "Besides, once the federal troops have their hands full with the demonstration, it will give the legislature some time to breathe." Another sip. "And come to its senses."

Whitcomb shook his head. He had never known a man as self-assured as Abner Bellamy, which was one of the things that attracted him to the young preacher. "Frankly, Abner, I think this plan warrants a 'maybe.' But what do you want me to do?"

"You can get on your phone and contribute to the demonstration," Abner replied without hesitation. "The voice of the people is a powerful thing." He stared into his glass for a moment. "Never mind that," he said abruptly. "What you can do is go visit your colleagues in the House and then the Senate and get this process back on track."

Whitcomb stared at Bellamy in disbelief.

"Look, Jeremy, the House here just did something historic, something it's been wanting to do for over a hundred and fifty years. It showed courage and fortitude in passing the resolution for secession. Maybe your colleagues in the Senate lost their nerve when the troops showed up. But think about it. Those state defense troops that Lewins had put together were just a distraction. He and Phillips thought they could muscle the legislature to do what they wanted. This is a better path. The US government can call those soldiers traitors or whatever else they want to call them, but the real steel, the real determination, comes from the legislature. So what you can do is take your focus off those Army troops out there and meet with your colleagues to get this thing done."

Jeremy Whitcomb's look of disbelief moderated just a little. He was thinking. There was something to what Bellamy was saying, and he was already in this so deep he didn't think he had much to lose. And he prided himself on his persuasive skills. He looked back at Bellamy.

"Okay."

"How can I assist you, Jeremy?" Abner asked.

Whitcomb looked at Abner for a long moment. "You can take care of McAuley." "Consider it done."

dam Wilson could feel the power of his personality when he dealt with his men. He knew he was the only person who could hold this group of dedicated, talented men together. As he walked away from the reenergized group, his cell phone rang again.

"Adam?" said the familiar voice on the other end of the line.

"David?"

"We need to talk."

"Yes, we do." Wilson marveled at the timing. Just when he was feeling the strength of his own leadership, David Blinder returned and addressed him as an equal. On the one hand, it had a "meant to be" feel about it. On the other hand, Adam Wilson was not sure he wanted to share his sense of personal potency with David Blinder or with anyone else. He was a little light-headed, as he smelled power coming to him. Power in the form of David Blinder.

"I am calling from a private plane, Adam. I want to meet with you and your group. I'll be there in an hour."

"Here?"

"In case you haven't been tracking the news, the feds invaded my home this morning. I managed to escape, but everyone else in the compound was detained." A hint of bitter resolve crept into his voice. "This is not over."

Wilson did not reply right away. He was listening intently and thinking as fast as he could, trying to make sense of what was happening. He had people tracking the news, and he was updated regularly. He had no news from the Texas compound where Blinder lived. The coverage was all about what was happening in the state houses.

The political landscape was shifting in Wilson's mind. It sounded as if Blinder were now a fugitive from justice, and he wasn't sure he wanted to host him here, even though he believed if the movement had any chance it was through the money, power, and influence of the man on the other end of the line. And his location was so secluded it was unlikely that anyone could track their meeting.

"We'll be ready," he said. "Is there anything you want me to do in the meantime?"

Silence on the other end. "Yes, I want you to prepare to evacuate your people and to make sure that when your group pulls up stakes, there is no trace of evidence." Blinder clicked off.

Wilson stared at his phone for a few minutes trying to digest what had just happened. Blinder wants me to destroy evidence. Of what? Of a group of guys who were meeting in the wilderness for a retreat? That was the standard cover story for what his men were doing. And there were no plans to leave until the secession succeeded or failed. Wilson didn't think he would know that for at least another day or two.

Blinder on the run was a new element.

Wilson stepped out into the cool mountain air and shook his head. He had a lot of questions. Was hosting David Blinder wise, given the fact that he was a fugitive? Was he still in control of the game? He said he was calling from his plane, but Wilson had no way to verify that, and Blinder knew it. He could have been calling from anywhere. For the first time since he met David Blinder, he labeled him "questionable."

On the other hand, Adam Wilson was feeling his own prominence grow, and he relished the eminence he had in his own group. The notion that he would not have to defer to anyone else or hand over that prestige to a more eminent figure caught his attention. Even if that figure made all this possible. Even if that figure was David Blinder.

The only thing he was sure about was that he had an hour to decide what to do.

avid Blinder clicked off and allowed himself an unusual daytime cocktail as he pondered his next step. The airplane that he had at his disposal was a well-equipped Learjet with all the accoutrements one would expect of a first-class private plane. For Blinder, it would now be his new command post.

He speed-dialed Bellamy's number. Georgia was key: if Bellamy could get Georgia back on track, the entire plan had better-than-even odds of succeeding. Bellamy's phone went straight to voicemail.

What now. His thoughts were interrupted by the flight attendant who was taking care of him.

"Mr. Blinder. The President is about to address the nation. Would you like to listen?"

David Blinder did not display any reaction. He knew he had to listen, if only to detect clues about what the federal strategy might entail. But he did not relish hearing from the man he had tried to kill not twenty-four hours before. "Yes, Spencer," he said.

The attendant turned and flipped a switch in the galley. Suddenly the room was filled with sound as the press secretary introduced the President of the United States.

The same message was being heard across the nation on all major networks.

When the President finished speaking, David Blinder took a sip of his cocktail and pondered his position. In his mind, he listed the assets still available to him. The Sovereign Citizen troops had flattened Fort Knox and were in possession of much of the nation's gold. The remnants of the Washington, DC, invasion were assembling at a new rendezvous point where they would combine with the eight thousand troops under Winslow Parker's command in southern Tennessee. There they would be available to any state that needed them to enforce resolutions of secession. That put the total number of troops at about twelve thousand.

Of course, the US Army was much larger, but it was top-heavy and could not be counted on to mobilize quickly. True, they responded with surprising speed in Washington, but that was the nation's capital, and plans for a rapid mobilization there had no doubt been in place for a long time. And in the end, it didn't matter. The SC troops, on the other hand, had the fastest vehicles money could provide at their disposal and could be inside the borders of any capital in the Confederacy within an hour and a half. David Blinder had great faith in Winslow Parker.

He picked up his phone and entered Parker's number.

Nothing. No voicemail, no response at all. Blinder shrugged and decided to start calling his assets in various state houses. His first call would be to Edwin Regis in Texas.

Then he hesitated. He put the phone down on the tray in front of him and found himself deep in thought. Why is Parker not responding? He began running through the possible scenarios. Could it be that Parker's been compromised somehow? He picked up his phone and hit the redial button.

Nothing.

David Blinder took a long sip from his cocktail, let the potent liquid swirl around in his mouth for a bit, and swallowed. He motioned for Spencer to bring him another. Then he picked up his laptop and went to the CNN website. He scanned the bulleted headline column. Turmoil in Atlanta. . . . Rebel troops surrounded. . . . Speaker of the House in Georgia kills himself. . . .

David Blinder stared at the last headline. *What?*

He clicked on the item to open the story. The video reel started immediately.

"In a move that shocked everyone," the reporter was saying, "Hugh Lewins, a longtime Georgia politician and Speaker of the Georgia House of Representatives, apparently shot himself this afternoon while talking to officers of the US Army, who were there to protect the gathering civilians around the Georgia capitol building."

David inhaled sharply. Lewins is gone. US troops are surrounding the capitol in Georgia. That means they're surrounding the State Defense Force troops who were supposed to be surrounding the building. He flipped back to the bullet points and saw a new banner across the CNN site: "Thousands of Americans Respond to the President."

He put down his laptop. Just then, Spencer arrived with his refreshed cocktail, and David took a big gulp.

He had one more play in Georgia, and that was to contact Abner Bellamy. David picked up his phone and held it for a moment before entering the number. If Abner is also compromised, he thought, the plan in Georgia is over. He took another long sip of his drink and entered the number.

Nothing.

Time to check in with Texas.

dwin Regis had a cell phone that was his exclusive link to David Blinder. So when it rang, he knew immediately who was trying to contact him. He had never not answered the phone when it rang. But now, even though he had been trying to contact Blinder all morning, he was suddenly paralyzed.

Images of the mayhem at the Blinder estate flashed through his mind. Although he hadn't been present for it, he had been hearing detailed descriptions all morning, and he knew that David Blinder was not in custody. He also knew there was a total news blackout on the events near Wichita Falls.

It was clear to Regis that no other state in the Union would secede if the plan in Georgia fell through. And even though the House there had passed a resolution, the Senate had not yet voted, and the Republican governor had been replaced by a Democrat. It did not look promising.

It felt like an eternity before the disposable cell phone in his hand stopped ringing. Fortunately, no one else was in his office at the time, so he knew it didn't make any difference. Still, he had no idea what Blinder was up to, what he was capable of, or what he would think of an unanswered phone. By design, there was no voicemail, as it was too easy to trace and there was no question about who would be on the other end of the line.

Regis took the small phone in both his hands and twisted it sharply. He pulled out what he believed to be the critical internal parts and broke them into smaller parts. He placed all the pieces of the shattered phone in his jacket pocket, knowing that he could not dispose of it in his office. He would do it later on his drive home.

57

Adam Wilson had a more moderate reaction. He heard the President's address, but it didn't bother him so much. Of course, he was not in federal custody surrounded by patriotic American soldiers. He was concerned about the success of the mission, but his concern was mitigated by the fact that he had taken great pains to mask his involvement and to give himself reasonable explanations for all his actions.

But nor had he lost confidence in the plan. He had his men and their considerable resources at his disposal. David Blinder was still in the game, even if he put too much store by his own judgment and the technology he so loved. Wilson also had confidence in Abner Bellamy and in Winslow Parker, both top-drawer talents in their respective fields.

He encouraged his group to contact as many people as they could to stage a demonstration supporting secession in Georgia. This was not so difficult as it might seem, as there were many long-standing discontented groups in that state that felt the War Between the States should never have ended in defeat of the Confederacy, a belief that was handed down through generations as it became more and more divorced from the actual circumstances on the ground in 1865. They were ready and willing to take to the streets to express their strongly felt but curious views.

Wilson wondered how this would look in the end, however. Most of these people were outliers, weekend warriors, rural discontents, often unshaven and unkempt. They were made up largely of the losers in the American economy. They hardly looked like Middle America.

Still, there were a lot of them in Georgia, and Wilson was more concerned with making good on his commitment to Bellamy than with the ultimate outcome. It was critical for him to look good in all situations, and this one was no different.

The plan for his men was to step into positions of leadership in the new order that was coming to North America, one that would be comprised of different nations rather than one overriding bureaucracy. Wilson saw this as a good and as an inevitable thing, and he wanted a big say in how the situation developed. He saw his group of committed religionists to be statesmen in the new order with himself as their head. He loved the feel of power; he could smell it.

He turned toward the table where men were on the phone, and he gestured for them to end their conversations and listen to him. He sent an assistant to fetch the rest of the men who were otherwise occupied in their remote hideout.

"Okay," he began. "We just heard the President call us traitors and fanatics. He declared war on us." Wilson paused for a moment and looked each man in the room in the eye. "This is just the kind of dictatorial behavior we have come to expect from US presidents: they will do nothing to curtail their power over the lives of good Christian men and women. And they will stop at nothing to push their secular agenda." He spat out the last two words.

"You all know where this will lead. If we lose this fight, government hubris will only increase. Good Christian values will be violated again and again and again, just as they have been for the last eighty years in this country." He looked around again. "And it is up to us to stop it.

"You will notice," Wilson added almost as an afterthought, "that the President made no mention of God. That man said that the US was a government of the people, not of God. But we know that relying on humans has failed. 'Put not your trust in princes, in a son of man, in whom there is no salvation,'" he bellowed, quoting one of his favorite scripture passages. "'Cursed is the man who trusts in man and makes flesh his strength, whose heart turns away from the Lord,'" he added for good measure.

Heads bobbed all around the room. Every man there knew what he was about and that this was his purpose in life. None believed that death or the threat of death could deter them from their mission.

Every person in the room knelt and prayed. Adam Wilson led the prayer: "All-powerful God, give us the strength to carry through your dreadful work and by your mighty hand deliver us from our enemies."

"Amen," responded the room in unison.

"Amen," repeated Adam Wilson.

bner walked slowly over to the Governor's office in the capitol. He needed time to devise a way to neutralize Jake McAuley before he reached his office. He considered his options: he could appeal to him as a native son of Georgia; he could threaten him if he tried to prevent secession; he could monopolize his time to prevent him from coordinating countermeasures against the resolution.

None of these seemed adequate. He believed that the state constitution did not address the issue of who would succeed a lieutenant governor who became governor, so he imagined that the legislature would have to decide. That worked to Abner's advantage.

But only if McAuley were removed or debilitated. Or killed.

Abner leaned against the corridor wall in the high-ceilinged hall down which he was walking. He could kill McAuley, but that would expose him to high risk if it became known. Abner had never killed anyone. He wasn't even sure how he could or would do it. He had not brought a gun, something he had considered doing only fleetingly, so he couldn't shoot him. Abner never thought of himself as a strong physical person, and he had no idea what kind of physical shape McAuley was in, so a physical altercation seemed impracticable.

He moved toward a window and looked outside at the federal troops arrayed across the capitol lawn. They were soldiers. Some of those men probably had killed people. Maybe I can get one of them to kill the Governor. But he quickly dismissed that idea as too risky. I could end up getting myself killed.

McAuley was someone Abner would classify as a liberal secularist. As such, he was part of the movement that led to the murder of Abner's father in a race riot in Macon, Georgia, when Abner was only fourteen. That led to his mother's fateful decision to send him away for the rest of his adolescence, a decision for which Abner had never forgiven her. He never saw her after he left home at that tender age. Even now, decades later, he felt sourness in his gut about how he was mistreated.

He began to think of McAuley as part of that same evil philosophy that led to his father's murder. Of course, he wasn't part of it, Abner thought, but he was cut from the same cloth. He would side with the "oppressed," which in Georgia meant African Americans. He would side with them against white people.

Abner's insides began to shake. All of a sudden, he began to feel the weight of the crushing stress of the past thirty hours. He had been forestalling it by bourbon, constant contact with team members, and sheer exhilaration at the breadth of what he was doing. Now he thought of Judith, his lover, who left him. He thought of his men, who had said they believed in him and had worked so hard up until now but seemed to be losing their nerve. He felt alone again.

His breathing became shallow, and he felt the color drain from his face. He shook his head to clear it and get back to the task at hand. He was still trying to think his way through the dilemma of what to do with McAuley. He remembered that one of the main reasons he went into the ministry was that he believed even as a teenager that reason had its limits in motivating people and dealing with situations. It was fervor that moved people. It was emotion and story and inspiration, not cold calculation.

He forced himself to get his breathing under control. Abner knew that his intelligence was helpful in planning recent events, but he also knew that the men he had assembled did so on the basis of the power of belief, not lifeless reason. Abner knew he could inspire people: he inspired his men; he inspired congregations; he inspired women. He knew the power of inspiration. Now he understood that he had one more person to inspire. That person was himself.

McAuley had to be stopped at all costs. Abner realized that trying to parse the situation in terms of who was stronger or whether or not he had a weapon or what the odds would be for success was just futile. God would provide him whatever weapons he needed; his passion would show him the way to end the threat he knew McAuley to be.

Abner stood up straight and took a long, deep breath. He knew what he had to do. He knew it involved risk, but what in life doesn't? His steps became more purposeful, the air cleared around his head. He always knew he had a mission, and now was the time to execute it. It all came down to him. For the rest of his walk down the long corridor, he prayed. He prayed as he had so often taught others to pray, even though he seldom prayed alone. It wasn't that he didn't believe; he just didn't believe the myths and stories of the religion he taught. But he believed in power, and as he advanced toward the Governor's office, he felt that power stir within him. "Though I walk through the valley of the shadow of death," he recited just under his breath.

He reached the door of McAuley's office. The usual guards were absent. Abner assumed, rightly as it turned out, that they had been reassigned because of the disturbing events of the morning. God is on my side, he thought as he approached the door to the anteroom.

After only a moment's hesitation, he turned the knob and pushed the door open. The secretary was on the phone; she smiled at him and motioned for him to take a seat. Abner smiled back and remained standing. He saw a brass letter opener on her desk, and as she turned away from him to continue her conversation, he picked it up and hid it up his sleeve, where he could pull it out on a moment's notice. He felt the cold metal on his forearm and the long and pointed shape pressing into his skin. God gave him the only weapon he needed to implement justice.

The secretary was clearly trying to end her conversation so she could ask the visitor what he wanted and what he was doing there. Abner motioned for her to take her time. She turned around once again, and he opened the door to McAuley's office, walked in, and closed the door.

The Governor was also on the phone. He did not recognize Abner and looked surprised that someone he did not know was in his office unannounced. His senses went on high alert. "I'll call you back," he said into the receiver. Then he turned and faced Bellamy across the desk.

"May I help you?"

"Governor," Abner began. "My name is Abner Bellamy. I am here to ask for your support in helping implement the resolution that was passed this morning in the Georgia House and that will momentarily be debated and voted upon in the Senate."

McAuley pushed the button on his intercom. "Sarah, get security in here right away."

Time slowed down for Abner Bellamy. In one mighty motion, he pulled the letter opener from his sleeve and lunged across the large room. Throwing himself across McAuley's desk, he held tight to the blade at the end of his straight arm and aimed for McAuley's chest.

Jake McAuley hesitated only a second when he realized what Abner was doing. As Abner approached, Jake slid his wheeled chair out of the line of attack and around to the other side of his desk. Abner skidded across the mahogany desktop and crashed against the wall behind the desk. His body was splayed across the floor and against the credenza along the wall. He was breathing heavily. His head was bleeding.

As he opened his eyes, he saw security guards racing into the room with their pistols drawn. They quickly came up on either side of Abner, hoisted him to his feet, and frisked him mercilessly. The letter opener was still in his hand.

"Get this man out of here," said McAuley.

59

J eremy Whitcomb was walking out of the office of a sympathetic senator with whom he had been discussing strategy. He thought there might be a chance that the Senate could be called into session and asked to vote on the resolution. He was counting votes in his head to see if they could take this over the top. Fleetingly, he wondered how Abner was faring with the Governor.

As Whitcomb walked down the corridor to another senator's office, he glanced outside at the US troops that were lining the street in front of the capitol, armed to the teeth, it seemed to him. He turned his head away: they were an obstacle he didn't want to think about just then. Not when the plan was back in play.

He heard a commotion outside as he marched past the windows that lined the corridor. He thought he saw movement out of the corner of his eye and he struggled not to look out the window. After passing just a few more windows, he could not help himself. He stopped and turned to face the outside straight on.

What he saw did not encourage him. The sound he had heard was the noise from horns honking. The movement was the arrival of more and more civilians. They were apparently honking their horns to get the attention of others, including those inside the building.

Whitcomb stared down the long avenue that fronted the capitol. It was lined with cars as far as he could see. He looked at the other streets giving onto the boulevard that ran parallel to the entrance: they too were packed with vehicles. He noticed that many of the cars had American flags on them. US flags.

He had to pull himself away from this inexplicable scene to attend his next meeting. He walked into the office of William Blakely, a senator from the low country of Georgia. He fully expected Blakely to be a supporter of the resolution Whitcomb was trying to resurrect.

Blakely's secretary was aware of the appointment and directed Whitcomb to go right into the senator's office. He was about to say something by way of greeting when he noticed that Blakely was standing at the window, staring out. He did not look pleased.

Whitcomb glanced at Blakely and then out the window and then back again. Outside he noticed the same kind of activity that he had observed along the corridor, except this time there were more people than cars.

He looked out the window again. He saw whole families—parents, children, grandparents—waving American flags and making some kind of noise he couldn't make out. He noticed that the Army troops were doing what they could to maintain order. The troops were engaging the crowd in a respectful way; armed sentries were facing outward, away from the crowd, as if protecting them.

"What's going on here?" Whitcomb asked.

William Blakely took a long breath and turned to look at his visitor. "What's going on here is that the people are responding to the appeal from the President of the United States to pressure their legislators to stop secession." Then he fell silent and returned his gaze to the window.

Whitcomb didn't understand what Blakely was talking about. "What?"

Blakely again turned toward Whitcomb with the air of a teacher trying to instruct a dull student. "I guess you didn't bother to listen to the President's address."

Whitcomb shook his head. "No, I didn't," he replied. It had completely slipped his mind. He realized it must have occurred when he was talking to Bellamy.

"Well, the President directed all Americans who wanted to preserve the Union to go to their state capitals and express themselves. And he promised them the protection of the US military to do this." He pointed to the window. "And, as you can see, the people are responding. So is the military."

Blakely turned toward Whitcomb full face. "It's over, Jeremy. It's not going to happen today in Georgia." He glanced out the window. "And if it doesn't happen today, it's not going to happen ever in my lifetime."

Whitcomb detected a tone of sadness in Blakely's voice. While he wasn't part of Bellamy's circle, Blakely was considered sympathetic to the Confederate cause. He even kept a small Confederate flag in his office on the credenza behind his desk. Whitcomb reflexively glanced over to the credenza. The flag was gone.

Blakely noticed Whitcomb's glance. "As soon as those cars started honking, I took it down. Now it's a matter of political survival."

Jeremy Whitcomb didn't know what to say. He could tell by Blakely's expression that there was no room for discussion or negotiation. Blakely was resigned. Whitcomb nodded, turned on his heel, and left the office.

When he got to the corridor, he was berating himself for missing the President's speech when he noticed several legislators chatting in small groups. He walked up to the group nearest to him.

"What's going on?"

"Haven't you heard?" one of the men said. "Somebody tried to assassinate McAuley."

Jeremy Whitcomb was speechless. The color drained from his face. It could only be Abner. He had said he would take care of

McAuley. Whitcomb did not think that included trying to murder him.

"Is McAuley all right?"

Heads nodded. "Yeah, he's okay. Evidently this guy, Bellamy, tried to stab him with a letter opener in the Governor's office."

It was at this moment that Jeremy Whitcomb realized there was another side to Abner Bellamy that had been invisible to him for all the time of their acquaintance. He had always seen Abner as an influential, intelligent, and powerful man who was focused on his single mission: to reestablish the Confederacy as a viable political unit. It never occurred to him prior to this moment that he might be deranged. But what other explanation was there for a person to attempt assassination of a sitting governor with a letter opener on the governor's home turf? It was insane.

Whitcomb walked back to his office to listen to the President's address and to make sense of what was happening. He needed to figure out a way to save himself from exposure and from being implicated in Abner's plan. This was a challenge. He had been collaborating with Abner for years now, and, while he thought he was always careful, he wasn't sure his care had been absolute. His anxiety level began to rise.

The Internet was lit up with the speech, so Whitcomb had no trouble finding it. He listened. It was noticeably short but potent. He could see why people responded. Damn, he thought, even I feel a pull to maintain the Union. .His mind flashed images of a younger, more idealistic, and more naïve version of himself. He felt a trace of shame.

He looked out the window. More people were coming. More cars were honking. More flags were waving. Jeremy Whitcomb was not given to despair, but he was given to realism, or so he thought. His new view of Abner Bellamy cleared his head, and he felt he had a better perspective. He had clearly been duped. He cursed the day he met Bellamy. He cursed his involvement with the group of rebels. He ran through his options: deny involvement, say nothing. But he had lobbied for secession and voted for it. He was, according to the President, suborning treason if not engaging in treasonous acts himself. His future seemed suddenly to dim.

eanwhile, Abner Bellamy was talking a blue streak. He was ranting against liberals, the North, his mother, the Governor, the Georgia legislature, Judith, his heretofore secret associates, his special mission, a monument to the Confederacy in Forest Park in St. Louis, the ministry, politics in general, and the need for atonement.

The officers guarding him kept him handcuffed as much for his own safety as for any other reason. They were, of course, videotaping the entire performance. One of the officers tried to get close enough to see if he could smell alcohol on Abner's breath, so inclined was he to believe that the man was drunk. But every time he got close, Abner looked at him with an expression of pure terror and crouched back into his chair, as if the officer were going to do him harm.

Poor crazy bastard, thought the officer.

After a while, a physician was called in to examine and, if necessary, sedate the prisoner. It took the doctor a while to arrive, so the performance went on. When he finally showed up, Abner was reciting a declaration of independence to the four walls of the interrogation room.

The good doctor did not need a great deal of time to finalize a diagnosis. He motioned for guards to come assist him in medicating the raving lunatic in front of him. Dr. Cambridge knew that was not an official diagnosis, but it pretty much described what he saw. *Acute psychotic episode*, he later wrote in the record.

After injecting Abner with a potent sedative, Dr. Cambridge helped the guards lay his weakening body on the table so he wouldn't fall and might be more comfortable in his drug-induced sleep. He told the officer in charge that they had to get this man to a hospital.

The guards, whose mood was jubilant as they learned of the arrival of the US Army and heard from the President why they were there, were happy to oblige. But they would not countenance letting the lunatic in question go or be harmed by some other fanatic. They found an old gurney used for moving records around and transferred Abner's limp body onto it. They wheeled him back through the same tunnel by which he had entered the building a few hours earlier and arranged for an ambulance to meet them at the Twin Towers building. They assigned four guards to stay with him the entire time. They did not remove the handcuffs.

Back in the Governor's office, Jake McAuley and Sarah, his secretary, were reestablishing order in the area of his desk and credenza. The police had been through everything, collecting evidence, but there was precious little of that in what appeared to be a deranged and ill-fated attempt on McAuley's life.

Considering someone had just tried to assassinate him, Jake McAuley's spirits were buoyant. Part of the reason for his mood was the realization that he had escaped a death threat, but he also drew encouragement from citizens of his state arrayed outside and the federal troops protecting them. The fact that this happened so quickly gave heft to the President's message.

In addition, he had spent some time fielding calls on McKenzie Phillips's private line from men who were apparently conspiring to destroy the United States. These men clearly felt they had a safe line of communication and often did not say much by way of introduction except their first and/or last name. Jake kept track of the numbers coming in and made notes of the conversations. He was a prosecutor by training, and those skills, he knew, were coming in very handy.

It was in the middle of one of those conversations when the attempt was made on his life. Since then, Sarah had been nothing but apologetic for allowing Bellamy into McAuley's office. As word began to spread about what happened, his official phone had not stopped ringing. It seemed everyone he had ever met wanted to be sure he was safe. Jake's first call was to his wife, who knew nothing of it and who almost fainted when he told her what had happened.

For all the stressful events swirling around him, Jake felt enormous relief. In the back of his mind, he wondered if politics was his true calling, but that was a decision he would have to postpone. For the moment, he had work to do, not only in getting Georgia back to working order but also in making sure those responsible for the day's events would not go unpunished.

He instructed Kurt Meaney to hold off on any announcement of the assassination attempt for as long as possible and to restrict physical access to his office. He wanted to give himself and law enforcement enough time to do the investigations that would be needed before arrests could be made. He asked Mercer Willoughby to send over assistants to comb through Phillips's files to find any links to insurgents or to Phillips's role in recent events. Jake didn't want to jail every person who voted for secession, but he wanted the ringleaders to be uncovered, and for that he needed some time.

Since his office was off-limits, he decided to make the rounds himself. He had a pretty good idea of where to start: the men and women who first raised the alarm that such a resolution was pending in the House. His first visit was to the office of Jackson Williams, the floor leader of the House, who was aware of the vote, crossed party lines by alerting the opposition, had voted nay, and who was at least as opposed to secession as Jake was. Jake figured, rightly as it turned out, that Williams knew exactly who voted for what, who had leaned on whom, and other relevant details of the vote in the House. Between Williams and Mary McDonald, the minority leader, he would be able to piece together a fairly compelling list of those he believed might be the ringleaders.

He was joined in this effort by the attorney general, who had played such an important role in galvanizing the opposition. McAuley knew that Mercer was a good balance for him: where he was inclined to forge ahead, Mercer was cautious and careful and thorough. Jake valued those tendencies in him.

When McAuley called Mercer a second time, the AG was reviewing the video of Abner Bellamy's "interrogation." In effect, it wasn't an interrogation at all but a movie of an obvious breakdown of Mr. Bellamy's mental faculties. Of course, Willoughby could not discount the possibility that it was all an act, so he had arranged for the video to be reviewed by a panel of mental health professionals. He liked being careful.

He also liked feeling relieved. He had not slept much in the past two days, and he was deathly tired. But the relief he felt at what looked like the end of these crazy activities compensated somewhat for the fatigue he felt.

At least, he hoped it was the end. The tide appeared to have turned—in Georgia, anyway—but he wouldn't be sure until his targets were within sight and the perpetrators were safely behind bars. Even though he was a lifelong Republican, he was relieved that Jake McAuley, a Democrat, was sitting in the governor's chair.

61

"How's it look?" the President asked.

"Here is where I think we are," said Valerie Escapan cautiously. "Georgia was a lodestone for most of the states of the old Confederacy. Since it happened that we made our biggest show of force there, it looks as if the other states are being more circumspect."

Circumspect is good, the President thought. "What about Texas?"

"Edwin Regis scheduled a press conference for this afternoon, sir. We're not sure what he's going to say, but I'd be surprised if he came out in favor of secession, given that his state hosted the mastermind of the operation and that person is still at large. All this follows an assault on his estate, which was defended by hundreds of insurgent troops."

Mr. Obama frowned. "The operation" was a dry way of describing the slaughter that had taken place in the nation's capital the day before and the bloodshed that followed in Fort Knox.

"And California?"

Valerie glanced at Joe Biden, who was sitting on the divan across from her, before responding. "It looks as if not one more vehicle could fit into the greater Sacramento area."

Obama looked at her quizzically for a moment. Then he smiled a small smile. "The people are showing up?"

"By the thousands, Mr. President. Maybe by the millions across the country. In states throughout the South, in Washington and Oregon, even in Vermont and New Hampshire. Anywhere that the threat of secession seemed real." She nodded with her head to the television. "May I?" she asked as she picked up the remote from the coffee table.

The President nodded, and she flipped on CNN, where reporters were struggling to keep up with the massive influx of Americans surrounding state houses across the country. US Army units were at each one, weapons at the ready and dead-serious looks on the soldiers' faces.

Mr. Obama glanced back at Valerie. "Makes one proud."

"Yes, sir, it does."

But the President had other things on his mind. He had to be sure that what he was seeing was not just a good sign but a turning point. He had to restore order and preserve the Union above all else. Next, he had to find and punish those responsible for this mayhem. He recognized progress when he saw it, but the knots in his back told him the process was still under way. He stood up to stretch his shoulders and upper back, even as the thoughts kept coming. He knew this movement had more than one center, and he intended to track down every one of them before they slipped back into the shadows.

To that end, he sat back down and called Max Grabel, the CIA chief. Max, he felt, had the best handle on what was happening on the ground, especially in Texas, where he was more or less in constant contact with Samantha and Marie, his operatives there.

"Talk to me, Max," the President said.

"Judging by the number of SC troops on the Blinder estate and his sudden departure, it is pretty clear that he was very important in the execution of the overall plan," Max replied. "We're pretty sure he actually masterminded the whole thing, but we're still working on the forensics.

"And he did a good job of covering up his tracks. He had his control room rigged with explosives. Our people just got into that room, and it doesn't look good. Plus, we know there are some other organizing points. One is a group of right-wing Christian fanatics who are working back channels to manipulate the states; another is a group headed by a man named Abner Bellamy who is focusing on the South."

"Bellamy is in custody," the President said. "He apparently tried to assassinate the governor of Georgia, who was against secession."

Grabel was surprised and mildly embarrassed that his boss knew that and he, the spy, did not. But he proceeded to update the President about the search for Blinder.

The President hung up the phone, stretched again, and turned to the men and women in his office. He glanced back at the television, where the volume had been turned down. "This media coverage can't hurt," he said.

"No, it can't," Valerie replied. "The events in Georgia have riveted the country via nonstop coverage from all the major networks and cable outlets. The news is about to break about the attempted assassination of Governor McAuley." She pointed to the screen on the far wall, where McAuley's face had just appeared. As she stared at the screen, she said to the President, "And we've been able to keep a tight blackout on Wichita Falls."

On the screen, McAuley's head shot was replaced by images of huge crowds of citizens waving American flags, responding to the President's appeal to make their voices heard.

As the reporter was describing events in Georgia, an announcement about an upcoming press conference with the governor of Texas scrolled across the bottom of the screen.

". . . and we take you now live to Austin, Texas, where Edwin Regis, the governor of Texas, is about to make an announcement," the news anchor said.

Short shrift for an assassination attempt, thought the President.

Then he saw Regis approaching a dais in front of the Great Seal of the State of Texas. Regis waited patiently as everyone settled down.

"As you know," he began, reading from a prepared text in front of him, "there has been a crisis of monumental proportion going on in our country over the past two days." Regis did not look up from the dais. "After close consultation with our political leaders here, the attorney general, and federal authorities, I have authorized the arrest of anyone in this state who is suspected of being a part of this conspiracy."

He looked up briefly to see the familiar faces in the capital press corps. Then his gaze returned to the paper. "I want to express my deep appreciation to the federal agents who participated in this arrest and whose speed and efficiency brought a swift end to the events in Washington, DC, yesterday. And I wish to express my deepest sympathies to the families of those patriots who lost their lives in this process."

He looked up again at the audience. With some effort, he put more determination in his voice. "And I want to assure the citizens of Texas and our representatives in Washington, DC, that Texas stands firmly with the Union against any attempt to destroy it. We are Americans first."

Edwin Regis walked away from the dais without taking questions, a deflated and chastened man.

The President turned to Escapan. "The tide may indeed be turning."

amantha and Marie found their way to the motel that had been commandeered by the Agency and, along with Cherie Keenan and Darrin McAlister, each found that a room had been assigned to him or her. Food and beverages were available in each room and the four of them were glad to have something to eat before they crashed in their respective beds. Never mind that it was the middle of the afternoon. The last news item they heard was the governor of Texas in effect throwing his support to the federal government.

Five hours later, there was a knock on Samantha's door. She was awake and reading. Looking through the peephole, she saw Marie standing on the other side of the flimsy wooden door. She opened it.

"Can't sleep?" she said to Marie, who looked roughly the same as she thought she herself looked: rested but disheveled and still keyed up.

"I slept for a while. But I can't help thinking this isn't over."

Sam nodded as she walked over to a small coffee pot in the room and began brewing two cups of black coffee. "Tell me what you're thinking," she said as the coffee percolated.

"I'm thinking that we're not going to get much from that sealed room," Marie said. "Even after they collect all the debris. It will take weeks if not months to come up with anything. This guy knew what he was doing. And I think it was very important for him to hide his connections, which no doubt would have been traceable if we had access to that room undamaged."

Samantha poured two cups of coffee and turned her head sidelong at Marie as she handed her a cup. "Go on."

"The thing that made this whole operation feasible was that Blinder was presumably able to gather different groups of discontents together and have them operate in unison. We know two of those centers: the Sovereign Citizens, who were able to put together and train a large military or at least a paramilitary force right under our noses; and Bellamy's group in the South, which twisted arms and thought they could generate successful secession votes." She took the coffee cup Sam was offering her. "And they got one from the Georgia House."

Samantha nodded as she followed Marie's thinking. She picked up the thread. "But there's been no sign of that group from the Midwest, the one that was inadvertently taped by a student who tipped us off at the beginning." She blew across the top of her coffee cup. "If we haven't located them, they are no doubt still hidden and likely operational."

Marie nodded. "That's the group that Cherie Keenan's husband was part of. They haven't shown up on anyone's radar since all this began. And I think that's because they do not want to be identified."

Sam thought for a while. "That may be, Marie. But the situation seems to be turning against the secessionists. Even the governor of Texas came out against it this afternoon."

"Yes, but there are other states that are still considering secession, and if one does, the tide can turn back pretty easily, despite what happened in Georgia."

Sam didn't dispute what Marie was saying. She nodded once again.

"Let's call Max," she said.

"No, wait," Marie replied. "Let's start with Cherie."

Sam's eyebrows lifted a bit. She had come to think of Cherie as

one of her team, not a person with any information about the conspiracy. She remembered one of her first conversations with Cherie,
when Cherie had said she didn't know all the members of the secret
group. But she did know at least a couple of them.

The two women looked at each other. "Adam Wilson," they
both said at the same time.

"He may be the key," Marie said.

"I think so," Sam answered. "Let's talk to Cherie."

They both put their coffee cups down and headed out the door
to Cherie's room, which was nearby on the same corridor. They
knocked gently.

The door opened almost immediately, surprising Sam and
Marie. Cherie was groomed and dressed.

"We were afraid to wake you," Sam said.

"I slept for a couple hours," Cherie replied. "Then I couldn't
sleep anymore. This is all so intense; it's hard to relax." She ushered
the two women into her room. "So I thought I'd just get cleaned up
and wait for you guys to get up." She smiled at both women now
standing in her small room. "Good timing," she added.

"Cherie," Marie said, seeing no reason to equivocate, "we were
thinking about the conspirators. A few days ago, you mentioned the
name Adam Wilson. You thought he may have had something to do
with your husband's death."

The reference to her husband made Cherie's stomach lurch.
She closed her eyes and took a deep breath. She realized she hadn't
thought of her husband much these past days. Intense indeed, she
thought.

She looked back at Marie. "What about him?"

Marie explained that a meeting of the group that Daniel Keenan
was a part of had been inadvertently taped by an undergraduate for
a school project, and that tape had made its way to the CIA. Max,
her contact, had shown it to her a few weeks ago, and it was the
trigger for the initial investigation.

As she spoke, Marie saw Cherie's eyes widen. Her face lost color. "You mean you knew this man was involved?"

"We knew that about a dozen prominent men were involved," Marie said. "But we haven't had time to process the particulars." Her look softened, and she touched Cherie's hand gently. "I do not mean to bring up a painful subject, but the members of that group are unaccounted for. We don't know where they are or what they are doing. But we know they pose a threat to the nation. And so long as they are off the radar, that threat remains very real."

Cherie glanced over at Samantha, whose look was also sympathetic. She was torn and wasn't sure why: she wanted to trust these women but was hesitant. Maybe it's a lack of sleep, she thought. Maybe I'm traumatized by all this killing. She started to cry softly. Even though she felt certain that her husband had betrayed her and her children and her country, she was beginning to feel the loss of a man she had loved and trusted and of a marriage of almost two decades.

She turned toward the window and let the tears flow. She wanted to be alone, but she also felt bound to the two other women who were standing in her small room, and she did not want them to think her emotional breakdown was somehow their doing.

She wondered why she still had a nagging sense of distrust. Maybe because I trusted Daniel. That didn't work out so well. Who could she really trust? She shook her head.

No, she admonished herself, do not go there. Plenty of people had proven themselves trustworthy in the past week—especially the two women standing in her room.

She turned back to face Sam and Marie. "How can I help you?"

Sam stepped up. "You can tell us everything you know about Adam Wilson and anyone else you know who might have been involved with your husband."

"With Daniel," Cherie interjected. "His name was Daniel."

"With Daniel," Sam said.

Cherie let out a long breath. "Tell me more about this meeting," she said. "Do you have the names of all the people who were there?"

"I can get that," Sam replied.

"Good," said Cherie. "I will tell you whatever I know. I am afraid it won't be much. Daniel told me these men were part of a prayer group. He did not say much about it until the very end, when he wanted us to leave town with him and go somewhere he would not disclose."

Sam nodded and went to retrieve her laptop and get the information Cherie wanted. Marie motioned to the single chair in the room, and Cherie sat down. Marie sat on the bed and took her hand. "You have been so brave during this, Cherie, I can't thank you enough for what you've done for us and for what you've done for your country."

Cherie nodded, but she didn't reply. The grief was just beginning, and she was trying to focus.

Samantha turned her laptop so that Cherie could see it. "Here is the list of men at that meeting."

Cherie scanned the names carefully. She did not want to miss any possible link, although the feeling of being less than useful was not far from the surface.

"This one," she said suddenly. "I don't know him personally, but I know someone who does."

The two women looked at her quizzically.

"He's an uncle of a woman from my church." She stopped herself. "From my former church."

"Would she have any idea of where he might be now?" Marie asked.

Cherie shrugged her shoulders. "I don't know, Marie. I guess I could call her and ask."

Marie glanced at Sam and they both nodded. "Would you mind?"

"Not at all."

63

A dam Wilson watched in disgust as Edwin Regis surrendered his dream of Texan independence without a fight. Coward, he thought.

He turned away from the video feed and walked out of the makeshift structure where it was located: a portable, lead-encased sheet-metal building that allowed only select, narrow-band signals in or out so as not to be discovered by anyone who might be searching for his group. And that may well include the federal authorities, he thought grimly.

Upon reflection, Wilson decided Regis must have been under pressure to throw in the towel like that, and no doubt from the feds. But he was certain Regis would have held out longer had Blinder been more firmly in charge. A thought crossed Adam Wilson's mind and his mood darkened. Blinder's estate had been attacked. Coupling that with Regis's surrender, Blinder's desperation would only increase. Who knew what he would do then. All of a sudden, Wilson was having a hard time seeing how the future of the movement could not be in jeopardy. He could check on the status of other states, but he had a sinking feeling that his participation in this massive effort was coming to an end much earlier than he had anticipated.

Wilson glanced at his watch. Another forty minutes before Blinder was to arrive. I don't have much to lose by waiting to see what he has to say, he thought. He could not imagine how even David Blinder could pull a rabbit out of this particular hat. In the meantime he would set about covering his tracks. He had gone out of his way to make sure that a path to him could not be traced, and he had supervised the ways his associates had covered theirs. Still, there were a dozen men and their wives who were in on the plan, and he wasn't sure he could count on all of them to remain quiet. They were, after all, solid Christians who got involved with him because they sincerely wanted society to reflect their religious values, not because they were a bunch of hotheaded malcontents. Their consciences just might require them to talk to the authorities. Sooner or later.

He thought of the men of his group. Successful to a person, they reflected a level of competence and intelligence that he could scarcely replicate in another group of people. It would be a shame for them all to die.

Wilson put that thought out of his mind, or at least out of his conscious focus. He had considered doing away with them all along, but it was at the periphery of his thinking, a final option if the plan he invested in went bad. It was still an option but not, he thought, an immediate one.

He had alternatives. One was to use his men to bring Wyoming into the fold of secessionist states. While the feds seemed to have prevailed in Georgia by force and Texas by intimidation, any state seceding from the Union could and probably would trigger the secession of others. Wyoming wasn't ideal: It was landlocked and had a small population. The terrain was rugged and the weather daunting. Still, it would be a relatively easy state to take control of because of those very features. Plus, he and his group were already gathered there.

He forced himself to back up and focus on the moment. He had made arrangements for mobs of people to show up in Atlanta to support secession, and they were scheduled to be on the streets in a few hours. It didn't matter what the President said; what mattered was what the people did. And his people were heading toward Atlanta in large numbers to make their discontented voices heard. Let's see what happens in Georgia this afternoon, he thought.

In the midst of these mullings, Aloysius Smitherin came up behind him and tapped him on the shoulder. "Adam."

Wilson jumped, but then tried not to act as startled as he was. He donned a smile and turned to face Smitherin. "Yes, Al?"

"We have information that huge crowds are surrounding state houses across the country. Not only in Georgia and in the other states considering secession but in all fifty states."

Wilson didn't say anything. He just looked at Smitherin and waited.

Smitherin was clearly anxious. His face was pale, and there was a slight tremor in his voice. He was having trouble speaking.

"What is it, Al?" Wilson said with as much solicitude as he could muster to mask his impatience.

Finally Smitherin was able to respond. "There's going to be a clash in Georgia. We contacted every secessionist group on your orders and instructed them to go to Atlanta to rally for the resolution of secession. But there are huge numbers of other Georgians already in Atlanta demonstrating for preserving the Union." He paused and looked directly into Wilson's eyes. "And they are being protected by armed federal troops."

To Wilson's mind, this was not a problem. It was simply a little more mayhem that would work to keep the insurrection alive. It would show that the federal government could not prevent American citizens from being killed on live TV. It would show how desperate the feds really were.

"Look, Al," he said soothingly. "This battle is not over. There will be casualties. We all knew that from the beginning. A new society can only be built on the blood of martyrs and heroes."

Smitherin looked down. Even though it felt and sounded hollow now, he did not disagree with what Wilson was saying; he had heard him say it often before. But the savageness of the attack on Washington dismayed him. The thought of more bloodshed was not sitting well with his conscience or the consciences of his colleagues.

"We could call them off, Adam."

Wilson knew the drill. "It is not in our hands, Al. And the fact is it wouldn't be easy to call them off. These citizens have been waiting for decades to do what they are going to do today. It is their time, and they are not likely to relinquish it by a phone call from us. Especially since we gave them the go-ahead in the first place."

Smitherin nodded slowly. What Wilson was saying was probably true. But it didn't seem right not to try.

"Pray with me, Al," he heard Wilson say.

Of course, he could not refuse. The two men knelt on the rocky ground and offered their prayers for the success of their enterprise.

When Smitherin returned to his duties, Wilson did something he had not done since he had to deal with Daniel Keenan: he began to wonder seriously about the loyalty of his men. If Smitherin were weakening in his resolve, others might be as well. Smitherin implied as much. He turned and walked toward the building where his men were.

He was met by a peculiar silence. Instead of the buzz of activity and conversation, he found his men sitting around in long-faced silence. No one was on the phone. No one was saying much of anything.

Adam Wilson knew that it was up to him to reenergize his men. No other member of the group had his prestige or presence. He walked to the middle of the room and turned to survey his men sitting around the cheap conference tables. All eyes looked up at him.

"My friends," he began softy. "This battle that we have joined, this battle for the soul and salvation of the country, has only just begun. I imagine many of you are discouraged by how events have been playing out today. There is more bloodshed than we would have liked; there is greater resistance than we anticipated." He paused and looked at each man, trying to make eye contact with those who would return his gaze. "But the day belongs to those who do not listen to the siren song of defeat or discouragement. The day belongs to those who believe. And each of you was chosen because your faith is strong. And despite whatever setbacks you see around you, we still have belief in our cause. Otherwise we wouldn't be here."

He continued in a louder voice. "Not one of you got here by an easy path. Every single one of you is a patriotic, freedom-loving American, responsible and successful and hardworking. And each of you places a high value on your faith. You knew that a strong faith was what built this country and sustained it. You only got here because you saw what was happening in the nation, how it was turning away from faith, from God. You feared for the country you loved. You came to realize that something drastic had to be done. Not in one case was this an easy thing to face. You chose to partici-pate in this project at great personal risk and at substantial personal cost. You came to believe that the costs and risks were worth it. Not one of you got here because you are the type of man who gives up easily. You are here because you are a true believer, because you know that if society does not change, our precious religion, our pre-cious values, will be tramped even more than before. God chose you. And God will not look kindly upon our failure."

Wilson paused to take the temperature of the men in the room. Some were shaking their heads; some were obviously praying; some were conflicted. Not the time to stop.

"This is not the time to stop our efforts," he said, increasing the volume of his voice once more. "This is the time to redouble them. We of all people know that it is God who directs our work, that it is God who supports our aims, that it is God who will show us the path to victory, even if in this moment, we cannot fully conceive what that might look like."

The feeling in the room began to shift. Wilson could see on the faces of a few that they were desperate to believe, that they wanted nothing more than to believe every word that came out of his mouth. "Amen," he heard from the back of the room. "Amen," he heard from another direction.

"Thou shalt not give up!" Wilson said at the top of his voice. "Thou shalt never give up!"

The amens became contagious, jumping from one tongue to another, until the whole room began erupting in amens and hallelujahs. Some people stood up. Someone started to sing A Mighty Fortress Is Our God until the whole room joined the chorus. Of course Wilson joined in. His voice could be heard the loudest. This was, after all, his show.

64

David Blinder's plane landed on a small airstrip in the vicinity of Wilson's encampment. He too had heard Regis declare for the Union, and he was running out of ideas. He was also concerned about Adam Wilson and his men. Religious fanatics cannot be trusted.

Blinder had arranged to be met at the airstrip by a local contingent of Sovereign Citizen troops, and they were there as directed. As he disembarked, a middle-aged man came up to him and saluted. Blinder nodded in return. The two walked silently to a waiting Humvee that was idling nearby. Blinder counted a total of three Humvees and a personnel carrier. He estimated there were about thirty to forty heavily armed men available to him.

Blinder knew that his options were vanishing before his eyes. Georgia was a loss; so was Texas. He doubted that even Wyoming, a sparsely populated state filled with freedom-loving individualists, could be persuaded to depart the Union at this point. He tasted the bitterness of defeat in his master plan, and he hated it. But facts are facts, and his job now was to take the escape path he had arranged for himself when this all started. First, however, he had some work to do.

"What are your orders, sir?"

Blinder did not respond right away. He was calculating the odds that thirty or so heavily armed men could eradicate forty or so unarmed civilians. He looked over at the driver.

"That way," Blinder said, pointing due north.

"Whatever you wish, sir."

"A couple miles from here, some dangerous men are having a meeting. We need to make sure they don't leave the mountain."

The man nodded.

herie telephoned Mary Applewhite and broached the topic of her uncle as Samantha and Marie had prepped her to do. Give no information. Inquire generally at first and then gradually get more specific. Keep the tone casual, but make it increasingly urgent. Appeal to her religiosity.

"Mary, do you know where your uncle is now?" she said after the preliminary pleasantries.

Mary Applewhite did not respond right away. The fact was she wasn't sure exactly where he was, but she had a vague notion that he was out west somewhere. Mostly, she was surprised to hear from Cherie Keenan. She was even more surprised at how—she couldn't quite put her finger on it—how calm and even sober she sounded. After the tragic and much publicized death of her husband. That poor woman, she thought over and over as she was talking.

"Mary, do you have any way of finding out where he is? I have some urgent business to discuss with him related to his work with Daniel. Do you know someone who might know where I could find him?"

Mary thought for a few minutes. Finally, she said, "I think our pastor might know. He was part of that prayer group for a while, and he let them meet at the church."

"Thank you so much, Mary. Be well."

Samantha had the phone number of the church written down by the time Cherie clicked off. "Pastor Wellington?"

"Yes, that's him." Cherie dialed the number and waited patiently until the church secretary picked up the phone.

"Annie," Cherie said. "This is Cherie Keenan."

At the sound Cherie's name, Annie inhaled sharply. "Pastor Wellington has been trying to get a hold of you. Give me a minute and I'll put you right through."

Marie, who was listening in on the conversation, raised an eyebrow at Cherie and then glanced over at Marie.

"Cherie," came the lugubrious baritone on the other end of the line. "I have been trying to reach you. How are you?"

"I'm okay, Pastor," she replied with a measure of guardedness in her voice. "It's been a trying time, as you might imagine."

Cherie Keenan did not dislike Thomas Wellington personally. She thought he was a sincere man who was a little unctuous for her taste. But he worked hard for his congregation. Nonetheless, the idea of reconnecting with any of these religious people made the pit of her stomach twist.

"Pastor, I've been trying to reach some of the men who were involved with the prayer group that my late husband was part of. I called Mary Applewhite because her uncle was part of that group, but she didn't know where he was. She knew he wasn't at home. . . ."

Cherie stopped because the silence at the end of the phone deepened noticeably. She waited, holding her breath.

Finally, Pastor Wellington spoke. "I do know where they are, Cherie," he said with a soft seriousness in his voice. "I'd been hoping you would call."

After another pause, he said, "Could we talk about this? I will be available any time that is convenient for you."

Cherie decided she needed to get straight to the point. "There's not time for that, Tom. I am not in town, and I need to know now."

Thomas Wellington was conflicted. Yes, he knew where the men had gone. And yes, he had some idea of what they were up to.

But he was torn. These were God-fearing men who were willing to take action on the basis of their faith. He wasn't sure he could give them up so easily, even to Cherie Keenan, who he knew suffered more than most because of the group.

"May I ask why this is so important, Cherie?"

Cherie took a chance. "I can't believe you would ask me that, Tom. You know what I've been through."

She heard a long exhale on the other end of the phone.

"I am going to tell you this in complete confidence," he finally said. "They are in Wyoming, at an abandoned mining camp about a hundred miles west of Casper."

"Thank you, Tom," Cherie said, looking up at Marie, who motioned to push a little more.

"Is there any other information you have that could help me, Tom?"

Another pause. "I think they are planning dangerous things, Cherie."

"What kind of things?"

"I can't say for sure, but I had a bad feeling when I went to a few of their meetings. They talked about extreme things, like fighting—actual armed struggle—for biblical values. And when Daniel was killed. . . . I don't know, I just feared the worst. Especially for you, Cherie."

"Thank you, Tom. You've been very helpful."

"I can't tell you how relieved I am you're still alive."

Cherie held the phone in her hand for a small moment. "Thank you," she whispered.

Cherie clicked off and looked at the two women. Marie was nodding and Sam was typing furiously on her laptop.

The Google Maps app made it easy to spot the location that Pastor Wellington had identified. Samantha picked up her phone.

"Get me the nearest airstrip to the following coordinates," she barked, typing a series of numbers into her computer. "And find me the fastest way there as soon as possible."

She clicked off and turned to Marie. "It will take us two to two and a half hours to get there. If they're still there, we can detain the whole group." Sam was thinking out loud. "If we surprise them, we can collect data."

"That may take too much time. Are there enough agents or is there a military base nearby?"

Sam checked her laptop. "Warren Air Force Base is outside Cheyenne. It's a missile base."

Marie was thinking hard about this when a knock on the door interrupted her thoughts. She went to open the door.

It was Darrin McAlister, who had obviously just woken up.

"I heard you guys talking," he said yawning. "I thought I might join you."

Marie said, "We found out where Wilson's group is. It's in the middle of Wyoming."

"Let's go get them," Darrin said, the sleepiness vanishing from his face.

"Not so easy," Sam said. "They are two hours by car outside of Cheyenne at an abandoned mining camp. And it will take us almost three hours to get to the air base near Cheyenne."

"So?" Darrin said.

There was silence for a while. Darrin looked from one woman to the next.

"What's the matter? Aren't you the people who just came to Texas and routed the man most responsible for what happened to the United States these past few days?"

Sam spoke up. "So the problem is that the situation is so fluid and things are developing so rapidly that we can't be sure we can make it in time."

"Only one way to find out," Darrin replied.

Sam looked at Marie and Cherie. "I guess so."

"Let's go," Marie said.

ax Grabel was running on empty. He had been awake for more than thirty-six hours, and given the constant flow of information, his brain was nearing capacity. He thought he was keeping everything straight, but he wasn't one hundred percent sure.

He was briefed by the Army about the recovery of the Fort Knox gold and the firefight between the SC troops who had participated in that raid and the regular Army. He was informed that Winslow Parker, thought to be the military mastermind of the attack, was dead.

Parker . . . Parker . . . Winslow Parker. Max kept turning the name over and over in his mind. It sounded familiar. He asked his secretary to do a search and within fifteen minutes, she informed him that there was a Winslow Parker who had graduated West Point twenty years ago, had spent some time in the military, and then just disappeared. Max figured that was where he had heard the name. His son had gone to West Point, so he must have heard it through him.

Max picked up the blinking phone on his desk. It was Marie, telling him what she and Samantha had learned from Cherie Keenan about Adam Wilson's group.

"We know where they are, Max. Or at least we have a very strong lead." She proceeded to describe the connection to the local pastor in Rolla.

"Are you sure he isn't in on this, Marie?"

Marie paused a bit before answering. "We don't think so, Max. And Cherie doesn't think so either." She paused again. "But we're concerned that we only have a small window before that group splits up and slinks back to wherever they came from."

"I don't think they'll be slinking," Max said. "These are prominent people. They will simply return to the lives they had before."

"And no one would be the wiser?"

"We need evidence, Marie. As much evidence as we can get our hands on."

"That's why we're heading in that direction now, Max. No time to lose."

Max chuckled. This was one of the reason he liked these two contract workers. They followed their often excellent hunches with few pauses in between. "Go," he said. "I'll get some satellite surveillance on that place. And maybe get some F-22s out of Warren Air Base to fly overhead and take a look."

After hanging up the phone, Max pushed back from his desk and turned to look out the window to clear his mind. Halfway through the turn, he felt a piercing pain in his arm. He grabbed his chest and opened his mouth, but no sound came out. In less than a minute, Max Grabel lay sprawled out behind his desk, dead of a heart attack.

His secretary heard a loud thump as the chair fell to the floor out from under Max's body. She took in a sharp breath, jumped up, and ran into her boss's office. She was so shocked she was barely able to stand, but long years of discipline enabled her to call for help. Medics came rushing in a matter of seconds, but no amount of reviving efforts mattered. Max was gone, and there was nothing anyone could do about it.

Marybeth Mayer, the young CIA technical analyst, was nearing Max's office when she heard the commotion. She ran in just behind the medics, who passed her in the corridor. Besides the secretary and the medical personnel, she was the first to see Max's body being carried out of the room on a gurney. She burst into tears. Marybeth knew how important Max was to the counterinsurgency operation, and she was fearful of losing the information in his head.

She had been with Max for most of the previous two days. She wanted to help, but she was unsure of the person to turn to. She finally found the presence of mind to ask Max's secretary, who directed her to the deputy chief, who was now the acting CIA chief.

Bailey Rutherford was winded from running to Max's office after the secretary called. While Rutherford was not without ambition, this was neither the time nor the place nor the situation to try to fill Max's experienced shoes. But he was a company man, and he knew the protocol. Until a new chief was selected, he was it.

Marybeth looked up at Rutherford as he entered the room. He nodded to her, not knowing who she really was. But she knew who he was and extended her hand. "I'm so sorry, Mr. Rutherford. I'm Marybeth Mayer. I just want you to know I've been spending a lot of time with Max since yesterday, and if I can be of any assistance . . ."

"Sit down, Ms. Mayer," Rutherford said, pointing to two chairs to his right. They both sat. "I want to know everything you know about what Max was doing."

So Marybeth told him everything she knew. She described Max's response to the attack on the CIA headquarters and how he masterminded the rapid response to the attack on the District. She told him he had direct access to the President and that the two had spoken several times. She also told him he had been working closely with Stanley Schindler, the FBI chief, in coordinating counterinsurgency activities. She explained about Samantha and Marie in Texas and what they had been able to accomplish. She didn't know exactly how thoroughly Max kept Rutherford in the loop, so she was as detailed as possible.

As she watched him stoically listen to the facts she lay before him, she thought she noticed slight shifts in the small muscles of his face. She interpreted this to mean that some, perhaps much, of this information was unknown to the new CIA chief.

When she stopped talking, Bailey Rutherford looked at her thoughtfully. "Thank you, Ms. Mayer," he said. "I want you to be my assistant. We will work together and pick up where Mr. Grabel left off."

Marybeth Mayer was stunned. She was just trying to be helpful. She was not looking for career advancement. "I will help you in any way I can, Mr. Rutherford."

Rutherford got up and walked over to the desk and picked up the phone. He scanned the recently called numbers and came upon the one he thought he wanted. He pushed the talk button.

The telephone rang in the Oval Office. The President picked it up personally; it was his direct line. He listened somberly as the new CIA chief told him what happened to Max.

"Mr. President," Rutherford said. "Is there anything I need to know from you to make this unfortunate transition seamless?"

Mr. Obama thought in silence for a moment. "It will be tribute to Max," he said, "if you can pick up right where he left off." Another pause. "As a nation, we owe Max Grabel a debt of gratitude. Just be worthy of him."

Rutherford's eyes rose slightly at this admonition, and he clicked off. He turned to Marybeth. "We have work to do."

67

Adam Wilson was feeling good about reviving the sagging spirits of his handpicked men. What he told them was one version of the truth, although no one among his group had any idea of how lightly he held his religious convictions. He learned a long time ago that religious people were easy to manipulate. And he loved to manipulate people.

Wilson walked dramatically out of the makeshift building where he had rallied his men and went to the small cabin that was serving as his bedroom and office. He had to find out who was still in operation, whom he could count on. And he had to make a decision.

He had insisted that all other members of his group relinquish their mobile phones and tablets connected to unapproved networks. They were to communicate only with the devices he had supplied them. This was a precaution against being traced. But he had retained his own just in case he needed them. He reasoned that a single person using a cellular network would be nearly impossible for the feds or anyone else to locate in a timely manner. Plus, he never figured that rules applied to him.

He took his tablet and logged on to major news networks, where coverage was fast-paced and changing rapidly. He saw the stats on the President's speech and was dismayed to find that the first polls gave it an approval rating in the eighties. He saw that someone had tried to assassinate the newly appointed governor of Georgia, but he was astonished to learn that Abner Bellamy was the principal, indeed the only, suspect, having been caught moments after what seemed like a foolish and impulsive attack.

This gave Wilson pause. Blinder is on the run, Bellamy is in custody, Georgia's lost, Texas conceded. The plan was in ruins. He kept scanning. An MSNBC news feed reported that at least some of the gold from Fort Knox had been recovered. He switched to CNN, which was also reporting on the issue, noting that "most" of the gold had been recovered. He switched through a half dozen other news feeds until it was finally reported that all of the federal gold had been recovered. Another loss.

There had apparently been a firefight in Tennessee and some Sovereign Citizen troops had been killed. No federal casualties.

Wilson shook his head. None of this was looking good.

He switched to a local news station that was reporting on events in Cheyenne, the capital of Wyoming. Since this was not a state targeted by his group or any group he was aware of, he wondered how open it was to seceding. Wyoming was full of hardy, independent-minded people who resented interference from the federal government or from anyone else, so he thought maybe there was a chance.

Nothing. Some citizens of the state had shown up in support of the President's speech, but otherwise there was no activity in the legislature. In fact, the governor had suspended all legislative activity and sent the legislators home to be with their families. Any activity on that front from Wilson's group was pointless.

Wilson pushed back on his small wheeled desk chair. This was it, he realized. His major allies had been compromised, the legislative push was moribund, and Americans were making their voices heard in favor of the Union. It was over.

And David Blinder was on his way to his location and would probably arrive within the hour. All of a sudden, Blinder's status in Wilson's mind went to zero. In fact, it may have been less. He may be a liability. Or a threat.

He considered his options. He had to determine if it was safe to allow members of his group to return quietly to their lives. After all, there was precious little indication that any of them had done anything wrong besides gather for a retreat of sorts. The most they could be accused of was supporting the activity of someone else, but Wilson was pretty sure this fell short of the kind of conspiracy charge that would land them in prison for the rest of their lives. Then again, he thought grimly, his knowledge of that part of the law was not complete.

Wilson checked his watch. In a couple of hours, secessionist groups would be arriving in Atlanta in large numbers, but not nearly so many as the pro-Union citizens who were responding to the President's call. They would no doubt clash with all those supposedly patriotic Americans who were filling the streets of Atlanta, citizens who were being protected by the US military. What just a few minutes before seemed like a hopeful use of chaos now began to strike Adam Wilson as a pathetic effort by some outliers to cause trouble. He had no doubt they would be efficiently managed through the good offices of the United States Army.

He wondered absently what had become of the Sovereign Citizens. He knew there were thousands of them across the country, awaiting orders that might well never come. Would they find a new leader among themselves? Wilson couldn't judge that. He had great respect for Winslow Parker, but if the successful assault on Fort Knox was followed up by the rapid retrieval of the gold, it was likely that Parker was in custody or worse.

Wilson looked out his window. He could see the wind blowing the scanty vegetation that graced the barren mountain. It felt as if the wind was blowing away his dreams. He could scarcely believe it. He had a long history of making smart moves, choosing winners rather than losers, and he thought he had winners in David Blinder, Abner Bellamy, and Winslow Parker, solid performers who could and would deliver on their promises.

Facing the fact that he was wrong shifted the landscape of his mind. He always knew he was cynical; that didn't bother him. What some people call cynicism was to him being realistic. But it is one thing to be cynical when your life is on an upward trajectory and praise and approbation are around every corner. Now he was in a position where he was left with his cynicism and where he had to watch his step to avoid prison. The gray sky out his dirty window took on a darker cast.

From the corner of his mind, a new thought inserted itself. Why is Blinder coming here? Is he looking for refuge? Or is he coming to take care of the loose end that Wilson's group might seem to him? Was he coming alone?

Adam Wilson took out his mobile phone and called his elderly mother. She was almost ninety and, though in frail health, her mind was sharp. He didn't know why he called her exactly. He wanted her to know he was okay. Or so he told himself.

No answer. The call went to voicemail after a half dozen rings. His own mother was not even available to him.

He looked around the shack where he found himself. What had seemed like a valiant place from which to launch the birth of new nations now seemed like the ramshackle collection of abandoned huts in the mountains it was. He was embarrassed that it would all come to an end in such a place.

But end it would. The thought of bearing the ignominy of reinserting himself into his humdrum life and loveless marriage and pretend religious allegiances filled him with bitterness. The grand project he had embraced was finished. He felt duped, perverted by smooth-talking men of wealth and power who should have known better. He did not want to play their game anymore. Images of revenge and hatred filled his mind. Blinder hanging on one of these windblown trees, Bellamy tortured by his handpicked group of fanatics: any torture or grisly death was what these traitors deserved.

He reached under his twin bed and pulled out a revolver he had placed there the day he arrived. If Blinder was planning on bringing harm to his men, he could at least discharge his responsibility by killing him first. That would bolster his stature among his group. It may even help turn him into a hero as the facts of Blinder's actions became more widely known. He smiled a sly smile at the irony of his getting a name as the man who took out the biggest criminal in America.

arie stood motionless with the phone in her hand as she listened to Bailey Rutherford tell her about Max's death. She was speechless. Tears rolled down her face. She silently handed the phone to Samantha.

"Oh, my God," Sam said, as she heard the news.

"One more thing, Ms. Stranger," Rutherford said. "When I spoke to the President, he told me to be worthy of Max. I want you and your team to know that from everything I have learned over the past hour, you have been worthy of him. It is my hope to be worthy of your work as well as his. Thank you."

The new CIA chief clicked off.

Sam turned to Marie who was still weeping quietly at the loss. Cherie and Darrin were in the room, and she turned to look directly at them. "Max is dead. He died of an apparent heart attack about an hour ago. Bailey Rutherford, his assistant, is the new chief, at least for now."

Neither Darrin nor Cherie responded, but the looks on their faces reflected the shock and grief they both felt as well as the fear of what this loss meant for them and their work.

"You will excuse me," Marie said. She walked out of the room.

Samantha followed her. When she caught up with Marie, she put her hand gently on Marie's arm. The two stopped midway down the corridor and looked at each other deeply, wordlessly trying to determine the next step. The silent conversation was *Do you want to be alone? I'm not sure. Neither am I. I am still in shock. What do we do now?*

With no clear path or plan, the two friends entered Samantha's room and fell into bed, holding each other close for several intense minutes. Then Marie got up.

"Max would not want us to stop." There was an edge to her voice.

"No, he wouldn't."

Sam got up, pulled out her phone, and called Rutherford back. "Max told us to sit tight, Mr. Rutherford," she said. "But we need to keep working. If nothing else, we need to finish this for Max's sake. If we don't have something to do . . ." She didn't want to say that she would just be overwhelmed by grief, but that was how she felt. Instead, she said, "We are in a pretty good position to move forward."

"Call me Bailey," Rutherford said. "What do you have in mind?"

"We know the rebellion had several centers. One was Blinder's residence here in Texas; another was in Georgia run by Abner Bellamy. But the third one, the one that had a big influence on keeping this all under wraps, was a group led by one Adam Wilson. He and his men pulled out of their influential jobs at the beginning of this and went into hiding." She paused for just a moment. "We believe we found out where they are."

Rutherford listened intently. He glanced over at Marybeth, motioning for her to pick up another headset. "Where?"

"Near Casper, Wyoming, a couple hours outside of Cheyenne."

Rutherford snapped his fingers at Marybeth, indicating that she should locate the town on the surveillance map arrayed along the east wall of the office. She began punching in information to the computer, and the large map shifted westward, pinpointing the small town of Casper.

"Got it," he said into the phone. "I'll get some surveillance drones in the air immediately. It shouldn't take them more than twenty minutes to get there."

"Keep us up-to-date in real time," Samantha said.

"Will do. And keep me posted about anything you find."

"Will do, Bailey. Thanks."

Bailey Rutherford got to work keeping his promises, and Sam and Marie went to work getting to Wyoming. They were packed in minutes.

Sam relayed the information Bailey had given her to the others. "Rutherford is sending in drones and some other surveillance mechanisms to gather information. By the time we get there, we should have a pretty good idea of what we're facing."

"What about you, Cherie?" Marie said. "Do you think you're up for this?"

Cherie turned slowly to look Marie in the face. "I have never in my life been exposed to so much death and destruction. I don't know how to feel about it. The truth is I don't think I feel much of anything."

Marie was not surprised. She could spot post-traumatic symptoms. "I understand," she said softly. "This has been more than most people are ever exposed to."

Darrin spoke up and turned toward Cherie. "You know, Cherie, there are three children waiting for you outside Chicago."

Cherie looked at Darrin with a startled glance; her face turned light crimson. She had forgotten about her children. She felt a painful stab of shame. "Oh, my God."

Marie looked Cherie directly in the eyes. "Cherie, you have served your purposes here. You have done more than we could have hoped for. And more than we had a right to ask. You do not need to continue."

Cherie forced herself to focus. She looked at Marie and nodded. "You are right, Marie. I think I have served my purpose here."

Then she turned to Darrin, who nodded back. "Of course, I will," he said, responding to the unspoken question of whether he would accompany her back to Chicago.

69

David Blinder sat in the rear seat of the Humvee that led the small convoy up the mountain toward to place where Wilson's group was carrying out their now-pointless activities. Blinder was angry—enraged really—but he tried to act as if he were calm. This was a challenge even for him.

The vehicle stopped at a small pull-off on the side of the mountain. The rest of the convoy came to a halt, blocking the entire road. The driver pulled out a pair of binoculars and surveyed the area beneath him.

"There it is," he said, pointing to a spot across a wide valley a little less elevated than the convoy was.

David Blinder reached for the binoculars and examined the site. It was much more rustic than he anticipated. This group did find one of the most out-of-the-way places possible.

Blinder put down the binoculars and looked over at the driver. "What kinds of weapons do you have?"

"Assault rifles, handguns, RPGs, even a couple shoulder-fired Stinger missiles."

"How many RPGs and Stingers?"

"A dozen RPGs, probably three Stingers."

Blinder picked up the binoculars and surveyed the area in front of the convoy. He studied the road around the mountain where they were stopped, looking for a spot that gave them closer access to the retreat.

He pointed to a rocky outcropping with abundant foliage near the edge about two miles ahead. "See that?"

The driver nodded.

"That's where we're going."

The convoy slowly started up again, lumbering along the side of the narrow mountain road.

The road was so desolate that it was easy to hear the low hum of drones approaching. David scanned the sky in search of them. They weren't difficult to spot, as the sun glistened off their shiny fuselages. He spotted two of them flying in from different angles.

So they found them, he thought. And they may have spotted us.

He put the glasses down and sat in thought for a few moments, trying to calculate his next move. It seemed to him that if they were relying on drones at this point, they either suspected that only Wilson's group would be there or their personnel was too far away to get there right away. Given how remote the area was, the latter possibility seemed likely.

Perfect. He turned to the driver. "Do you have a high-powered sniper rifle?"

The driver nodded.

Then the drones have served their purpose, Blinder thought.

n Washington, Bailey Rutherford leaned back in his chair when Marybeth gave him the information coming in from the drones. He shook his head. "This is good, but what kind of satellite surveillance do we have available?"

"We have a satellite coming into range in about forty minutes."

Forty minutes seemed like an eternity to Bailey Rutherford.

"What are we looking for exactly?"

Marybeth shook her head. "We're looking for some kind of structure that holds between twenty and fifty people—the suspects themselves and their spouses." She paused. "But it could be anything or anywhere within two hundred miles or so of Casper."

He looked up at the still images sent from the drones. Several structures spread out along the side of a mountain. He knew the satellites would provide more useful information, but he had to admit this seemed like a promising lead.

Rutherford grimaced but silently. He had to report to the President in fifteen minutes, and he wanted to have more definite evidence.

He turned to his young assistant. "So what do I tell the President?"

Marybeth shrugged. "Tell him we believe we have a general location and that we're working on pinpointing the suspects' safe house." She wondered if she was overstating their progress. She was an analyst; she wasn't supposed to give political advice. It just seemed obvious to her.

Rutherford didn't seem to care. "Of course. Put a team on this. It has priority. We want to track down all the ringleaders, and this group is high on our list."

Marybeth nodded and turned and walked out of the room.

71

At about the same time those conversations were going on across the country, Aloysius Smitherin was getting antsy. He was nervous about the upcoming clash he foresaw in Atlanta, where self-appointed militia were heading toward what he believed would be an inevitable conflict with the US Army. It would not be pretty, he thought gravely.

The bloodshed weighed on him. He understood in the abstract that war meant bloodshed, and he was aware that in its history Christianity was filled with the horrors of armed conflict. But that was long ago, and the thought of people getting killed for something he was a part of was wearing on his already battered conscience.

Plus, he hadn't had a chance to talk to Adam Wilson after Wilson rallied his men earlier. For a while after that, everyone settled down and got back to work. Contrary to orders, they began monitoring news outlets with their own contraband devices, trying to gauge the direction the pendulum was swinging. It didn't take long for most of the men sitting around the tables to see that things were not going their way. Despite their earlier enthusiasm, a sense of dread began to descend once again on the tables where they were working.

Smitherin was drumming his hands on the tabletop where he was sitting, and he felt anxiety surging through his body. His hands and feet were cold, and his stomach was roiling. When he decided he couldn't take it anymore, he shot up from his chair and went looking for Wilson.

He walked around the building he was in; then he went outside. Wilson was nowhere to be found. He surveyed the mountainside where he was standing, wondering where he might have gone. He decided to walk down to his cabin, which was set about forty yards away from the main building. Once there, he knocked on the heavy wooden door.

No answer.

He pushed on the door to see if it would open. No luck; it was locked. He leaned over and peered inside the one-room cabin through a dirty pane of glass. He spotted Wilson sitting in a chair, staring out the far window of the cabin.

Smitherin knocked gently on the wooden door.

No answer.

He knocked again, this time more loudly. He leaned over to see if Wilson had heard him. He wondered absently for a moment if Wilson were alive.

But then he saw Wilson's head turn. Smitherin waved to him through the window, motioning for him to come to the door. He noticed Wilson slide something off his lap into an open drawer next to him. Then he watched Wilson slowly make his way to the door.

Wilson did not speak. He just looked at Aloysius Smitherin expectantly with an upturned nose and a raised eyebrow, as if the other adult had interrupted him needlessly.

Smitherin sputtered. "Um, um, um," he began. "The others and I, we were wondering about the plan." He shook himself to calm down. "We want to know what to do now."

Wilson lowered his head, turned his head to the side for a moment, and then turned back to look directly into Smitherin's eyes. "Now, we wait, Al."

Smitherin wasn't sure how to respond to this. He thought for a few moments.

"We've been tracking events through the media," he said at length. "It's not looking good, Adam."

"Not, it's not, Al," Wilson replied, ignoring the fact that Smitherin was admitting to having devices he wasn't supposed to have. "Sad to say, I think we're losing this round."

Smitherin did not say anything right away. "So . . . what? We pack up and go home? We abandon our dream, our plan?" The irritation in his voice surprised even him.

"There is a time to advance and a time to withdraw," replied Wilson vacuously. He looked at Smitherin, who was getting visibly more agitated. He reached out and put his hand on his colleague's shoulder. "I'm waiting to hear from some of our other contacts, Al," he said soothingly. "We'll know where we stand in about an hour."

Smitherin nodded but his eyes averted Wilson's gaze. He did not know how to respond, so he just said, "Okay, Adam," pulled his shoulder out from under Wilson's hand, and turned and walked back toward the compound.

Adam Wilson stood on the small porch of his cabin and felt anger rise up inside him. Who does he think he is to walk away from me without a word? He turned and walked back into the cabin. He sat back down but could barely contain his anger at what felt like insubordination. But he also recognized that he was anxious about the arrival of David Blinder. Too many factors beyond his control. He reached back into the drawer of the small desk and pulled out the revolver once again. I'll kill them all if I have to, he thought bitterly. He looked at his watch. It had only been thirty minutes since he had spoken to Blinder on the phone. Thirty minutes to go.

arybeth Mayer kept studying the video and images coming in from the drone surveillance. She had ordered the drones to make several passes over what appeared to be an abandoned mining village on the side of a mountain outside Casper. The more she watched it, the more she felt convinced it was the likely hideout for the subversive group she was looking for. As the cameras zoomed in at her command, she could see that it wasn't abandoned, that there were people, both men and women, walking in between the buildings. She wished she had the more sophisticated satellite coverage, but that would be another twenty minutes. When she wasn't giving orders, she stood impassively staring at the large screen, as did the technicians in the viewing room.

On the third drone pass over the mountainside, she noticed something at the bottom of the screen. "Hone in on that," she said, pointing to the movement on the lower edge of the screen.

She waited, feigning patience for the few minutes it took to redirect the drone. Then all of a sudden the screen went blank. *"What happened?"*

Hands and fingers started flying across keyboards and joysticks and toggle switches and buttons on the large console. The technicians were frenetically but methodically evaluating their options, attempting various fixes to get the images back up on the screens.

"Major malfunction," said one of them. "Or it crashed." Pause. "It may have been shot down."

Marybeth glanced at her watch. Another fifteen minutes before the less vulnerable satellite comes into view. Damn!

★　★　★　★

In Wyoming, David Blinder looked over at the young sharp-shooter. "Damn fine shooting, son."

"Thank you, sir."

"Damn fine shooting," he repeated. "Keep that rifle handy." He turned to the driver. "Let's get our men and equipment up to that outcropping."

The young soldier got back into his vehicle with his sniper rifle at his side; the convoy proceeded up to the designated spot.

★　★　★　★

Back in Virginia, Marybeth was steely in her determination. "Get more drones up there," she barked. "And get some F-22s in the air!"

The technicians did as they were told.

"What's the ETA for the drones?"

"ETA twelve minutes."

Not so bad, Marybeth thought. The destruction of the drones confirmed her suspicion that they were on the right track. She tried to make that satisfy her as she waited for the new drones to arrive.

"What's the ETA for the F-22s?"

"Eight minutes, ma'am."

We can't fire on them without verification, Marybeth realized. Still, the show of force would rattle the most self-assured rebel.

Time slowed down. She waited.

Meanwhile, the Sovereign Citizen troops now led by David Blinder were not waiting. Everyone knew that Warren Air Base was a scant two hundred miles away, and they were certain new drones and perhaps even warplanes would be arriving within minutes.

As the vehicles got to the outcropping, they aligned themselves behind the brush on the edge of the outcropping to mask their presence from the Wilson compound across the valley. Blinder stepped out of his vehicle and started barking orders. "Get those Stingers in place. And get those RPGs ready along the ridge."

He took a deep breath. This was almost as rewarding as orchestrating mayhem from his now destroyed command post.

He turned to the troops manning the Stinger missiles. "If you see a warplane overhead, shoot it down." He figured he had enough RPG firepower and other weapons to take care of Wilson's group across the valley.

The driver wasn't so sure. "Those things have a range of about a mile."

"And it's about a mile across the valley," Blinder replied.

The driver shrugged. He thought of informing his new commander that the RPGs were less accurate the farther they went. But he turned to look across the valley and saw that the targets were probably big enough to bear the tolerances. He walked back toward his men to help them finish setting up.

Hyperalert, David Blinder heard the first F-22s overhead. He turned his binoculars skyward to pinpoint them. The sky had some clouds, but he saw two planes flitting in between them. "There they are," he shouted.

The men with the Stingers looked at each other. Neither of them believed they would even get close to the warplanes, which were too fast, too advanced, and too well defended to allow a single Stinger to get to them. But they had observed how Blinder had run over their boss when he made a sensible objection, and no one wanted to be humiliated.

Blinder kept focusing on the warplanes. "Get ready."

The troops aimed their weapons as best they could.

"Stop!" cried the driver suddenly. "Don't you understand that if we miss, which we are likely to do, those planes will retaliate within seconds?"

David Blinder stopped. He was not accustomed to being spoken to in such an aggressive manner, but he had to admit that the driver had a point. He crooked his head to the side and turned his gaze across the valley. Those missiles will go to a better use than drawing fire onto themselves.

On the other side of the valley, Adam Wilson's anxiety was not abating. He got up from his chair, stuffed the revolver in his belt along his backside as he'd seen done in dozens of movies, and walked out to his front porch.

He heard a rifle shot and saw the first drone crash; then he looked up and saw the second one hit a mountainside. "Oh, shit!" A cold sensation ran down his spine. He walked back into the cabin to get his binoculars and began scanning the horizon.

That someone was out to do him harm was now a fact. Who that person might be was still to be determined. Two choices: either the feds or Blinder. Obviously it was not the feds; they wouldn't shoot down their own drones. That left Blinder, who was clearly not acting alone.

He scanned the ridges of the mountains around him. The anxiety he had been feeling faded into a deeper awareness that his life was in danger—as were the lives of all the people with him. He stopped trembling, but he could feel the blood abandon his extremities to protect his internal organs. He was having some trouble breathing.

Then he heard warplanes above him. He shifted his binoculars to scan the sky. He saw them at the same time the first rocket-propelled grenade exploded into the large building where most of his men were gathered. He stood in shock as the building exploded into flames. He heard screams and saw people running away from the explosion.

Another building burst into flames. Wilson, fearing his cabin would be next, jumped off his small front porch and began running away from the mayhem. He heard people behind him but they were farther back.

As he ran, he heard gunfire crackling across the valley, and he heard the groans of men and women in his encampment being hit. He didn't turn around but kept moving down the mountain.

From what he believed to be a safe distance, he turned and saw that his personal cabin had been hit and was now aflame. Screams and moans of the wounded and dying rang out, but he was safe.

Adam Wilson continued to believe he was safe up until his last moment, when a sniper bullet hit him directly in the side of his head, splattering the other side against the mountain. His lifeless body quickly followed suit.

"Damn fine shooting, son," David Blinder said. "Damn fine shooting."

n the late afternoon in Atlanta, the crowds surrounding the capitol were in a festive mood. They could sense that their presence made a difference, and it began to seem that the insurgency was on the run. They sang patriotic songs, they hugged and saluted the troops who protected them, and in general they celebrated the triumph of the people over the forces of destruction.

Jake McAuley sat in his new office and watched the festivities. "I think we should send the legislature home," he said to Mary McDonald, who was standing by the window. "It would be a sign that those people out there had been heard."

Mary nodded. She was feeling almost giddy relief that the crisis in Georgia appeared to be over and that many of the people responsible were in custody or otherwise accounted for. She felt no grief at the loss of her colleague Hugh Lewins when she heard about his suicide. As far as she was concerned, Lewins had selected himself out of Georgia politics, and that seemed to Mary McDonald to be a good thing for the state.

McAuley's phone rang. It was Agent Withers, the special agent in charge at the FBI's Atlanta headquarters.

"Governor, we have been informed that several hundred citizens who are sympathetic to secession are converging on Atlanta." He paused a moment. "You're about to have even more company."

Jake McAuley sighed. He thought this was over. "How long before they arrive?" he asked.

"Best guess is about an hour."

"Thanks for the heads-up," the Governor said, and he hung up the phone.

He turned to Mary McDonald. "More trouble. A couple hundred of our outlying citizens are on their way here to make their views known."

Mary sighed. She too had been hoping that the worst was behind them. "What do we do now?"

Good question, Jake thought. He was quiet for some minutes while he considered his options.

"First of all," he said at length, "we need to let the military know. They should be prepared." He thought some more. "Then we need to contain them at the earliest possible time, preferably before they enter the area around the capitol."

"Are they armed?"

Another good question, Jake thought. "I'm not sure."

He picked up the phone and pushed the last number received button. He relayed Mary's question to the agent in charge.

"Yes, they are," the agent replied. "Rifles and handguns, by the looks of it."

Jake stood up while still on the phone. "Advice?"

"Alert the Army," Withers said. "We'll gather as many agents here as we can to assist. But I think a show of military force would have the strongest deterrent effect."

Jake nodded and pushed the intercom for his secretary. "Find out who is in charge of the military out there."

"That would be Major Sheridan, sir."

"Get him on the phone now."

Within sixty seconds, he was talking to the ranking US Army officer on the capitol grounds. He explained the situation.

"Where exactly are they now?" asked Sheridan, after listening to Jake describe the information.

"I'm not sure, Major."

"I'll get back with you shortly." Sheridan clicked off.

Jake was anxious. He silently reprimanded himself for being lulled into thinking this was all over because of the overwhelming numbers of Army units outside his window.

Mary McDonald was more hopeful. "I imagine we still have numbers on our side, Jake."

The phone rang. It was Sheridan. "Yes?" Jake said.

"Governor, I dispatched several of our helicopters to determine their exact position. They will be arriving here in about twenty minutes. What would you like me to do?"

"I want you to protect those citizens who are protesting peacefully in front of the capitol building."

"Yes, sir," said Sheridan. "I have already started placing units to act as a buffer between the people here and the newcomers."

"Thank you, Major. Keep me posted."

After hanging up, Jake turned to Mary. "They are close, about twenty minutes out. Sheridan is putting up a buffer between them and the people outside."

Mary could feel Jake's anxiety. She stood up and put her hand on his shoulder. "That's what they are here to do, Jake. Let them do their jobs."

Jake put his hand on hers. He knew she was right, but he hated being an observer.

74

Within ten minutes, US Army units had taken up positions along Martin Luther King Drive and nearby streets, blocking intersections and funneling the demonstrators away from the capitol and the huge crowds gathered in front of it. Their new route enabled them to see the building from a few blocks away but provided enough distance so as not to spark a conflict between the armed demonstrators and the peaceful ones.

Major Sheridan observed the progress of the new group via his binoculars. He was also in constant contact with the helicopters that were observing their movements from above.

Without taking his eyes off the glasses, he continued giving orders. "If any one of those people brandishes a weapon, raise yours. Let them know you are serious. If they fire, return fire."

There had been little time to erect safety barriers, so the soldiers on the street had positioned armored personnel carriers to block off intersections. Then they stationed themselves behind them and other parked vehicles, using whatever obstacles they could find. Despite the makeshift nature of the blockages, there would be no doubt where the Army wanted the demonstrators to go.

Twenty minutes later, the first vehicles in the caravan started arriving. They included mostly pickup and flatbed trucks with heavy-set, bearded men in the back. Each of them was clutching a long weapon, a rifle or a shotgun, in his arms; some had handguns tucked into their waistbands.

"Raise your weapons!" Sheridan ordered his men. After Lewins's suicide, he was not in the mood for surprises. "Let them pass peacefully. But if they shoot, return fire."

The soldiers did as they were told. The men in the trucks glared silently at them.

The convoy proceeded slowly past the soldiers. The first turn-off was two blocks away, and Sheridan, along with his men, assumed that if they were going to make trouble, that would be the place.

"Major Sheridan?" said a voice next to him.

"What is it, son?" Sheridan said.

"The Governor is here to see you, sir." .

Sheridan put down his binoculars and turned toward the young officer. As he turned he noticed a tall man in a blue suit and red tie a few feet away. He nodded to the officer and took a step toward McAuley.

"Governor," he said as he saluted.

"Major," replied McAuley. "I apologize if this is an inconvenient time, but I wanted to be on top of things and to help any way I can."

Sheridan turned back toward the incoming demonstrators and proceeded to bring McAuley up to date. He motioned for an aid to get McAuley a pair of binoculars. "It looks as if we have about thirty vehicles, each carrying a dozen heavily armed men. My men are stationed at each intersection where we can direct their progress."

There was a pause, and the air felt heavy. "If they challenge the blockade, we think they will do it at the intersection of Martin Luther King Drive and Washington Street. That's the first blocked intersection that will lead them away from the capitol."

Jake followed the Major's description with his binoculars. He then turned back to survey the incoming trucks. "Jesus!" he said softly.

Sheridan put his glasses down and turned to McAuley. "We're not giving them much wiggle room, Governor. If any of them pulls a trigger, my men have orders to return fire. I don't want to give them the idea that we will back down." He glanced away briefly. "Because we won't."

McAuley nodded. He did not relish the prospect of a firefight in front of the capitol of his state, but neither did he wish to have those patriotic citizens who showed up to support the nation suffer at the hands of hot-headed reactionaries who couldn't bear the thought of government. "I understand."

As the convoy approached the intersection, it slowed down but did not stop. Several of the men in the first truck raised their weapons in the air and shouted something Sheridan couldn't make out. He listened for a moment to his earpiece, where the squadron leader was in direct contact with him.

"What did he say?" asked Sheridan.

"'Georgia forever,'" said the squadron leader.

Amen to that, Sheridan thought.

He and McAuley watched as the convoy followed the direction of the Army and headed northward, away from the capitol. McAuley noticed that, in the distance, black SUVs were taking up positions. No doubt FBI, he thought, waiting to monitor their movements until they were safely out of harm's way.

s the satellite passed over tiny Casper, Wyoming, fires in the mining camp were burning full blast, sending clouds of smoke billowing into the sky. Marybeth stared at the screen and gave direction to the technicians who were controlling the angle of view and the onboard equipment of the satellite.

She strained to recall what she had seen a few minutes earlier. Something at the bottom of the screen. She directed the technicians to refocus on that side of the valley. As the satellite zoomed in, she saw a convoy of military vehicles going slowly down the mountain, away from the mining camp still burning bright.

"Zoom in."

The obedient satellite did just that in response to commands from the ground. The highly sophisticated machine, which could read a license plate from a thousand miles above the earth, easily snapped a photo of David Blinder riding in the front seat of one of those vehicles.

This information was shared immediately with Samantha and Marie, who were disembarking from the plane at Warren Air Base about the same time. All relevant data, including descriptions of the vehicles, estimated number of personnel, and the presence of David Blinder, were reported in a calm, bloodless manner.

"Too many well-equipped troops for us to attack without help," Marie said needlessly. The others nodded.

The pair found their way to the command center of the air base with assistance from a young lieutenant. When they got there, Brigadier General Herman Hughes, the base commander, came out of his office with an outstretched hand.

"Fine work in Texas," he said, smiling.

Samantha and Marie nodded and shook hands.

"Let's get you guys briefed." General Hughes led the two women into a conference room adjacent to his office. He motioned for them to take their seats. He remained standing and turned to a large electronic map arrayed along the wall at the end of a long conference table.

"Here's what we know," he said, facing the group. "About thirty minutes ago, there was an attack on what was thought to be an abandoned mining encampment. It had apparently been taken over by a group of people who were using it as an off-the-grid command center. Just prior to the attack on the encampment, two of our drones were shot down. We sent up new drones and dispatched two F-22s to fly over and take a look."

He turned back to the map. "The F-22s got there first and filmed the attack. It was clearly an effort to wipe out whoever was in that encampment. We have a team headed in that direction now. They should be there is about another hour."

He looked at his watch. "We don't have high hopes for survivors. They apparently laid waste to the area with RPGs and Stinger missiles. They also used small-arms fire to eliminate anyone the bombs may have missed." His tone was even, but his audience could feel the anger beneath it.

"CIA in Langley and our intelligence officers here have been tracking the movement of the attacking convoy. Our intel suggests that it includes about thirty troops and an unknown supply of weapons. We do not know where they are headed, but we are tracking their movements from the air."

Samantha was the first to speak up. "What's the plan, General?"

General Hughes did not hesitate. "Our plan is to stop that convoy at any cost and if possible detain the people in it."

"If possible?" Marie asked.

"We've been coordinating with Langley and they want us to stop the convoy and if possible detain those inside. But stopping it is the primary objective."

"Dead or alive?"

"Dead or alive."

"Is there anything we can do to assist, General?" Samantha asked.

General Hughes shook his head. "I don't think so. We all know how crucial your role was in figuring out who was behind the insurrection and the events in Washington, Fort Knox, and elsewhere around the country. And we know you took the lead in attacking Blinder's compound in Texas." He looked at Samantha and Marie. "There is no need to place yourselves in danger now. We have this."

A sense of relief swept the room. Though Sam and Marie were more than willing to do whatever duty demanded, the carnage and sheer stress of the past few days was finally catching up with them.

"Okay," said Marie. "We appreciate that."

General Hughes continued. "You can, however, have a front-row seat."

He motioned for the civilians to follow him and led them to a room down the hall. It was dark, save for the bright computer screens. The General proceeded to explain what they were looking at. "This is our real-time tracking squad."

The two women and two men seated at the consoles nodded to the visitors. They did not seem surprised that they were there.

The General explained drones were taking video of the convoy being followed, the troops assigned to reconnoiter at the mining encampment, and the contingent sent to intercept the Blinder convoy.

"ETA to convoy is seven minutes," said one of the young technicians.

No one in the room made a sound. Everyone watched as the Army contingent broke single-file formation. One personnel carrier turned sideways to block the road several hundred yards in front of the convoy. Other vehicles spread out to flank it. Samantha wondered absently where they were going.

As if reading her mind, the General said, "We think they're headed to an abandoned mine about thirty miles away. We discovered activity there this morning and have dispatched a unit to investigate. We are holding back so they can't warn the convoy and so we can reinforce the squadron we sent there. We presume they are in radio contact." He continued speaking in a matter-of-fact tone.

All of a sudden, a burst of noise came from a loudspeaker atop one of the Army vehicles and was picked up by the video feed.

"By order of the United States Army, stop your vehicles," a booming voice said.

Helicopters appeared in the sky over the Army vehicles, guns trained on the slowing convoy.

76

David Blinder heard the announcement from the Army vehicle. He looked up and saw the helicopters aimed directly at his convoy. It did not take him long to assess his situation. Pleased as he had been feeling by the destruction of Wilson's group, he was more than dismayed that his movements had been tracked so quickly by federal authorities. He knew he had little choice. If he wanted to live.

"Stop the vehicle," he said to the driver.

The driver did as he was told. Because they were first in line, the entire caravan came to a slow stop.

"Tell your men to stand down," Blinder said. "I'll handle this."

The driver picked up the microphone from the dashboard and gave the order to stand down. "No resistance or engagement," he commanded.

David Blinder took a deep breath, opened the door of his Humvee, got out, and surveyed the area around him. The foothills of the mountains looked oddly beautiful to him. He started walking slowly toward the personnel carrier that was blocking the road. He did not raise his arms in surrender. He approached the vehicle as if it were just another business conversation.

As he got close, the door opened, and a sergeant got out of the personnel carrier. He trained his M-16 straight at him.

"Mr. Blinder?"

"Yes."

"I have been ordered to take you and your men into custody. Please instruct your men to lay down their arms."

"I've already done that, Sergeant."

The sergeant did not move. Blinder finally realized he was waiting for him to comply with his order, so he turned back toward the convoy and motioned for his men to put down their weapons.

"Tell them to disembark."

This time Blinder did as he was told. Men started exiting the vehicles.

In the meantime, US Army troops exited their vehicles, weapons at the ready. They collected the men, searched the vehicles, and confiscated any weapons they found.

David Blinder was filled with an unfamiliar feeling—the feeling that he had lost.

"I want to speak to your commanding officer," he said in an authoritative voice to the sergeant who had the gun aimed at his chest.

The sergeant did not reply right away. He kept his gun aimed at Blinder but was following the movement of his men and the detainees with his eyes, glancing back and forth. After a while he turned to Blinder. "Your request is noted, Mr. Blinder."

"Look here, young man . . . "

The sergeant tightened the grip on his rifle and looked David Blinder straight in the eye. "If you step away I will shoot you." The look on his face demonstrated that he was serious. "I suggest you remain silent."

Blinder felt the ground beneath him tremble. He looked down. He could see that it was not moving. It was his legs that felt as if they were about to give out. Is this what defeat feels like?

After all the Sovereign Citizen troops were loaded onto Army vehicles, a reconstituted convoy formed and headed back to Warren Air Base. No one spoke.

Back at the air base, the stress level in the intel room dropped. No more bloodshed, at least for now.

Sam and Marie looked at each other. So this is the mighty David Blinder?

General Hughes looked at the two women and spoke up.

"It's over," he said. "No other states passed secession resolutions. And Georgia rescinded the one the House passed the other day. All the gold from Fort Knox has been recovered. The United States remains intact."

77

From the Oval Office, President Obama and his team followed the events in Georgia and in Wyoming. All major news outlets were covering the events in Georgia, and the sky was swarming with news helicopters. No news teams were covering the events in Wyoming.

Mr. Obama had a phone in his hand that was directly linked to Stanley Schindler, the head of the FBI, who was filling the President in on the likely movements of the armed demonstrators.

"Far fewer than we anticipated," Schindler said. "It looks like they're heading back to where they came from, Mr. President."

The President could see from the video feeds that the trucks bearing the armed men were entering an interstate that led out of the city. He let out a small sigh of relief.

Then he spoke into the phone. "What's the status of those men in Wyoming?"

"We believe all the members of the team led by Adam Wilson were killed by a contingent of Sovereign Citizens led by Blinder."

"By Blinder personally?"

"Yes, sir. He apparently hooked up with SC fighters after he escaped his compound in Texas."

"Survivors?"

"None so far, Mr. President. The fire crews can't get close enough to the fire to put it out. They are just trying to make sure it doesn't spread."

Schindler continued. "Blinder and his men are in custody."

"All of them?"

"The ones who were with him, sir. We're working on identifying the rest of them." The FBI director paused. "That's going to take a while."

"Thanks, Stanley. Keep me posted."

"Will do, Mr. President."

The President hung up and looked around to his advisors. "It looks like this is over. I need to talk to the people."

Heads nodded all around.

Within half an hour, an unscripted Barack Obama sat at his desk and faced the cameras arrayed in front of him.

"My fellow Americans," he began. He paused for a few moments to gather his thoughts. "In this country, every child learns the Pledge of Allegiance," he said. "Every day, thousands of elementary students pledge themselves to one nation, indivisible, with liberty and justice for all.

"Today, we have seen that allegiance in action where it matters most.

"Over the past two days, we have endured the gravest threat to our democracy since the Civil War. It now appears that the threat has passed. The United States of America remains intact, despite the considerable efforts to destroy it."

He stared hard-faced into the camera. "Our successful response to this outrageous crime is due to the proficiency of federal agencies and the professionalism of key politicians who responded with courage and tenacity in countering this assault on our nation.

"It is also due, however, to a greater force. That force is the voice of the American people, those elementary students who grew up and kept their promise to the nation. They— You are the ones who recognize that this country is not for sale, that it is not something to be treated like a commodity that can be cut up and sold off to the highest bidder. This country—our country—is for all of us, not just the rich and comfortable, the religious and the pious, or the hotheads. It is our country to preserve and protect, just as previous generations of Americans have preserved and protected it and bequeathed it to us.

"Let there be no mistake or misunderstanding: The United States of America is an idea that is larger than any individual citizen. American democracy is our gift to the world, and over these past few days we have renewed that gift by demonstrating to the world that we will not tolerate those divisive forces that would tear our nation apart for private gain.

"I want to thank every American citizen who showed up at their state capital today and stood up for their country. Let us join together and celebrate the victory that is ours today, and let us honor those who lost their lives these past few days in defending this great nation. Let us never lose sight of the fact that freedom comes at a cost, at the cost of vigilance which preserves and protects the precious gift that has been given us and which we now pass on to our children and their children's children. God bless you and God bless the United States of America. One nation. Indivisible."

The End